Trilemma

Trilemma

A Novel

Jennifer Mortimer

Oceanview Publishing
LONGBOAT KEY, FLORIDA

TO MY SISTERS

Anne, Gilda, and Claire

Rowena and Alex

Jane and Georgianne

trilemma: 1 : a choice among three favorable options, only two of which are possible at the same time **2 :** a difficult choice from three options, each of which is unacceptable or unfavorable.

trilemma in computing: fast, cheap, good: pick two

Trilemma

Prologue

I wake in darkness, curled like a fetus on my left-hand side and take a breath—and a vile sweet stench explodes in my nostrils, in my throat, and I gag and retch and thrash out with all my panicked strength, but my arms, my legs, they are caught, trapped, buried, I can't get away from it, I can't move at all— *oh God, trapped in a hole—my worst nightmare*—My mind explodes in blind irrational terror and all goes blank.

Part I

This Land of Hope

Chapter 1

I am a loser when it comes to love and family. I have no husband and no children. My birth mother left when I was a baby and my father died when I was twelve. Now Mom, too, is leaving me, inexorably, one marble at a time.

When I discovered my father's papers in her desk, I thought they might hold some clue to his New Zealand family. And so it turned out. I found an address in Wellington, New Zealand, on the back of a photograph, and when I Googled the address, up popped an apartment to rent. How could I not take it?

My old professor taught that good decisions are made from good logic and good information; a and b therefore c. You can write it up in a formula. So long as you know what a and b are, and your formula is right, then c is an obvious answer.

Sometimes the factors are way more complicated, but they say the human brain can process a mass of information and instinctively come up with the best decision, even though you can't trace the logic. I'd like to think that's true, but how would you know it's the right decision if you don't know how you got there?

Fifty years ago, my father followed a pretty girl home to New Zealand and found love, family, and a career, although he lost them all when he met my mother.

Fifty days ago, I decided to follow in his footsteps.

Now I pause and look at the tall villa crouched amongst blossoming trees and wonder what the hell I'm doing. The wind catches my hair, blowing it over my eyes, blinding me until I catch the errant strands and tuck them behind my ears.

Then I grasp the handle of my battered suitcase and step onto the path.

A small boy rushes past, tugging a fragment of cloth attached to a set of dog's teeth, followed by what at first impression seems to be a golden sheep but is a large woolly dog.

They stop when they see me. The dog drops the cloth and barks. *Rowf, rowf, rowf!*

I stand my ground. "Hello Rowfer, good boy!" I hope.

"Her name is Polly, not Ralph," says the child. "And she's a girl."

The woolly beast wags her tail. I offer my hand. "How do you do, Polly?"

She gives me her hairy foot. I shake it solemnly.

"Rowf!" she says and wiggles her bottom.

"Indeed. And I am Lin."

The boy looks at me. "Top floor?"

"That's me."

He sticks out his own grubby paw. "I'm Michael."

"Pleased to meet you, Michael."

A statuesque woman with long, fair hair emerges from the ground floor apartment. She examines me with shrewd green eyes edged by laughter lines and dark brows that curve up at the outer edges.

"You must be our new neighbor," she says. "I'm Sally Trumpet. I see you've met my son."

"And his trusty companion," I reply, and offer my hand. "Linnet Mere."

Sally shakes my hand and asks, "Why don't you pop in tomorrow night for a drink?"

"Thank you. I'd like that."

The penthouse smells of the lilies squatting in a vase on the table. The card says "Welcome! Alienne," which strikes me as a little impolite until I recognize the name of the company that rented me the apartment.

I touch the soft gray leather of the sofa then walk to the window. Puffs of white cloud break free from the eastern hills and scud across the azure sky, while in the harbor yachts dart across the sea.

Although I had traveled New Zealand several times before, I always flew direct to Queenstown and missed one of New Zealand's best-kept secrets. You can't beat Wellington on a good day, they say, and today is one of those days. Glistening in the sun, nestled in tall green hills, and cradled by the cobalt sea, Wellington is absolutely, positively gorgeous.

The hot sun streams in the window and warms my skin. Below in the pohutukawa tree birds twitter, and faint music meanders up through the streets as someone practices piano. A lawn mower drones in the distance. A feeling of gentle well-being washes over me.

I made the right decision.

Like my father I might find love, and like my father, I might find a family in this land of hope and plenty. The first country to give women the vote and where they say the glass ceiling is thinner. A Pacific island with a fair and open culture that looks both to the East and the West.

The land where I was born and the land where Ben lives.

So while you might say it was fate that led me to the house where my father once lived, I know it was logic.

Chapter 2

I love wandering the aisles of supermarkets to see what special foods the locals eat, what fruits and vegetables grow here, and what kind of wine they make.

I buy grapes and strawberries, Agria potatoes, wild rocket, baby carrots, and Cardrona lamb cutlets. I pick out fresh Zorganic milk, cheeses, a dozen bluff oysters, coffee from L'affare, and a jar of Marmite spread. New Zealand fancies itself as a maker of excellent wine, I know, so I meander through the shelves and load up twelve different bottles to try.

When I get back to the apartment, I eat the oysters with a glass of Sauvignon Blanc at my table looking out over the city, and then I descend to the ground floor bearing a gift of cheese.

Sally opens the door and surveys me with a friendly smile. The fair hair is now bundled into a coil that slips down one white shoulder.

"Right on time," she says. "I've just finished reading Michael his bedtime story. I hope you like wine."

Do bears defecate in the woods? "I love wine."

Sally's living room is like a Wedgwood bowl; high ceilings, pale green walls, and ornate white woodwork. Polly hastens over and thrusts her head under my hand. I rub the tight gold curls on the top of her head, which causes an ecstatic wiggling of the back end of her body. I like dogs but I've never been able to own one. It wouldn't be kind to keep leaving a dog behind whenever I move on. I couldn't do that to a dog.

"What breed is she? Or is she a mongrel?"

"She's a Labradoodle—a cross between a poodle and a

Labrador, very fashionable at the moment because they don't shed hair. So fashionable that she cost more than buying both the poodle and the Labrador."

"So she's a mongrel."

"A *designer* mongrel."

I must remember that one. I am a mongrel myself, but an accidental one. As if she has heard my thoughts, Sally asks where I'm from.

"I can tell from your voice that you are American, but your eyes are from somewhere else."

"I grew up in America." She lifts an eyebrow and waits for me to complete the answer. "My mother was Chinese."

"Do you see much of her family?"

"Nope."

I hate talking about my mother. I hate admitting that she left while I was still only a baby. When I was a child, I felt ashamed because she must have decided I wasn't worth sticking around for. I don't care now, of course, but it is still sad to know your mother didn't love you enough to stay.

"Are you a Wellingtonian?" I ask.

"I grew up here, but I lived in Christchurch for a while. We came back after the quakes. I work at the hospital," she says, tilting her head at one wall as if the hospital were just through there. "What about you?"

"I'm looking for a job," I reply.

"What are you?"

I smile. "Hard to say. But I'm looking for work as a project manager."

I don't tell her I was born here and I don't tell her I'm looking for my sisters. That quest is too private, and I *am* looking for a job.

She refills my glass with a practiced twist of the wrist. "I like the color of your hair," she says. "Nice shade of red."

"Thank you. I chose it myself."

She laughs. I don't tell her I was trying to match my father's hair color. He used to call me his little hothead and ruffle my thick brown mop of hair. Just like your dad, but you don't show it, he'd said. That's good.

Suddenly a stuffed duck sails through the air, closely followed by Polly the dog. She catches the duck and skids to a halt, then returns her prey to the little angel in white pajamas who is standing by the bedroom door.

"Back to bed!" calls Sally. Michael giggles and returns to his room.

"Is Michael's father around?" I ask.

"No. At least I don't think so. I don't know who he was."

"Oh."

"Don't look so ridiculously impassive!" she says. "Artificial insemination from an anonymous sperm donor. I found myself pushing forty with no man and I wanted a baby before it was too late."

It has taken me years to perfect my carefully constructed poker face but I give her a genuine smile, wide enough to show my crooked tooth, because you have to let your guard down, don't you, if you want to make friends.

"He's a cute kid."

"He's a monster," she replies proudly.

Sally swings her legs up and settles herself on the sofa with her feet up on one sofa arm and her swan neck tilted back over the other.

"Damn," she says. "I'm getting fat."

How can you respond to a statement like that from a woman you barely know?

"Mmm?" I murmur.

"What keeps you so thin?" she asks. "Bitch."

"Stress. When I get busy I forget to eat."

"That reminds me—" She goes into the kitchen to fetch the cheese, and when she returns, she talks about art.

I start to relax. The room is warm and the sofa comfortable. In the corner an iPod plugged into an elegant white speaker system is playing Aimee Mann. Sally tells me about a band she likes. I tell her about a concert I went to some months earlier, and wince as I remember my companion on that night, the profile of his face against the sky as we sat on the walls and watched the spectacle.

I remember his laughter when the fat lady sang and the scent of his skin as I leaned my head on his shoulder. The taste of the cheap red wine when I kissed his lips.

Sally asks about the music, but I talk, instead, of books I've been meaning to read. We kill the bottle and consummate our tentative new friendship with a promise to meet up on Friday night.

My ears sing from the wine I have drunk. I press my fingers to my temples, but I can't stop the memories flooding back. Images of Ben, dreams dreamed and lost.

My father never talked about New Zealand. I think that's why Ben intrigued me when I met him that first time. I wanted to know all about the land of hope and plenty. He took his time telling me and, like Scheherazade's sultan, by the time the last story ended, I was hooked.

"Lucky at cards, unlucky in love," the proverb says, although I work for a living rather than playing cards. The work gives me a good life and, yes, I would say I've been lucky in the jobs I've had.

But love? That's another story.

Chapter 3

Friday nights can be lonely in a new town. You don't want to go looking for Mr. Goodbar by yourself, so you sit at home with your table set for one and try not to finish the whole bottle of wine.

I have friends—Facebook tells me so. Every month or so, when I remember, I log in and post a message. But most of my Facebook friends are as busy as me. We don't engage in witty repartee across the Internet, just the occasional check to see who has changed jobs, or country of residence, or partner.

Sally shows promise as a friend. I like the gleam in her eyes when she pours another glass and that she knows a little about a lot of things. It is a myth that strong, successful women automatically like each other. We don't. If Sally and I worked together, we'd probably hate each other. But with the separation in our working lives, maybe we can manage some kind of friendship.

Sally says she has a great group of friends and I should come meet them. Perhaps I will find that sense of community I've seen in other people's lives, those people who have parents and brothers and sisters and cousins and aunts and uncles and nieces and nephews and friends and family friends and friends of family friends.

I find her sitting at the long bar, wearing a red velvet dress with a low neckline that shows off her shapely figure and white skin. She smiles and waves me to a seat beside a gorgeous young man with a halo of wild dark hair, who leans toward my neck and introduces himself as Karim. Loud music is playing, so it is hard to hear. I ask him what he does for a living, and he tells me he's a nurse.

"I was a doctor, but they do not recognize my qualifications," he says. "I must sit examinations to requalify."

"Where are you from originally?"

"Pakistan. My parents thought I would have better opportunities here, but I don't know. Sometimes I think I should give up and go back home."

The bar gets busier and my glass is filled again. I haven't eaten all day, so I think about slowing down, but then a waitress walks up and taps Sally on the arm and points. We head for the table, which is in an open-air atrium deep in the stomach of the restaurant. Fortunately, there are heaters because today is not one of the good days in Wellington. I find myself sitting next to Karim, with a new man on my other side. This one is older, with a receding hairline and spectacles, and has been quiet so far. He introduces himself as John from gastroenterology.

"Are you a specialist?" I ask.

He stares owlishly at me through his glasses. "I'm a nurse."

I eat carpaccio of yellowtail kingfish with rhubarb, grapefruit and ginger buckwheat, elegant but miniscule. The noise of happy eaters rings in my ears, and I am transported back to another meal in a place far away, in different company, a magnificent meal with too much wine—just like tonight.

I remember the bad call I made that night and think about slowing down, but the bottle in Sally's hand intervenes.

"Come on, Lin, finish this off, and we'll get another."

I ask her the question I should have asked when we first met. "What do you do at the hospital, Sally? Your e-mail said Ms. S. Trumpet, so I assumed you were a nurse."

"Doctors are such snobs," she says. "I'm a specialist, darling. We refer to ourselves as Mr. or Ms. to distinguish us from the GPs."

"I suppose you're a brain surgeon." I say, only half in jest.

"Me mum said with my clever hands I'd either be a seam-stress or a surgeon. But I chose pathology. The hours are better."

"And you play doctors and nurses with nurses?"

"That's how it works. Doctors don't like competition. We prefer the deference of a sosh—socio-economic subordinate. Don't you?"

"I don't think I'd put it that way."

"No one does. We're all hyp hyp . . . hypocrites."

She's not wrong. High-flying women may fancy alpha males, but we can't stay with one for long. We rip them to shreds when they annoy us and then they dump us for a gentler, sweeter model. If we're wise, we find a gentle, sweet man ourselves.

But I'm not going to think about that.

Sally pours the rest of the wine into my glass, pats Karim on the cheek, and sends him to fetch another bottle. John scowls at Karim's back and turns to me. He has been getting drunker as the night progresses and is now relaxed enough to speak. He comes from Palmerston North, he tells me belligerently when I ask. Now it is I who do not understand, so I force a smile and say, how nice.

"Are you taking the piss?" he asks.

I look at him blankly, and he turns away.

Later, we spill out of the restaurant and onto the street where there is a fountain made of large, colored buckets of water tip-ping into each other with a splash. I must be drunker than I thought because I seem to see a hobbit pissing in the fountain. He turns and yes, dammit, it is a hobbit, Frodo I think, although he is dressed in jeans rather than a hobbit cloak. I shake my head and follow Sally up the road to a doorway guarded by two ostentatiously large men. Sally hands them money and they step aside to let us enter.

The room at the end of the corridor is dark apart from the lights pinpointing the musicians and the strip lighting over the bar. The place is throbbing with sound, like the blood pumping through my head, thud, thud, and thud. Sally disappears into the gloom. I push through hot bodies to reach the bar, but she isn't there, so I order myself a cocktail. Something with chocolate in it I say and turn back to the crowd, running my eyes over the dim shapes to see if I can find her and the others who were supposed to join us.

After five minutes of fruitless searching, I give up and prop myself against the bar, hoping that I will be found, trying to look nonchalant. The alcohol has caught up with me and my head fills with haze as the music thuds on through my brain.

A familiar face swims into view. After a moment's puzzling, I recognize the man who showed me around the penthouse. *What was his name?*

"Nice to see you again," he says. "Out on the town tonight?"

"I'm with friends," I reply. "But I seem to have lost them."

He glances at me sideways. "Has anyone told you what beautiful eyes you have?"

I gaze at him with my beautiful eyes and wonder where the nearest taxi stand is.

He moves close and puts his hand on my thigh. "My friends call me Nick."

The night is a confusion of intimate connections of flesh; hot, hard, rough, wet, slippery, and urgent.

I fall asleep and wake in the dark an hour before dawn, alone. I am naked. My nipples are sore. There is a damp stickiness on my thighs. My head aches. I remember, and a wave of disgust washes over me, leaving my skin crawling and my stomach sour.

Like I said, good decisions are based on good information and good logic; not just acting without thinking or you might wake up and realize you've made a really bad mistake.

I blot out the memory and sink back into the abyss of unconsciousness.

Chapter 4

When there is a knock on my door the following morning, I assume it is Sally, whom I haven't seen since last night.

But it isn't Sally.

"Lin!" he says, showing his teeth. "How are you?"

I pull my robe close around my body. "Fine."

"May I come in?"

"I was just about to go out."

He raises his arm and leans against the door jamb, smiling, and flicks his gaze down my body, as if he knows what I look like naked.

"I'd like to see more of you," he says.

I shake my head. "I'm sorry, but it was a mistake."

"Didn't feel like a mistake when you—"

"Sorry," I say, and start closing the door. "I'm not interested."

He puts his foot out and stops the door half closed. He is no longer smiling.

We stare coldly at each other, like sphinxes at the entrance to an innermost courtyard.

"Remove your foot. Now."

He shrugs and steps backward and I slam the door closed.

I am angry with myself for succumbing to the alcohol and the music and his insistence. Because it didn't work. Another man's meager body and second-rate sexual skills couldn't replace the memories of Ben.

•   •   •

Another knock comes that evening.

"Come for dinner? I've got a huge roast," Sally says when I cautiously open the door. "Pork. You've got to help us eat it."

"Okay."

"What happened to you last night?" she asks when I join her and Michael downstairs. "I turned around and you weren't there."

"I could say the same of you."

"We were in the back bar."

"Oh, now she tells me there's a back bar! I got stuck in the front one, with the property agent."

"Handy Nicholas? Poor you."

After dinner Michael goes to bed, where I read him *Hairy Mcclary from Donaldson's Dairy* while Polly lies snoring on the floor pretending she's asleep. But I can see the stealthy eye that opens every few minutes, waiting for me to leave so she can steal up onto the bed.

Back in the living room, his mother offers me a Kiwi version of *affogato* with vanilla ice cream and Dark Spice liqueur, doused with hot, strong, fresh espresso.

"How is progress on the job front?"

"A guy I used to work for wants to talk to me about a job at a new telecommunications company."

"Bloody hell, do we need another?"

"If you want to keep the prices sharp, you have to give Kiwicom more competition."

Kiwicom, the incumbent telecom company, is especially adroit at keeping politicians happy and customers on their books.

Sally sits up and refills our glasses. "Is it a fair life for women in your IT world?"

I shift my glass around in my hand to avoid the lipstick mark I have left on the rim. "It's fair up to a certain level. Above that, it becomes pretty tough and you have to act like a man to survive. What we might think of as considerate behavior, the corporate Mafia would consider softness."

"Uh-huh."

"Some women treat their femininity as a weapon and use all their wiles to get their way with the men they deal with."

"Yep, seen it."

"I don't do that. Probably because I still think of myself as a geek rather than a girl. Once a geek, always a geek."

"You've scrubbed up pretty well for a geek."

"And you for a cutter up of dead people."

"I don't tell people that's what I do. Tends to put men off."

"Who did you enjoy yourself with last night?"

Her mouth gives a little quirk. "Karim, actually."

"He seems a nice guy."

"He is a lovely guy. But Karim will qualify as a doctor soon, and I expect he'll head off into the wild blue yonder with a pretty young wife of his own culture at his side. Not some old Anglo-Saxon atheist like me."

"There's always John, although he seems a bit morose."

"He's got good reason to be morose. Once upon a time he used to run an investment company."

"How did he end up as a nurse?"

"When the economy took a dive, the company he ran took some hits, and he took a risk that the dip was temporary and propped it up with his own money. When they found him out, he got the sack and was lucky not to be sued for making fraudulent statements. Lost all his money and his trophy wife. She kept what was left of the family assets and sued him for support."

"There must be some kind of work around for a secondhand executive."

"In New Zealand when you fall from grace, no one will touch you," Sally says. "He couldn't get even the lowliest of accounting jobs. Then he thinks, well, he's paid a few million in taxes over the years and so perhaps the Government will help.

And they did. On their terms. Work and Income told him it was either nursing or cleaning toilets."

"You'd think they'd show a little more sensitivity."

Sally chortles. "Sensitivity? For a white middle-class, middle-aged male? No way. I'm sure they rubbed their hands together with glee when he sold his city apartment and his Mercedes in a fire sale and moved into a cheap studio."

"Poor guy."

"Yeah. I feel sorry for him."

"Not much to build a relationship on."

"Who's looking for a relationship? And he's terrific with Michael."

"You're not looking for anything permanent?"

Sally looks into her glass. "We'd all like something permanent. Handsome, well paid, interesting, kind, but there just ain't so many of those sorts around, are there?"

"Nope," I reply. "It's a hard road finding a good man."

I glance at Sally. Her eyes are fixed on her glass and she has that half smile on her generous mouth. I feel a rush of warmth toward her. Sally is everything one could want in a friend.

"I had a good man, but I screwed up."

Now she looks up. "Screwed up how?"

"Slept with someone else."

"And he found out," she prompts, her green eyes aglow with interest.

"I told him."

"Oh, big mistake."

I sigh. "Yes."

"Telling him, I mean. Was your man American?"

"Kiwi."

"Fantastic! Where does he live? Here in Wellington?"

I shake my head. "In a small town south of Queenstown, near Invercargill."

"Invercargill? Well, I'm sure he's very nice, anyway. Any chance of making up?"

"I—don't think so."

"There are other fish in the ocean. You'll have to come out with us. What was your bloke like?"

"I thought he was good looking," I tell her. "Brown hair, blue eyes. Strong tanned arms."

"Mm-hmm!" she says.

"But he didn't earn much."

"Interesting?"

"Very interesting. And nearly always kind."

"Wow, Lin, three out of four! What a catch."

"But also very irritating."

"Duh? He's a guy, right?"

"And far too attached to his daughter."

"He sounds better and better. Give me his e-mail address! I'll call him in for an audition."

I laugh and throw a cushion at her. "No way!"

"I should organize a dinner party where you can meet some interesting people."

"That might be fun," I reply, and try to smile a genuine smile.

"We'll make it fun," she replies. "Shall I organize you a man too?"

"No thanks."

"I'll ask the gay guys from upstairs then. They get back from Hobbiton next week, I think. You'll like them, they're Americans too."

"I'm not—okay, whatever."

On the roof terrace I lean on the railing sipping my wine and looking out over Wellington. There is a full moon tonight, tipping the roofs and treetops silver.

Suddenly, the metal bucks in my grasp and the railing peels away from the terrace and falls down the side of the house. For a moment I teeter on the edge, undulating, like a fish trying to swim backward. My glass flies from my hand, splashing red wine into the air, then wine and glass follow the railing down.

I gasp and clutch at the pillar that had been anchoring the balustrade only a few seconds before, and manage to hold myself back from slipping over the edge.

There is a clang as the railing hits the wall and a crash as the wine glass falls onto the concrete beneath the trees at the base of the house.

The blood pounds through my veins, thud, thud, thud, as I look at the swathe the railing has made in the branches of the cherry tree below. It is a long drop down.

Then I pull myself back onto the safety of the terrace and slump into the deck chair. The wind has cooled the sweat on my skin and my pulse has slowed almost to normal when I notice the blood.

Goddammit! There are bright red smears all over my white trousers. I twist my right arm and see the long gash running from elbow to wrist.

After I have cleaned my arm and thrown the trousers into the washing machine, I go back out onto the terrace. When I run my hand lightly over the side of the pillar I can feel the jagged edge of torn metal.

Well, that could have been nasty, I think, and return indoors to call the property agent.

Chapter 5

In Courtenay Place the streets are full of inward-facing bars and fast-food joints. The wind seems to funnel through the grid, tossing garbage in the air and across the roads. My eyes quickly fill with grit, so it is a relief to reach the Museum Art Hotel where I am meeting Robert.

When I first met Robert Smith he was running a small software company near Tunbridge Wells. I had just completed my degree in Computer Science, which I'd switched to from English Literature when I realized I preferred logic to language. He was feeling nostalgic for America and liked my accent, and that is where my career began.

That first job is always special. Robert had a small team of clever oddballs working on the software. God, we were heroes! They don't write software now as easily as we wrote it then. When Robert sold out, I was so angry I broke it off with him, but by then he'd started looking at the sweet young Jamaican girl who did our accounts the way he used to look at me, so I knew it was ending. I got out first, pretended it was my choice, pretended there weren't any scars.

The company that bought us laid us all off pretty damned quick and moved the software, and we never heard about it again. They swooped in and took all the tapes away and cleaned out the off-site backups too. I wished I'd kept a copy, but you never think that the security risk is from the owners, do you?

I didn't hear from Robert for a couple of years until he recommended me to a company in London looking for a development manager. And we kept in touch after that whenever he visited England—he was living in Vegas by then—and eventually I forgot we'd ever been anything more than occasional work colleagues.

Earlier in the year, he contacted me when he needed some help and so I worked for him for a few months. That job ended, and when I decided to come to New Zealand, Robert told me he had a venture starting up in Wellington and there might be an opportunity for me.

I thought about it long and hard, but you have to utilize favors, don't you, to keep climbing the ladder?

In subdued lighting Robert can still look like a catch. His hair is a subtle shade of bleached blond and his tan speaks of some place where men are not afraid to use a sunbed. Only his chicken-skin neck betrays his true age.

He rises to greet me, blinking in the dim light of the lobby bar, blue lenses circling his irises before settling into place.

"How are you, my dear?" he asks, and smiles his shiny triangular smile, like a discreet shark.

"I'm well. Can I get you another drink?"

He finishes his glass. "Whiskey."

"I know."

"The good stuff."

I order him the best they have and a glass of Chablis for me.

"No Moana?" Moana was Robert's aide, in more ways than one. A big beautiful island girl.

He glances up but doesn't meet my eyes. "I left her in Hawaii. She doesn't need to come on all my trips." Then he says, "Caught up with lover boy yet?"

I put my glass gently down on the table. "That's all over. So, you're setting up a new telco to compete with Kiwicom?" I ask.

Robert smirks but lets me change the subject. "Indeed. The company's called Hera. We've got an international set of investors as well as the usual local suspects."

"There's a lot of Government money sloshing around for broadband." I have done my research. "Are you looking for a slice?"

"The Government is letting us join the Broadband Consortium on the condition we prove our commitment by launching a pilot service by March."

"Less than six months away!"

"We're slipping badly behind the plan. The guy running the project had a nervous breakdown or something, so we need another project manager urgently."

The project manager is the person who works out what needs to be done and when it needs to be done and chases everyone to make sure it is done. Of course, it's more complicated than that, and a lot of it involves writing up plans, reporting on status of tasks, and meeting to discuss issues, risks, and constraints. And, hopefully, find solutions.

"So are you interested?"

"I am very interested."

"They're not expecting to pay expenses so you'd need to find your own accommodation."

"I already have an apartment."

"So you're already committed to living here, huh?"

"I like Wellington."

He smiles his small, expensive smile. "Don't get too comfortable, Lin. In this country you're the alien."

I take a sip of the wine and look around the bar at the other guests. This is one of Wellington's top hotels, so you can expect there will be a few foreign visitors. The woman talking to the bald man, for instance. The way she is dressed, the makeup, and the perfect hair don't look local. And I can easily recognize the origins of the Asian women sitting at the table beyond us and the beautiful South American girl at the bar.

Everyone is an alien somewhere, but I seem to be an alien every place I go. If it isn't the Asian eyes, it's the American accent. If it isn't how I look and sound, then it's because I am a thirty-nine-year-old woman working at a level more commonly occupied by middle-aged men.

I lean back in my chair and scrutinize Robert's face. "I never told you I was born in New Zealand, did I?"

Robert's eyebrows rise slightly, but it is hard to tell the difference from his carefully cosmetically tightened forehead.

"I thought your father was British."

"He immigrated here in the sixties. He had this romantic idea that New Zealand was a South Seas paradise and took a job as professor of English Literature at the university."

"Must have been a shock when he arrived in a Wellington southerly."

"It's still sunnier than England. Most of the time. Anyway, I was born in Wellington, but when I was a toddler, he took me to the States."

God knows why my father hooked up with Mom. They never talked to each other beyond a grunt from him and "uh-huh" from her. Maybe she thought Dad was a tasteful accoutrement for her décor, and maybe he thought she was an easy way to keep him in comfort once his career had collapsed.

But it wasn't a comfortable household. I can still remember the fights my stepbrother, Steve, had with Dad. Mom always used to take Steve's side; "he's just a boy," she'd say, and it would always be Dad who left. "Another conference," Mom would explain when I came down and he wasn't at the breakfast table.

Looking back, I think he'd just take off whenever he couldn't stand living with us any longer. That last time it turned out he'd driven off the road on one of those long stretches between the mountains where you can't take any risks or you end up down a cliff. Mom kept saying he wasn't drunk, but it was a while before they found him, so who knows?

"You might say I'm a Kiwi."

He snorts. "Don't delude yourself. You are what your accent says you are. In your case, a Yank."

The South American girl shuffles on the bar stool, crossing and re-crossing her legs. Robert's attention wanders.

But I am not a Yank, although I grew up in America. My stepsister, Hilary, used to call me "Cuckoo" which was cruel, especially since no one could have pushed Steve and Hilary out of the family nest if they didn't want to go. Like Mom they were large blond people with blue eyes and a lot of gleaming white teeth. I was little, with brown hair and the dark slanting eyes that marked me as different. A small brown cuckoo.

I am not the Brit my father was either, even though I followed in his footsteps and studied at Oxford and have worked in London on and off for years. I am not French, although I've lived there too, nor Australian. And, although my birth mother was Chinese, I know nothing of that heritage.

I think about the alien I have always been and I decide it will be different this time.

Although I've searched all the directories and the social media sites, I haven't found any trace of Vivienne or Alison Mere. My sisters from my father's first marriage.

I guess both must have married and changed their name. No matter. From past experience, I knew it wasn't going to be easy. But one way or another, I plan to belong in this country.

I want to be a kiwi and not a cuckoo.

"When can I start?"

Chapter 6

Five percent of the population are psychopaths, or so the article says. Psychopaths are often confident and articulate. They lie with ease, they feel no guilt, they smile and smile and yet are villains.

According to the writer, the modern psychopath typically doesn't kill—why take that kind of risk? They don't even break the law. The modern-day psychopath can gain everything they want through legal manipulation of the world they live in. If you're not encumbered by self-doubt, consideration for others, or the inconvenient need to be truthful, what can you not achieve?

The writer states that being a psychopath is a genetic predilection, unlike the sociopath who is likely to have suffered neglect, abuse, or some major trauma that has damaged their humanity.

Seek out the untruthful, self-serving egotist when you look for your five percent, the writer says. Psychopaths always focus on their own best interests.

The article deteriorates into emotive claims that such people lack "souls," and I stop reading. But that doesn't mean there is no truth in the conditions described, and it makes me wonder how many of the people I meet might be a psychopath.

I consider myself adept at reading people; it is a useful skill for a manager, and I pride myself on being able to read the truth or the lie in a person's eyes. But I wonder what you can read in a psychopath's eyes?

I put away the paper, stretch, then roll out of bed and prepare for my working day. Washed, dressed in black, and made up in the immaculate image of a career woman, I climb into my car and drive down the hill into the city.

At the office, I add the final touches to our presentation on the status of the launch for this afternoon's Board meeting. The elevator arrives, and Hera's chief operating officer Tom Heke emerges; tall, dark, and self-assured, striding across the office like a warrior coming to battle.

Tom and I are metaphorically circling; not in a sexual way, well, yes, there is something of a sexual element to male-female interaction when you work together, but this circling is more about who is going to be top dog. Tom is used to being the leader of the pack and he doesn't like giving ground.

Neither do I.

He places a firm hand on my shoulder and smiles at me with warm brown eyes.

"How are the plans going?"

I shrug my shoulder to dislodge his hand. "They'll go better once you decide on the location for the operations center."

"I'm getting another opinion on the fault line in Petone," he replies. "And we're still working out how to get network across the rail yards if we go for the port site."

"What's wrong with Seaview?"

"Nothing's wrong with Seaview, but we need to look at all our options."

"We need to get started." I relax my mouth into a small polite smile of encouragement. "When can you make the decision?"

Tom smiles widely back. "Don't be so impatient."

His eyes are so self-assured. *Oh, man, don't you ever wonder if you're wrong?*

"We're running out of time —"

Tom pats my shoulder lightly. "We need to do this right," he says, and strides away before I can answer.

I watch him pace across the room with my eyes calm, my anger hidden. The decision on where to locate the operations center is on the critical path for the project. The location has become less important than the delay in starting the build.

I've reasoned, I've cajoled, I've pushed, but Tom still won't commit to a choice, and Adam listens to Tom.

Corporate testosterone has a smell of its own; a subtle blend of cologne with high notes of expensive soap from the executive washroom where they wash their hands of responsibility for any mistakes, a touch of cigar smoke, maybe a whiff of the bouquet of a fine wine, a soupçon of eau de secretary's perfume. There is never any stink of sweat. Never the stale odor of well-worn shoes nor the whiff of wet wool from walking the streets in the rain.

I sit at the foot of the table with Hera's chief executive, Adam Challoner, wearing the calm and confident mask I present to the corporate bosses.

It's best, I've found, to show no emotion at all. If you smile, they think you want to be liked and mark you down as needy. If you frown, they think you're at a loss as to what to do and mark you down as indecisive. If you narrow your eyes, they think you're challenging them, and they'll huff and they'll puff louder to make you back down. I prefer to keep them guessing. My father's little hothead keeps her temper well hidden.

Robert, representing the American shareholders, sits on the nearest side of the boardroom table. Alongside Robert is Quon Dao from Hong Kong who heads up a Chinese company that seeks to invest in New Zealand. Dao has short, thick, ash-colored hair and eyes like mine.

On the other side of the table is gray-suited, gray-haired Stewart Hobb, CFO of Australian shareholder Ozcom and chairman of Hera's Board. Beside Hobb is plump and pleasant Pita Lane from Christchurch representing the *iwi*—the term for a Maori tribe, and Mark Stanton, a lawyer from Auckland, who is the independent professional director who ensures good governance and proper bureaucracy. There's something of an Old Boy and Old Girl network of directors in New Zealand, I'm told. Same as anywhere, I guess.

Stanton is white-haired, red-faced, and pleasant when the going's easy, gruff when it's not. Right now he's gruff.

"That is not acceptable," Robert states after I present the plan. "The launch date is not negotiable."

"Okay," I say. "Then working back from the March launch date, we'll need to start the build by this date," and I point at the chart. "Which means we need to complete the design by this date, which means we need to make the decision on the operations center by—"

"This week!" snaps Robert.

"This week?" asks Lane.

"This week." I confirm.

After the Board members have gone, the management team arrives for a debrief. Adam slumps amongst the clutter of papers, teacups, and leftover food, dark rings around his tired eyes. Hera's head of human resources, Marion King, glances at him before taking her seat. Fred Mitchell, head of IT, and Ian Green, our marketing guru, help themselves to the leftover sandwiches and Tom snags the last sausage roll. CFO Deepak Gupta hurries in last and closes the door.

"They've told me to go with the Seaview site," Adam tells us.

Tom splutters pastry crumbs on the table. "But—"

"No buts," says Adam. "That's the decision. Let's get on with it."

Tom glares at me. I gaze steadily back.

He turns to Adam and lifts his chin. "Okay, boss. I'll call the agent and make the final arrangements for Seaview."

"We need to talk," Marion says to me. "Let's go to my office."

When we reach her office, she closes the door, picks up my

working visa application from her desk, and places it on the table. She tilts her elegant, silvered head toward the papers.

"You didn't tell me you were actually born in New Zealand."

"I didn't think it was relevant." I pause. "And I'm illegitimate."

Marion snorts. "Haven't heard anyone call themselves illegitimate for a long time. No one here cares whether your parents were married or not. You could probably get citizenship since you were born in New Zealand," she adds. "But it would have been even easier if you still had family here."

"Oh?"

"That would make it a dead cert."

"Actually, I do have some family in New Zealand."

"Fantastic! Give me their details, and we'll include the information in the application."

I mutter something noncommittal.

I can't tell her I don't know where they live. I can't tell her that they have never wanted to know me, that every time my father tried to make contact, they sent back a reply that always had the same theme.

Fuck you and the horse you rode in on.

Chapter 7

When the weekend arrives, I sleep in and it is late morning by the time I get up, shower, pull on jeans, a shirt, and my most comfortable shoes. I make coffee and toast with Marmite. The first time I tried the stuff, I slathered it on thick like Nutella and it made me gag. Ben laughed until he fell off his chair. Now I dab it delicately in dainty dots like a Pissarro.

Outside in the bright sun Michael and Polly are chasing each other around the house. They stop to wag their tails at me and then take off again, giggling happily.

I love to walk. I don't care whether I walk the busy streets of a city or the alleyways of old stone villages, shady forest paths, or wild and lonely beaches. It's the act of placing your steps one after another, letting your eyes see whatever the world has to offer, your ears hear the sound of the birds or the buzz of foreign-sounding voices, and your nostrils smell the earth or the food cooking in some back street café.

I head down the road and turn onto a path through a forest. I could be in another world. The trees are tall and their foliage is dense and green and lush, full of hidden birds who twitter, honk, ring, screech, cry, and sing. A jogger jogs past, panting, sweat glowing on his pink skin, feet slapping the leafy carpet as he thrusts himself onward. A man walking his terrier greets me with a polite nod. The dog sniffs my leg and passes on.

When I emerge from the trees, ahead lies the city, glinting in myriad shades of black, white, gray, and green. The jagged shapes of buildings rise up from streets that are neither boule-vards nor alleys but somewhere in between. Every building is a different height and shape, and every street emerges on an angle.

I walk down a steep hill and arrive at the top of Cuba Street. I pass art galleries and boutiques of handcrafted clothing, a New-Age gift shop, a fish shop selling dozens of varieties of fish and shellfish, a coffee roaster. To my left and right are cafés of all types; rich ones, poor ones, Italian, Malaysian, Thai, Chinese, Indian, Mexican, Turkish, French.

Young girls strut past in laddered tights and short-skirted dresses alongside boys with pants falling off their behinds. A middle-aged woman sits at a table on the pavement drinking coffee and reading a book. A couple walks by carrying bags of shopping and arguing over where to stop for lunch. I count three street performers—an Asian boy playing violin, a hippy with a guitar, and a Maori couple singing to a boom box. "How bizarre" he sings in a beautiful tenor while she warbles the chorus and taps her tambourine.

I collect a baguette from a French deli and a fillet of local fish, *hapuka*, I am told, from the fish shop. On my way back up the street, I pause outside the window of an art gallery. Inside are canvasses in black and white, with Maori words scattered across them in red. I don't know what any of the words mean, although I am starting to recognize the language.

Reading the words, a sudden thought strikes me.

I remember playing in the sand of Cannon Beach back in Oregon, years ago, just my father and me. We built a hill out of the damp sand, with a castle at the top where I buried gold-colored candy wrappers. My father marked the spot with a *Z*, and then he named our castle "Ngatirua," creating the word out of small pieces of gray driftwood.

"Who lives there, Dad?" I'd asked.

"A prince used to live there, but he escaped."

"Is there a monster?"

I remember him laughing. *"Maybe there's a monster. Or a wicked witch."*

• • •

I turn back to the road and walk briskly up the hill. When I reach my apartment, I retrieve a large envelope from the battered leather suitcase under the bed. On top is a photograph of Ben and Emmy standing in front of Ben's studio, but beneath is the handful of old photographs I'd found in Mom's house.

I take out the first clue I found in my father's papers, a photograph of an infant lying asleep in a buggy. On the back of the photo is a scrawl, saying "Linnet," the year of my birth, and the address of the house in which I now live.

I pick out another photograph, this one of my father. Behind his head is a painting of a Maori warrior so the photograph must have been from when he lived in New Zealand. On the back of the photograph is a word; "Ng" then a squiggle then "rua," it says.

I had thought Ngatirua was a funny made-up name, but now I realize it might be a real place.

Clue number two. I type "Ngatirua" into Google. No locations come up, just a jumble of similar words. I scroll through the results. The last is an image of a painting, called: *The Road to Ngatirua*. The painting is of a road zigzagging up a hill, tan and ochre with touches of green.

Then I see the artist's name. Rose Mere. *Mere!*

I type in "Rose Mere." And at last I strike gold, of sorts. I find an article on a Hawke's Bay artist who painted in the fifties and the sixties. She died the year I was born. Married, two daughters.

I continue reading. Now when I bring up the maps, I search the hills of Hawke's Bay for a road like the one in the painting. After half an hour of careful examination, I think I have found the road to Ngatirua.

I make a pot of tea and take my cup outside onto the roof terrace, where the break in the railing stills gapes like a hasty exit. The breeze has stiffened and tugs at my hair. I gaze to the north, beyond the harbor, where steep green ridges march into the hazy distance.

A precious feeling of happiness washes over me, the first time I've felt hopeful since the day I lost Ben.

Somewhere beyond those hills must be a trace of my sisters.

Chapter 8

It has rained overnight and the sky is hovering between gray and blue. When I look to the north, I can see the long white cloud hanging over the hills.

Should I, shouldn't I? What's to lose?

The edgy charge of anticipation suspends rational thought. Half an hour later I drive alongside the river to the top of the Hutt Valley. The road narrows and becomes a single lane to climb the Rimutakas, turning and bending and turning again to reach the summit, high in the mountains and covered with dense native bush and trees. Going down the far side is easier and ten minutes later I emerge into a small country town. One blink and it is gone.

The next place arrives with a prettiness of flower baskets and a charm of colonial architecture, and is bustling with people. I drive on, deeper into provincial New Zealand, where the flat lands are stocked with dairy cows, the hills in sheep and beef. Higher up, the grass turns to bush and higher still there is a scattering of snow on the otherwise bald peaks.

I see the road sign and make the turn.

In front of me a range of steep hills towers above green pastures dotted with sheep. Climbing the hill, cutting left and right into the green land, runs a zigzag road. I stop the car and take out my copy of Rose Mere's painting.

It is the same shape. This is the road I seek.

What am I going to find at the end of this road? A haven amongst my long-lost family? A pot of gold? A weird castle with a monster in the dungeon? Or nothing at all?

I shake my head, smiling at my foolish fancies, downshift, and drive slowly up the switchback to the top of the hill. The rise is steep and the corners are sharp. The car strains and chokes and splutters as I reach the summit. Five minutes later I see a corridor of tall trees to my left. At the roadside is a mailbox large enough to hold a sheep.

I stop and read the inscription.

There are two sets of names, not one. Christopher and Vivienne Marchmount. Walter and Alison Repati. I have found both of them.

Do I stop now and return to Wellington?

The blood races through my veins in anticipation. I lift my foot gently from the brake and turn up the driveway.

Invisible dogs bark as I drive up and stop the car in front of a sprawling farmhouse of gray clapboard with white window frames. A battered SUV is parked in the car shed and a dirt-embossed motorbike leans against a water tank.

I pause with my hand on the door lever, and then I press it down, push open the door and step out of the car.

Gravel crunches beneath my feet as I approach a porch adorned with Wellington boots, a basket of wood, two cat food bowls, a walking stick, and four umbrellas in various states of disrepair. When I reach the door, I knock lightly, three times. It seems appropriate. I wait, listening, but there is no noise from within, no patter of feet across old wooden floorboards coming to meet a long-lost prodigal sister.

I knock again, loudly this time. Still nothing. I walk around the back. The dogs start barking again, more of them joining in, until there is a crescendo of dog noise coming from the hill beyond the house. On the far side is a large veranda facing north to capture the sun, with doors opening from the house, but all are closed today.

The house has a sleepy air, as if it waits like a faithful dog for its owner. I want to walk up to the glass and peer inside, but I am not certain it is empty, so I look from afar, but see nothing.

I circle around to the entrance and knock again, but there is no response.

Back in the car, I reverse down the driveway and pause. The driveway goes around a rose garden and up a hill.

There must be another house farther in. I drive forward, past bluebells pushing up their petaled heads amongst the ferns beneath the trees, and climb to the top of the rise.

To my left, now, is a grassy tennis court. To my right, a swimming pool, an elegant structure of red metal and glass and terra-cotta tiles. Ahead lies a beautiful country house. Not a castle, not a villa, but a colonial mansion built on a grand scale. Trees frame the house, and flower bushes spill out of the beds that fill its many crevices.

I drive up to the porch. Pots in rich shades of blue and red are artfully placed on the terra-cotta-tiled steps. The door is wide open.

As I sit in my car anticipating what might come next, a man emerges from the house, a dog at his side. I get out of the car and walk toward him. He is younger than I expected, tall and handsome, with fair hair, dark glasses, and a tanned face.

"Can I help you?" he asks, staring at the car.

I can't see his eyes behind the dark lenses.

I clear my throat. "I am looking for Vivienne or Alison. Is either of them at home?"

He drops his gaze to my face.

"I am Christopher Marchmount. My wife is shopping in Hastings and Alison and Walter are at the dog trials," he replies. "Perhaps I can help?"

I don't want to speak of who I am to anyone but my sisters.

"Will Vivienne be home soon?"

He leans down and touches the dog's head. "I don't expect her back until this evening. And Alison and Walter are in Wairoa so they won't be home until late. What do you want with them?"

"I've seen one of their mother's paintings," I tell him. "I was wondering if there were any available to buy."

It is a lie, but I do need a painting or two for my office wall. Although I'm not sure I would want a painting by my father's spurned first wife.

His jaw moves into a smile, showing a set of even white teeth. "Come in," he says. "I think Vivienne has some of her mother's pieces in the hall."

He stands to one side and puts out his hand, brushing my shoulder as I pass. I flinch involuntarily.

"They are here somewhere," he says, as I stand blinking in a large hallway. "But I cannot recall where."

I walk up the hallway, looking at the artworks on display. "I can't see Rose's signature on any of these," I say.

Still wearing his dark glasses, he seems to gaze right through me. I start to feel uncomfortable.

"Perhaps they are in the studio." He walks past me and opens a door to the outside. "Follow me."

He leaves the house and crosses the lawn to a gate beyond. The dog paces silently beside him.

He fumbles with the gate. I look back at the house. We are now on the northern side, and as with the farmhouse below, there is a wide veranda built for the sun. The house looks beautiful from this angle as well, with its deep windows, gray-painted wood, white walls, and the profusion of flowers bordering the deck. There is a scent of lavender in the air.

"Come," Christopher says and so I follow him through the gate and into a paddock.

Now the air smells more of rural countryside; grass and earth with a hint of dung, a waft of decay.

My cell phone rings and I stop to answer it. "Hello? This is Lin."

"Where are you?" asks Sally's voice.

"I'm at a place called Ngatirua," I reply. "In Hawke's Bay."

Christopher has paused to wait for me.

"That's a bloody long drive," she says. "Anyway, I've asked the gay guys for dinner tonight. You okay for that?"

"Sure," I reply. We say good-bye and hang up.

"Sorry," I say.

Christopher is standing facing the paddock but turns back to me, his gaze fixing just above my forehead. "Actually, I don't know if there are any of Rose's paintings in the studio either," he says. "I can't find them for you. You see, I am blind."

"Blind?" I feel foolish for not having realized his odd manner was due to lack of sight. "I am sorry, I didn't realize."

"You should come back when my wife is here." He turns and walks back to the house, with me trailing along behind.

"So this was the family farm?"

"Rose's parents' farm, yes. Vivienne and her sister inherited it from their grandparents."

"Nice that they still live so close to each other."

"They have always been close," he says. "Since they were children and their mother killed herself."

"Oh?"

"Vivienne said that Rose was devastated when her husband left her for another woman. And when he had a child with the new woman, Rose broke down completely. Vivienne found her body."

"Oh."

"Vivienne has never been able to forget her mother's agony. She hated her father. Never mentions his name." Christopher says this as he ushers me back to the front door and stands at the entrance, waiting for me to go away.

"Well, thank you for letting me take a look. I'll call," I reply.

My blind brother-in-law closes the front door, and I return to the car.

The house sits in the sun looking like a painting of a perfect home. I let out my breath in a long sigh, turn on the ignition, and wend my way back out of the hills, onto the highway again, pointing the nose of my car toward Wellington.

If I could just meet them, with a hand held out, surely there would be some kind of feeling between us, a warm feeling, of family and everything that family meant? Or did they only see me as the indirect cause of their mother's death?

The road home is long and dull. As if in sympathy with my mood, the rain starts when I reach the Rimutakas, and I slow to a crawl behind a stream of trucks grinding their cautious way up and over the pass.

When I reach the harbor, Wellington itself is gray, the clouds mirroring the grayness of the buildings and the gray sea. My car swishes along the motorway, through the wet streets, and up the hill to home.

By the time I pull into the garage I have decided to let sleeping sisters lie. For now, anyway, until I work out how to get through to them. I don't want to take the risk and hold out my hand only to see them turn away.

I walk up the path to my father's old home. All the anticipation and the enthusiasm I had been feeling have fizzled out in the rain.

I wonder, again, what the hell I am doing here, following my father's cold trail.

Chapter 9

Dirk is a big man with sandy hair and freckled skin and Jiro is small and dark and has a Japanese cast to his features.

Their accents are pure American. We play the game of establishing whereabouts in America we are from. Jiro and Dirk are L.A. from the top of their well-groomed heads to the pointy tips of their elegant footwear.

"I grew up in Portland," I say.

"Do you get home often?" Dirk asks.

"I stopped in to see my stepmother a month ago," I say. "But I wouldn't call Portland home."

"So," interjects Karim, "what movies are you guys working on?"

"*The Hobbit*," Jiro replies.

Bloody hobbits, can't get away from them.

"And where is home?" Dirk asks me.

"Ah. Home is where my clothes are. Last year Sydney. Right now, Wellington. Next year, who knows?"

"What do you think of New Zealand?" asks Jiro.

"Don't you guys start! Of course I think it's beautiful. And friendly."

"New Zealanders are the most gay-friendly people we've ever met," Jiro says. "People dislike the fact we're American more than that we're gay."

Dirk laughs. "Yeah, Kiwis think it's okay to trash Yanks. That's not being racist, is it! Not like saying anything negative about the Maori. You get crucified for criticizing Maori."

Karim frowns. "I don't find it so racist. I am doing very well."

"New Zealanders don't much like people from the countries they think are doing better than they," says Dirk. "Americans. Australians. Increasingly, the Chinese. Kiwis call it the tall-poppy syndrome. We call it small-dog syndrome."

"Although they wouldn't recognize my qualifications," says Karim.

"In America, we worship the successful and it's the poor who are disliked—especially the Mexican poor," says Dirk.

"And it was hard to get a place to rent," says Karim. "But apart from that, New Zealand has been fine."

"It could certainly be a lot worse," says Jiro. "The Japanese don't like any other races at all."

"I guess everyone is a little racist, against somebody or other," I say. "But admitting it is taboo."

Sally joins us. "What's taboo? Enjoying anal sex?"

"No, no, no!" Jiro's face flushes. "We're talking about having racist thoughts."

Dirk's eyes rest on Sally with an expression of anticipation. "And about how Kiwis suffer from small-dog syndrome. You guys are ankle biters with a chip on both shoulders."

"Americans," Sally shakes her head. "At least we are brave little dogs who do our humble best to fight back. Your lot are raving paranoids, so scared of being attacked you have to carry a gun to protect your sissy arses."

"Oh, not the gun argument!" Jiro says hastily. "Can I get you another glass of wine? What shall we open next?"

Dirk laughs and holds out a bottle. "This is a five-year-old Chardonnay from the Napa Valley."

"Damn, it's got a cork. Screw caps are easier. And they keep the wine fresh and crisp," says Sally. "At least that's what the local winemakers tell us."

"More like raw and sharp! I'd rather drink mellow and

smooth. Which means a few years under a cork so the oxygen can dribble in," Dirk replies and removes the cork for her.

I find myself relaxing with these people, interesting people, who don't notice the color of my skin, the angle of my eyes, or how I talk. I take another sip of the smooth, yellow Chardonnay.

"Have you met Peter Jackson?" asks Karim. "Is he cool?"

"In a hairy sort of way," Dirk replies.

"Do you get to meet all the stars? What are they like?"

"Like normal people," Dirk says. "They eat, they drink, and they shit, just like the rest of us."

Michael darts back into the room with napkins and lays them carefully on the plates. He has laid the tables with the knives and forks reversed. At least I hope it was Michael. I'd hate to think our resident pathologist doesn't know her right from her left.

Sally has roasted a large piece of lamb, with potatoes and *kumara*, the sweet potato they eat here, and cauliflower with cheese and peas. Sally carries in the lamb. Polly pads hopefully behind her and lies at our feet, licking her chops.

The meat has a hot kick. "Cayenne pepper smeared over the surface," says Sally. "The gravy is made with butter and red wine."

"Butter?" asks Dirk anxiously, holding the gravy boat as if it is poison.

"Don't be afraid," coos Sally. "It won't hurt you so long as you drink red wine as well."

I pick up the red wine bottle to examine the label. "Martinborough. People keep telling me I should visit the wineries."

"Are you going to the Martinborough Wine Festival?" asks Sally.

"I'd like to see more of New Zealand," I say. "Ask me again, closer to the date."

Michael carefully clears away the dishes. Polly scoots into the kitchen before him and waits by her bowl, tail high and eyes alert. She is rewarded with the scraps, makes a strangled yelp as the cayenne hits, and submerges her nose in her water bowl.

Sally brings out a large white dessert covered with fruit, sitting on a crystal platter.

"Pavlova!" she cries, brandishing a butcher's knife.

She cuts portions and slides the slices onto our plates. The meringue has a soft marshmallow center, a chewy outer layer, and a crisp shell, and is piled with fresh whipped cream, raspberries, slices of green kiwis, and chunks of yellow pineapple. Silence falls, eventually broken by the sound of spoons scraping on empty plates.

Sally takes Michael to his room, and Karim heads out to a night shift, leaving the Americans alone at the table.

"What do you think of Kiwis?" asks Jiro.

"They're—I was about to say nice, but that's such a favorite Kiwi word!" I reply. "I'm slipping into Kiwisms."

"*Nice* reflects the Kiwi very well," says Dirk. "*Nice* has a connotation of pleasantness in a modest kind of way, a way that doesn't aim for anything outstanding."

Jiro adds, "If you want to please a Kiwi, you don't compliment them on anything special they've achieved as an individual, all you need do is tell them what a great country it is."

Dirk laughs. "Yeah, they love being told New Zealand is beautiful. It's easier than complimenting people on how they look. The women wear too much black—black tops, black trousers, flat black shoes. All Blacks, eh? Nothing too distinctive. And the men make no effort at all. Gray, gray, gray."

"It's a good lifestyle, though," says Jiro. "Good wine and food, not corrupt, safe."

"But expensive," adds Dirk. "Everything is expensive to buy." He looks at me with a slight smile. "Are you thinking of settling here, Lin? Do you think you can hack it?"

"Maybe. As you say, they are very friendly people. They make you feel at home."

"At home? Yes, but only if you keep telling us we're wonderful," Sally returns to the table with a platter of cheeses.

"You're wonderful, Sally!" I reply, and smile up at my wonderful Kiwi friend.

Upstairs I put the leftover piece of Pavlova in the refrigerator to eat for breakfast and sit gazing out on Wellington. Okay, so I've found my sisters, but I can't see any way to meet them that will work out well. I think I'll just have to park that possibility for now.

Instead, I open up my laptop and start an e-mail. I write that I've got a job in Wellington, a good one, for six months anyway, and that I've applied for a New Zealand passport.

I write how I am enjoying the city and my friend Sally, a pathologist who drinks a little too much. I write that I have found my sisters but I haven't met them yet.

I'm making myself a home here, I say.

I read the email, make a couple of corrections, push the cursor up to the SEND icon, and pause.

The wine sings through my brain, telling me to reach out and take the risk. I read the draft again but it isn't quite right, or maybe I'm just not ready.

Instead of pressing SEND, I save the draft, close my laptop down, and head to bed.

.

Chapter 10

Projects have three parameters—money, time, and functionality. If you're good, you manage to hit one of these. If you're very good as well as lucky, you might hit two of them. But never all three. So, as in life, something has to give, and you have to compromise.

Sometimes you have to spend more; sometimes you have to take more time. Sometimes you reduce the scope of what you're trying to deliver, or defer parts of the functionality until a later date. Sometimes the best solution is to accept lesser quality in areas where quality is not so critical.

The hard part is knowing which compromises to make and what risks you can afford to take. That is where my skill comes in.

In the boardroom, chief consultant Scott Peake is presenting his summary of the support systems options to Hera's executive team. He smiles widely as he turns from the screen to face us. He is a great smiler, is Scott.

"The first option, from VNL, is what we call the 'Best of Breed' solution, based on the leading packages in each of the areas and integrated using an enterprise service bus."

His eyes move from Ian to Fred before finally resting on Tom's face. He doesn't look at me or at Deepak. I don't take it personally. He hasn't liked me ever since I asked him to explain the figures in the summary and then asked for the source documents so I could check what he said. I haven't liked him since he refused to give me the documents, telling me it was important to interpret the information correctly, and he didn't want any misunderstandings. I looked into Peake's eyes then and saw what lay behind. Dollar signs, mainly, for himself and his consulting firm.

"These are the costs."

All told, the costs total $20 million, which made me want to do a bit of interpreting myself.

"That is far higher than we were expecting," says Deepak.

"We can't afford to cut corners," says Tom.

"I am very sorry, but it is way over our budget," Deepak says.

"We can do anything we want with these packages," says Ian, his head bobbing excitedly as he speaks.

Deepak looks down at his hands, and Peake moves on.

"The second option is based on a version of Kiwicom's systems," he says. "Their vendor, LCNS, has proposed a lease arrangement. The costs look like this," and he shows a different set of colored slides.

Deepak's face is anxious. "Not as expensive," he says. "But still beyond our budget."

Tom says, "The technology is proprietary. We would be locked in."

"And it's a really old system," says Ian. "We wouldn't be able to differentiate ourselves from Kiwicom."

"Is there a third option?' I ask.

"No," says Peake. "The other proposals are from the individual vendors of the packages, so each only covers part of the picture."

Fred blinks rapidly behind his gold-rimmed spectacles, opens his mouth, then closes it and stays silent.

"So we're agreed then," says Tom. "We go with VNL's proposal."

"Hear, hear," says Ian.

Deepak hunches his shoulders and says nothing. Fred blinks again and looks down.

"Great, I'll get the contracts started," says Peake.

"Just a minute," I say, raising my hand in a gesture that says stop. "I don't believe we have enough information to be confident we're making the best decision. I'd like to go through the detailed proposals."

"We completed the evaluation against the agreed criteria using the weightings that were signed off," says Peake. He doesn't look at me, he looks at Tom.

"I'm not confident we established all the options."

"That was the process we agreed," Tom says, frowning.

"But the proposal is costing far more than we budgeted. I'm not comfortable with the recommendation, Tom. I'm not prepared to present it to the Board until we've done more work."

Peake heaves a gusty sigh and closes down the presentation, still without meeting my gaze.

"Thanks for the preso," Tom says. "Let's talk about where to next."

As they leave the room together, I hear Peake say, "Another hissy fit from the prissy chink," and I hear Tom laugh.

Peake glances back and smirks when he sees I heard him. My blood starts pumping faster, but my face is calm, my Asian eyes still. His smirk widens to a triumphant grin.

Tom calls me into his office. "Scott's pretty upset with your attitude, Lin." When he leans forward, a manly scent of pine and spice tickles my nostrils. "They've spent a lot of time on the evaluation."

"I'm not impressed with how much time and money has been spent on the evaluation just to propose an outcome we can't afford."

"There are no other solutions."

"There have to be," I reply.

A rare uncertain expression flickers across his face. "I'll talk to Scott," he says.

"Scott is a—" I almost say cocksucker but I'm not going to descend into the same behavior.

Tom's smile is perfunctory. "Don't get hot under the collar."

I pause, my blood starting to race, but he just nods and turns back to his PC, so I leave his office and head up the stairs. I hesitate at the door to the level where my own office is located, and examine the gray-green linoleum of the stairwell floor, scuffed with the scurryings of a thousand workers' feet. Then I sigh and carry on up the stairs to Adam's office two floors above.

"They'll have to increase the budget," he says when I explain our dilemma.

"They may not be prepared to," I reply.

Adam rubs his eyes. "We'll let them know the situation and see what they say."

"We start pouring concrete next week," I tell the Board. "If all goes according to plan, we should have the switch building ready by mid-December."

"Scott tells me you're making some questionable compromises," Stanton says.

I slip my right hand onto my left wrist. Calm.

"These are the plans we've worked on as a team," I say.

Stanton and Hobb exchange glances.

"On the next slide we have the systems implementation," and I bring up the next Gantt chart.

"Cost is the major issue," I say. "We're still pulling the figures together on the various options, but none of the proposals fall within our budget. The consultants are going through everything line by line to see what we can do to bring the estimates down."

"We're not increasing the budget any further." Robert is looking grim. "It's already higher than the original business case."

I look around the table to gauge the atmosphere. All faces look stern.

Stanton scowls. "Do you hear? Get the costs back down."

The dark rings under Adam's eyes seem to deepen. He opens

his mouth, but no words emerge. Sweat bubbles on his forehead.

"There might be some options we can look into," I say hastily, distracting the eyes of the Board from Adam's face.

"Then look into them, but don't let us hear you're taking any risks," says Stanton.

Yeah, right! As they say here.

Corporate Kiwis are much the same as other corporate cultures, I've found. The risk averse always seem to outweigh the risk takers.

Perhaps a little more so here, in Wellington, seat of the Government. And in New Zealand if you take a risk and succeed, they eye you with suspicion, because you might be that dangerous thing, a tall poppy.

But if you take a risk and fail, they crucify you.

Chapter 11

Self-serving, sparing with the truth on the rare occasions he's acquainted with it, Scott Peake preys on my sleep for the next few nights.

If I complain that Peake insults and undermines me, they'll be reassured in their judgment of women as needy, whiny, de facto hysterics. Moreover, in the ways of corporate politics the fact Peake has insulted me makes it more difficult, not less, to challenge his arguments. There will be an assumption of automatic bias, as if my anger must cloud my judgment. Particularly as a woman. Anger in corporate men shows strength; anger in corporate women just shows hysteria.

I could talk to Robert, but he'll tell me to suck it up, and he'll consider me weak and not put me forward for the tough jobs again. You can't expect kindness from Robert, I know that.

It is just words, and I'd rather be judged by actions or inactions than by that which is merely spoken, so I decide to say nothing about Peake's snide attacks.

But I can't put aside my concern about the consultant's approach to our systems. We can't afford to spend the money in Peake's plan. There's got to be another option or Hera is doomed.

If you challenge a powerful man, you're more likely to be labeled "not a team player" than admired for your courage. If you're a woman, you'll be labeled "a bitch" as well. It is the way of the corporate world. And there are quite a few outstandingly awful corporate bitches who have prepared this path for the rest of us.

I try hard not to be a bitch. I'd rather be called a bastard than a bitch, because, of course, I am a bastard. So what?

Adam has been looking even more stressed of late. I wish I could help him cope with the conflicting pressures, the dilemmas he's constantly facing as Hera's chief executive, but he's not the sort of man who takes advice from a woman.

In her role as director of human resouces, Marion managed the process to select Hera's executive team. She'd chosen a group of people with different skills and different personalities, but who all had one thing in common. Like her, they all had hearts—or that empathy and care for others that we think of as coming from the heart and which, according to the article, psychopaths lack.

Having a heart is not necessarily a common trait amongst leaders. It is remarkable how often leaders are selected first on their self-confidence and ability to talk. The top-dog attitude is so often based on arrogant self-satisfaction, and not the natural confidence that comes with achievement. Caring about people ranks farther down the list, especially for roles in the commercial world where they want you to be strong and sharp and focus on the bottom line.

Adam, our chief executive is a nice man, a decent man, but maybe not quite tough enough to make the hard decisions that need to be made when you face the challenges Hera faces.

Adam's blocky figure is encased in a tight t-shirt, baggy shorts, and brand-new sneakers.

"Is this a bad time?"

"Not if you're quick," he says. "I'm going for a run."

"We need to go through the costs and find some ways of bringing them down."

"Not quick then." He sighs. "Can you come back at two?"

We walk to the elevator together, although I plan to take the stairs. "Where do you run?" I ask.

"To the waterfront and around the harbor. Running is

great," he says. "Makes me feel so alive! You should try it some-time."

"I prefer to walk," I reply. "I only run when I'm scared."

Adam's face relaxes in a smile. "And not much scares you, does it, Lin?" The elevator doors open and he gets in. "I'll see you at two."

It is true that not much scares me. When it comes to conflict, my first response is fight, not flight. I am not afraid of people, perhaps because I've never been physically hurt by anyone. While I wouldn't claim my childhood was close and loving, I wasn't beaten or abused, no stranger attacked me on the way home, and no date raped me in my room.

My greatest fear is irrational—being enclosed in a small, tight space. I hate elevators, and you would never catch me canyoning, one of this country's more adventurous sports. I much prefer to stick with the wide-open spaces. And so instead of joining Adam in the elevator, I walk down the stairs to the company's kitchen on the first floor. The office provides a coffee machine, teabags, and, of course, fresh milk. The Kiwis are very precious about their milk, like the French about their baguettes. Not for Kiwis the white paint mix that Yanks use to color their coffee.

I make myself a flat white, slide a coin into the chocolate machine, and smile at the workers sitting at the tables eating their packed lunches. Conversation stills for a moment, but then Helen shuffles along.

"Join us, Lin."

I smile and sit beside her. Helen is eating a large bowl of pasta with walnuts, drowning in oil.

"You like dressing?" I ask.

She laughs. "It's the Mediterranean diet. I make sure I have lots of nuts and olive oil every day."

The woman beside her opens her plastic container, which has two compartments, one holding pie and the other a stick of celery and a morsel of ham.

"I'm on one of the fasting days for my five-to-two diet," she says, her expression morose. She tilts her wrist to look at her watch. "But in another thirty-five minutes, I'm eating the pie."

They look at my Moro bar. "What diet is that?"

"The I-left-too-early-to-make-lunch diet," I reply. "Works for me."

When I arrive back at Adam's office, Helen is still on her lunch break. His door is slightly ajar. I knock and enter the room. "Boss?"

He is not in his chair. I look beyond the desk to the view over the harbor. The weather is mixed today. The sky is a pallid blue and a long cloud hovers over the hills. As usual, the wind is blowing. I can see yachts out on the water, their sails billowing in the breeze.

On Adam's desk are three photographs. A beautiful young Asian woman smiles out of one. Filipino, perhaps? The second is of Adam holding a baby wrapped in a long white shawl. I look closer at the third photograph, which shows Adam with the beautiful woman, this time dressed as the bridal couple. So it must be his baby then, not a grandchild.

A common story: a rich and successful older man snaring, or snared by, a much younger woman. Did he dump a first Mrs. Challoner for this gorgeous Asian beauty? I wonder idly before turning to leave the office.

I catch my breath. Adam lies curled on the floor behind the door, still in his running clothes. His head is twisted to one side, his face flattened against the pale carpet. His right eye stares blankly at me. I kneel down and take his wrist, feeling for a pulse. But there is none.

I stretch out to brush the hair away from his face. *Poor man. I am so sorry I couldn't help you.* Then I put my lips to his mouth and try to blow life into him, then I press his chest to make his heart beat again.

"Helen!" I call out, hearing the bustle of her return. I sit over him, shielding her from him, or him from her, I don't know. "Call an ambulance. Adam's had a heart attack."

"Ohhh," she says, covering her mouth with her hands. "Is he all right?"

I press his chest again and shake my head.

Chapter 12

The funeral is held at Old St Paul's Cathedral on Mulgrave Street. I pity the young widow sitting by herself in the front pew, veiled and silent. Afterward, when the casket has made its stately way down the aisle on the shoulders of Adam's first family, she seems uncertain what she is supposed to do next. When I approach and introduce myself, she thanks me for trying to save him and starts crying. I look around desperately until Marion comes over and takes the sad girl into her kind arms.

Tom and I flee to the foyer to drink stewed tea and eat sweet, dry biscuits.

Marion arrives ten minutes later.

"Is she okay?" I ask.

She shakes her head. "She is lost without him."

"Adam's child bride," says Tom, and shakes his head as well.

As I sip the harsh tea, I push away the memory of Adam's dead eyes, and try instead to remember the photographs on his shelf, the beautiful bride and the baby wrapped in white.

In them, he looked happy, before the stress built up and stopped his heart beating, leaving a young widow alone in a strange land and yet another child to grow up without a father.

Now we sit in Tom's office wondering what kind of leader the Board will choose to replace Adam. Ian flings his arms about like Laurence Olivier and talks of discussions with the agency over Hera's brand. Fred sits at one end of the table and Deepak at the other, wearing matching worried frowns. Tom leans forward, his hands moving restlessly across the papers, but his dark eyes are hooded. Marion smiles her calm smile and nods as each person gives an update on the week's work.

I look down at my charts and worry about the time passing. We are in limbo. Nothing is going to get decided on the project while there is no chief executive.

After an hour, the Board calls me in. The atmosphere is cool. All five men sit a yard apart from each other, faces unsmiling.

"We need a fresh pair of eyes," Robert says. "I've told them I think you're an excellent judge of people. Tell us what you think of Hera's executive team."

I gaze around the faces for a moment, reflecting on what I should say.

"Ian is everything you need in a marketing director," I tell them. "Imaginative, enthusiastic, optimistic. But he is only thirty and has limited experience in the rest of the business."

"Young," says Dao. Hobb grunts in agreement.

"Deepak has extensive business experience, and an exceptional grasp on how best to deploy money. I've found his judgment to be very sound. I guess if he has any fault it's that he's not forceful enough."

"Lacks confidence," states Stanton.

"He is a very courteous man. Marion is—"

"I don't think we're interested in Mrs. King," he interjects. "A good woman, no doubt, but hardly of the stature we need to be chief executive."

"Fred is an excellent IT manager," I continue. "The best I've worked with. But I doubt if he'd be remotely interested in taking on the CEO role. He is just too *nice*."

"And Heke?" asks Lane.

"Tom is a very good operations manager," I say. "He is confident, and he knows the technology very well."

"But?" asks Robert.

I pause before replying. "I don't think he is very good at making tough decisions. I think he is out of his depth in any project that requires a major leap into something new."

"But if he has Green for new ideas and Gupta for the financial analysis?" Lane asks.

"And Lin to drive things along," adds Robert.

"Don't get me wrong," I add. "Tom is a terrific manager and for any organization in a more stable situation he would be an outstanding chief executive. But I don't think he is the best candidate when the role requires stepping outside of standard practice and into the unknown."

The men fall silent.

"What about that woman who used to run the local telco?" asks Stewart Hobb.

"Tania Gates? No," says Stanton. His nose curls with disgust. "Too emotional." He glances around the table. "I have several good candidates in mind. Men I know well.

"Linnette, you can go now," he says.

"It's Linnet."

"Whatever."

Tom, Ian, and Deepak are hovering around my desk.

"Did they say anything about who will replace Adam?"

"I think they're looking at some mate of Stanton's," I reply.

"Shit."

"Bummer."

"Blast."

"Yeah."

When the Board breaks for tea, Robert says he wants some fresh air and tells me to join him. We walk across to the civic center and find a coffee bar.

"What did you decide?" I ask.

"We haven't," he says. "Stanton's mates will take too long to come on board. We can't afford to be without a CEO for two months or more. It is too critical a period."

"I guess you could appoint someone to act in the meantime."

"We could."

"Who? Tom?"

"Maybe. He's offered to step in. Do you think he could handle things for a couple of months?"

"Perhaps."

Inwardly, I wince as I think about Tom's conservative approach. And then I let myself think about how it might feel to be the chief executive of Hera. Being a chief executive wasn't something I'd ever considered. Oh, of course, you dream you might climb that high, but so few do that it's not an ambition I'd ever dwelled on. And yet, and yet, why not?

I could make the decisions I knew had to be made. *I* could lead the way I thought a leader should lead.

Did I know enough? But the rest of the team was strong. Anything I didn't know was well covered by Deepak, Fred, Ian, Marion, and Tom. We were a perfect team.

Tom! How could I do this to him? He had the best right to this job. And yet I knew, I knew he could not bring Hera to the launch date as well as I. I knew he could not achieve as much with our few resources as I.

Sometimes there's a time and tide in your life that waits for no man. Or woman.

"What about me?"

Robert sips his coffee. "You?"

"I'm smart, I'm decisive, and I've got the right experience. And I know what needs to be done and how to get it done. Why can't I throw my hat in the ring?"

"This is a hard job. Are you tough enough?"

"I'm strong."

"Not quite the same thing as being tough. And you're a maverick, Lin. Useful when the going gets rough, but a liability when you have to deal with the Government, and the media, and all the other players in this game."

"I can be diplomatic when I need to be," I say. "Haven't I

been polite to Adam and Tom and to the Board even when I thought they were goddamn fools?"

"It's a thin veneer," he says. "And the job will require absolute commitment."

"I don't have any family," I reply. "No husband, no children, no parents. No distractions."

"I'm not sticking my neck out for you on this one, Lin. Don't go expecting that."

I've pushed too hard. Time to back off. I shrug. "I expect nothing, Robert. All I ask is that you consider me as another option."

Robert's eyes lose focus. He puts down his empty cup to look at his watch. "I'd better get back to the meeting."

I try to focus on the financials in my spreadsheet, but when I think about the opportunity to be chief executive, to be right at the top of that ladder, my heart starts beating faster and the blood pumps thud, thud, thud, so I get up and pace back and forth across the room.

I want the job. I *want* it.

Chapter 13

Why is it taking them so long? I send Robert a text asking him how much longer. He doesn't reply.

I get up and pace back and forth, sit down, try to work, give up, stand and pace again. I'd been in my profession for seventeen, going on eighteen years, climbing that ladder, rung by rung, success by success. I'd moved rapidly into being a manager, not because I was one of the effortless confident leaders who could always assume they would be the one people would follow, but because I was damned good at what I did. I never failed to deliver. I argued for what I thought was the right way, and then proved myself correct. I recognized good people, listened to them, and made sure to pull them together into a team.

Robert used to complain I argued too much, but if you know what to do, it's your duty to make sure it happens. Not for me the political silences and the working through others and the patient oblique influencing. I preferred blunt talk and direct action.

And that is what Hera was going to need if we were to have any chance of building our business from the bare earth of the switch site on the Petone shore, through the streets of the Hutt Valley, and into Wellington and this office.

I'm still at my desk when Robert finally reappears. He stands beside me, looking over my shoulder at the figures.

"How are the finances tracking?"

"This month is okay, but once the software project kicks in we'll have much more of a challenge staying within budget."

Robert sighs. "This business keeps getting more expensive. Sometimes I wonder whether we should have stayed out of it."

"Do your investors have big pockets?"

"Big pockets but small stomachs."

"Are you going to back out?"

"Not yet. We made a decision on Adam's replacement."

"It took you guys a while," I say. *Come on, Robert, spit it out.*

"Stanton was pretty keen to go with his Old Boy network."

"It's a specialized business," I reply. "Telco knowledge is important."

"Hobb wanted to bring in one of his executives from Ozcom. Obviously, with a lot of telco experience."

"The challenger culture is different. I doubt if any of the Ozcom managers would know how to move fast and with so few people."

"More relevant is that Lane is from the South Island and the only people South Islanders dislike more than Aucklanders are Australians. Lane preferred your friend Heke."

"Tom would be a good choice." *Although not as good as me.*

"The three of them ended up deadlocked. Dao, on the other hand, liked the look of you, Lin, probably in more ways than one. He said you would best represent the multicultural aspect of Hera."

A man with excellent judgment. "Et tu, Robert?"

"I thought any chance of meeting the deadline would be screwed if we lost momentum by bringing in someone new. And yet I wasn't confident Heke could do it."

"So?"

"Then Lane realized he didn't have enough support for Heke and changed his choice."

"And so?"

Robert picks up the box of business cards I have on my desk

and takes one out, examining the company's logo. "I hate the color," he says. "It's so—purple."

"Violet," I correct him.

"I bet you had a hand in choosing it, Lin. Nothing too dull for you, eh?"

I wait impatiently while he toys with me.

He tosses the box into the wastepaper basket. "You'd better get some new business cards. The job is yours."

"Cool," I reply. But it is a warm sensation that fills my body, from my stomach out to the tips of my fingers and toes.

"For the next six months you're going to have to eat, drink, and breathe Hera. No running back to lover boy."

Robert and I share stares. "I told you that was finished," I say.

"And if he calls to tell you he wants you back?"

"*I* don't want *him*!" I reply. "It's over."

"You'll be a target, you realize? A foreigner and a woman? If you have a weakness, they'll find it. If you make a mistake, they'll crucify you for it."

"I will be Caesar's wife."

"There's always something, Lin, that can bring you down. Maybe in the job, maybe in your private life. The trick is to see it coming and get it before it gets you."

"I promise you, *nothing* will bring me down."

The management team gathers in the boardroom and Robert makes the announcement. They take it well, even Tom.

He puts his hand on my shoulder and says, "Well done that girl!"

Suddenly the glow dims a little. Then I tell myself, *all's fair in love and war* and *the best man won* and other sad clichés to make myself feel like I didn't just shit on him. But my intentions are good. *My intentions were good.*

I dress carefully in conservative black linen. When I enter the restaurant, five pairs of eyes observe me critically as I walk to the table. Lane stands and holds out his hand to congratulate me, then pulls out a chair.

Dao gives me a smile and a small nod of his head. Hobb also nods but without the smile, and Stanton shows me his teeth.

"Well done, Linnette, I'm sure you'll do an excellent job."

Robert pours me a glass of wine and they toast me.

I put on the polite smile, supping on the French chef's filet and sipping on a single glass of Pinot Noir that smells of sweat and saddles, and leave them to their port when the jokes become too masculine and the laughter too loud.

When I arrive home, I take out the bottle of bubbly and slip into the Jacuzzi. I lie in the steaming water, drinking my wine, smoking a cigarillo, and looking out over Wellington.

Tonight the water and the wine don't relax me. Instead the blood pumps fast through my arteries. Fantastic opportunity. Terrific challenge. Huge responsibility. Thud, thud, thud through my neck, my head, my brain. Eat, drink, breathe Hera. There will never be a chance like this again. Thud, thud, thud.

Eventually, I clamber out of the water, pull on my robe, and sit down at the table. I open the draft of the e-mail I have been writing to Ben. I read my words again, but this time there are no improvements to make.

I hold my head in my hands while the sky spins slowly and my stomach churns.

I could send the email. Tell Ben I love him and ask if we can fix what went wrong. Ask him to forgive me.

Instead, I delete the e-mail.

Part II

Woman at the Top

Chapter 14

At night and in the morning, before the meetings start, my brain is full of ideas and options and plans for what to do. It is as well I have that time to think because during the day and into the evening I meet with staff, our lawyers, the public relations agency, the accountants, and barely have time to clear my e-mails before nine p.m.

In the brief moments between meetings, my gaze returns to the corner where Adam died. If I close my eyes, I can see him, the sparse gray hair messed up and his eye staring into nothingness. They said it was fast. I hope he didn't feel any pain.

I pace the room before making up my mind. The desk is heavy, but I tug and twist and shuffle it around so the window is beside my chair and I won't be staring at that corner. Instead, I will gaze out at the sea. I shift the bookshelf behind the door to cover the spot where Adam lay. Then the table has to be moved as well to balance the space.

I sit down at the desk and run my fingers across the golden wood, shot through with flecks of caramel, then glance around the innocuous room.

Better.

Two days later, I get in to the office early, open my laptop, and sip on my take-out coffee. While I wait for my overnight emails and my day's appointments to appear, I glance across at the corner where the bookshelf now stands. Instead of family photographs, three large glass bowls adorn the shelves; one in chartreuse and lavender, one in shades of pink and cobalt, and the tallest an acid-yellow mixed with violet.

This is *my* office now.

I wash my hands in the executive bathroom; *my* bathroom, the toilet seat firmly set down, and stare at my face in the mirror. Framed by shoulder-length red hair my dark, slanted eyes gaze back without expression. I stretch my mouth into a polite, executive smile. I practice my smile again, and then for a third time. The eyes stay still. *Good.*

I tuck the ends of my hair behind my ears. *Better.*

Then I fish out a smart set of red-framed spectacles and put them on. This is my new image: chief executive Lin. *Perfect.*

That night I leave early and get home just before seven and turn on the television.

Men in black appear, moving in slow motion and in soft focus across the screen. It is an advertisement celebrating New Zealand's beloved All Blacks, the national team for the national sport of rugby. Although from what I can see they are nearly All Brown. Now they are taking off their jerseys. I watch, entranced, but they go no farther. Teasers!

Finally, the ads end and the current-affairs program starts up. The presenter is a pretty boy who wears nearly as much makeup as they put on me. But I'm not complaining because he was really *very nice*. The camera zooms onto my face.

Wearing my specs and with my hair drawn back behind my ears, I think I look intellectual and authoritative. And less Asian.

"Welcome to Linnette Mere, the new chief executive of Hera, the international company that is trying to join the broadband race," he says, cocking his head to one side. "Congratulations on the new job!"

I watch myself smile politely back. Smiles are important on television, but you have to get it right. Not too wide, not too small. "Actually, my name is pronounced Linnet," I say. "The little bird with a sweet voice."

"Sweet, sweet. As a woman, were you surprised to get the nod?"

"New Zealand has a great record where women are concerned," I reply. "The first country to give women the vote." I don't mention that several American states beat New Zealand to this; no one likes a smart-ass, especially New Zealanders. "And, of course, not long ago women held most of the senior posts in this country: prime minister, governor-general, chief justice, CEO of the second largest company—"

He nods, happy to hear about Kiwis leading the world in something or other. Then he assumes a serious expression. "Why do you think a foreign company should be allowed to be part of New Zealand's new network?"

The image of me again smiles politely. "Hera is a New Zealand company, Barney, staffed mainly by New Zealanders."

Barney looks at me sternly. "But partly owned by foreigners. How do we reconcile selling our assets to overseas companies?"

"Hera is looking forward to investing in building those assets in the first place, Barney. We're very excited about the chance to be part of another world-leading initiative by New Zealand."

He leans forward and fixes me with what he probably thinks is an eaglelike stare. "Your appointment took many commentators by surprise. Why do you think an American got the job instead of the position going to a New Zealander?"

"Well," the image of me is saying, "my father taught at one of the universities here and he told me so much about this beautiful country, that when the opportunity arose, I jumped at the chance to see New Zealand for myself."

I didn't admit he'd got one of his students pregnant. I certainly didn't tell them he was a hothead, a drunkard, and a philanderer.

"Your dad lived here? That's fantastic!"

"And, actually, Barney, I was even born here."

I didn't mention that after I was born, his wife killed herself, and my mother went back to Macau.

Barney's eyes goggle. "Linnet! That makes you a Kiwi!"

"I'm not sure if it does or not. I left when I was a child."

I didn't describe how he was accused of murder and, although the coroner concluded Rose's death was suicide, he was sacked and hounded out of the country by the media, his academic career in tatters.

Barney is now beaming at me. "So our very own Linnet Mere has been chosen to head up Hera. How are you enjoying being back in New Zealand?"

"I love being here. It's such a beautiful country, and everyone is so friendly."

Barney turns back to the camera and says, "Well, we're certainly pleased to have heard from Linnet Mere, the new Kiwi chief executive for Hera. Thank you, Linnet."

And the cameras cut and the light was turned back on, and Barney dropped his smile and I rubbed the space between my eyes where the spectacle frames were pinching, and then everyone smiled again and someone said "that went well" and I vanished behind the scenes while Barney interviewed the aunt of some murder victim bewailing—whatever.

I lie in the Jacuzzi, smoking and sipping Sauvignon Blanc, still feeling charged about being on TV.

Look at me now, Steve and Hilary; not such a sad little cuckoo after all, huh? Look at me now, Ralph, Mike, Ted, and Sean. I'm famous. Don't you wish you'd stuck with me?

But I can't tell the person I most wish to about my success. She wouldn't understand.

When Mom stopped replying to my e-mails, I assumed it was because Steve and his young wife, Mary, had just presented her with twin grandchildren and she no longer had room for the little cuckoo she'd nurtured for so long. When my birthday passed and no present arrived, I thought she'd finally decided I was too old for gifts. When I telephoned and she didn't answer, I assumed she was away visiting Steve or maybe staying with Hilary in New York. I left a message, but she didn't call me back. To my shame, three months passed without hearing from her before I contacted Steve to ask if she was okay.

Nah, he'd said. She's lost it.

I flew over to see her in the home they'd put her in when she'd started wandering to the shops in her nightdress.

Dear Mom. I can still see her anxious face when I came into her room. She knew she was supposed to know me, but the memory of my name was gone. "It's Lin," I said. "Your step-daughter."

"Lin!" she cried, and her eyes relaxed and she smiled happily. "Of course, it's you. How are you, dear? I like your shoes, are they new?"

"No, Mom, I bought them a while ago, but they are nice, aren't they?" I'd said, and gave her the Swiss chocolates I brought.

"Thank you, dear," she said. "I like your shoes. Are they new?"

The next time I visited there was no light in her eyes at all. She didn't notice my shoes. She didn't notice anything at all. I seldom cry, but that day I wept all the way to the airport. Very little of Mom was still there. Her body now grown frail and her mind mostly departed, I felt I'd lost my only family.

Dear Mom. I took you too much for granted. I wish I'd told you how much I loved you before it was too late.

It was then I decided to find my sisters, so I wouldn't have to feel so alone in the world. Vivienne and Alison, did you see me tonight? Did you hear me stake my claim to our father?

•　　•　　•

I drag myself out only when my eyelids start to droop. Although I long for the embrace of the crisp white sheets of my bed, I stop at the table and check my e-mail.

In my in-box are notes from Marion and Ian and from several other members of the staff. Two suppliers obsequiously register their congratulations. A request for an interview from a journalist from a business magazine. Three salespeople wanting to sell me something.

And—an e-mail from Emmy. The last wisps of alcohol vanish from my brain. Little Emmy, half brat and half sweet kid. Growing up in leaps and bounds, faster than her father could bear. I couldn't help resenting the hold she had over him. *What's that hanging off Emmy's little finger?* I'd ask. *Oh, it's Ben,* I'd answer.

Although I admired his devotion to his daughter, I wished he had more for me.

I open the message.

> Dear Lin, I just heard that you're down here in New Zealand! I hope you're going to come and visit. Dad didn't say what happened, just that you and he had broken up and he didn't know if we'd see you again.
>
> Anyway, I just wanted to say hi, and that Dad misses you and I do too, so I hope you can visit us. Maybe you and Dad can sort it out?
>
> Love, Emmy

Now, how was I to reply? Insult her with prevarication or hurt her with the truth?

Chapter 15

In the room the men come and go, talking of ultrafast broadband.

For my first public event as Hera's CEO, I wear a dark-gray suit with a skirt that ends just below the knee and a pair of modest heels. No cleavage, no thigh, no toes, nothing see-through and nothing too tight. Definitely nothing that says "fuck me." Women chief executives do not seek to be fucked.

There is a crowd around the chief executive of the country's incumbent Kiwicom. Although run by foreigners and owned by mainly foreign investors, they are still considered "the local" telco. As Tom and I pause at the entrance to the room, a short man with a thick moustache peels away from the group and approaches us. Tom introduces him as chairman of the Telecommunications Forum, but I am so busy basking in my new title I forget to listen to his name.

Another two men leave the group and join us. Their eyes quickly skim my figure before settling on my face. One is partner-manager for Kiwicom, and the younger of the two is a management consultant specializing in transformations, he tells me. He has a quick line of banter that breaks the ice.

I practice my executive smile. Although I know these men are not interested in Lin the person, only in Lin Mere, chief executive, it is hard not to enjoy the attention.

A young waitress holds out a tray and offers me a miniature hamburger, an inch in diameter, stuck on a toothpick flying a Kiwi flag.

"Pretty," I say, and take one. I try not to eye the tray too eagerly. I missed lunch and I'm hungry.

"Yes, they're from Ruth Pretty Catering. Top up?" she gestures with the bottle. I shake my head. I will wet my lips, I will not drink.

A fair-haired man with a hawkish nose and a square jaw greets me. "Luke Holden," he says and reaches out a well-manicured hand. "You must be Linnette Mere." He holds my hand a second too long.

"Linnet," I reply. "Are you in the telecommunications business too?"

He smiles ruefully. "Afraid so. Is your husband with you?"

"I don't have a husband."

"Boyfriend?"

I shake my head. "Not even a cat. And you?"

Luke is signaling the waitress. "Let me get you a drink," and he places a glass of red wine in my hand and smiles down at me. "Bit of a crush tonight. Do you know many people here?"

I am whisked around the room to meet more guests. Tom catches up with us and takes my arm.

"I must take Lin to meet—" he says and starts to move away.

"So you'll join me at the ballet?" Luke asks, his eyes creasing into a smile just for me.

"I would like that."

I smile back with a real smile as Tom pulls me away.

"Henry, meet Lin Mere. Lin, Dr. Grey chairs the technology committee."

A thin man holds out a limp hand and gives mine a perfunctory shake.

"American," he says, accusingly.

"Nice to meet you," I reply.

Dr. Grey grunts. "Tom, give me a call next week," and he moves away.

Luke appears beside me and puts his hand on my arm. "Do you want to meet Wilson?" he asks.

"Does he still have any power?"

"Not much," says Tom, glaring at Luke.

"But his opinion influences others," Luke says.

So we thread our way through the gaggle to where an older gentleman with a lined face, hairy brows, and a tired brown suit, is accepting homage by the window. He does not look out onto the city that sparkles beneath us. Instead, he looks down at his hands, busy demonstrating the latest technological masterpiece given him by some sycophant.

The old guy looks at Luke and nods in recognition but does not relinquish his new toy. Luke introduces us and Wilson studies me briefly.

"Do you know Larry Ellison?" he asks.

"No," I reply.

"Bill?"

Which one? Although it doesn't matter because I don't know either Clinton or Gates. I shake my head. "No."

Wilson grunts and turns back to his toy.

"Sorry," says Luke with a quick smile as we move away and leave the aging politico to the admiration of his cronies. "He's a bit of a fame groupie these days."

Tom takes my arm, swinging me away from Luke's genial presence and leads me to a tall woman with a calm face and dark hair pulled back in a small bun that rests on the back of her neck.

"Georgette Meyer," Tom says. "This is Lin Mere, our new chief executive. Georgette is the associate minister for the broadband initiative."

Georgette gives me a large hand to shake.

"Congratulations on the new job. We're looking forward to Hera's involvement," she says. "We need more international investment."

"But as a junior partner," I say.

Georgette nods. "As a junior partner. No selling off the crown jewels to foreigners. How are you enjoying New Zealand?" she asks.

"I spend most of my time in Wellington," I reply. "But what I've seen is very beautiful."

"You have to get out into the countryside," she says. "That's where the real New Zealand lies."

I nod and give her my polite smile. "I'm hoping to find the time to do a hike."

"Tramp," says Tom.

"Pardon me?"

"We call it tramping, not hiking."

"I'd like to do a—whatever."

We move away and into the path of a platter of small fritters. "Whitebait," says the waitress. Eight hands reach in, octopuslike, to secure a fritter. They are white and soft. So are the fritters.

"Where are the rest of the women, Tom? I thought New Zealand was full of senior-level women?"

"They're still running half the Government departments, but since Tania left Kiwicom there are fewer senior women running the tech companies. Jane Kelly from VNL is over by the bar, the blond woman talking with Scott. She's keen to meet you."

I gaze across the room at our lead consultant and his companion. So he's in bed with VNL, just what I should have expected.

"Your new friend will, of course, try to persuade you to go with LCNS."

"Luke? He's with LCNS?"

"Director of sales."

Huh. Conflict of interest. Damn.

The laughter has grown loud as the guests avail themselves of the free wine. The men start talking about rugby, and then about the property market. I smile politely and nod in the right places. Eventually, the room empties out of the senior people, only the juniors and the freeloaders remain, settling in to drink the free booze as long as possible.

Tom checks his cell phone and tells me he needs to be home in time to watch the fireworks display, so shall we go?

I am barely inside the apartment when my telephone rings.

"Hello? This is Lin Mere."

"I want to eat your pussy."

"What?"

"I want to eat your pussy!" the female voice repeats.

I slam down the handset.

Well, that was a first. A dirty phone call from a woman.

Typical. If a woman is single and in a position of power, there's always the assumption that she must be like a man and therefore a lesbian.

As I gaze at the telephone handset, I wonder who she was and why she thought she could just ring a stranger and speak like that. My guise of being Caesar's wife is still in place. Why would anyone think I was interested in sex?

The telephone rings again.

"Hello?" I say, tentatively. "This is Lin."

"It's me."

The skies explode and I drop the phone. Outside, fireworks commemorating Guy Fawkes have started with three balls of gold that splatter into myriad fragments before my eyes.

I retrieve the phone. "Ben."

"Emmy showed me your e-mail. How are you?"

The skies now fill with multiple silver flares.

"Fine."

Multiple skyrockets bursting into stars of many colors.

Ben is silent. The shreds of light fall down into the sea.

"I hadn't heard from you," he says. "As far as I knew, we were finished."

More balls of golden fire, exploding into red hearts that evaporate, just like they do in real life.

"You didn't make any contact, Ben. You made no effort at all."

"I think it was up to you, Lin, to make an effort. It was you who slept with whatshisname."

Green lights, yellow lights, red lights.

"I did make the effort! I came all the way to New Zealand!"

"No doubt you came down here at whatshisname's call, Lin, for your brilliant new job!"

Lights are now exploding all over the sky.

I regain control of myself. "Don't throw that back at me, Ben. Robert offered me the job after I got here. So. What did you call me for anyway? Do you want something?"

"No, I don't want anything! Just to set things straight with you."

"Consider them set straight."

The explosions continue to dance in front of my eyes, blurred now. It is too much. I switch off the phone and put the handset back on the table, blink my eyes clear, and watch the fireworks without seeing a thing.

When Robert asked me to help him set up a new company in the Channel Islands I was happy to agree. Ben had refused to join me, and it looked like I was on my way to another split. Was it because I wanted to get in first and avoid that loss of face that came with rejection that made me sleep with Robert?

Who am I fooling. It was just another of those stupid decisions you make without thinking, fueled by too much wine.

The fireworks finish with one last crescendo of sound and light. I sit staring down at the nightscape punctured by the scattered windows of the city buildings and the golden trails of streetlights, then I turn back to the documents lying on the table and force myself to scan each page, but my brain is not taking in the words.

Whenever I close my eyes, I can see Ben's face before he turned and walked away. I can't get that image out of my head.

It is hot tonight, humid and sticky. Not enough wind. I rub the back of my neck and write a note in the margin of the report.

I am the chief executive of Hera. I don't need a man to complete me.

Chapter 16

When I open the door the property agent is there, carrying a bag of tools and a section of wrought iron railing. I had put off calling him week after week, and then he rang to ask if everything was to my satisfaction. No, I'd said, not at all.

"I'm about to leave for work."

"No problem, I've got all the keys," he says.

Nicholas struts in as if he owns the place and pauses in the middle of the room. "Coffee would be nice."

"I'm out of milk."

"I'll take a short black for a change." He smirks. "Bit of variety is always nice."

His eyes hold mine and it is me who looks away. I turn to the kitchen and make his coffee very short.

On the terrace, he is banging the new section of railing in place.

"Coffee."

"Thanks!" He slurps the dark stuff down and smiles, his thin face creasing into lines and his eyes sinking into their sockets. His pupils are tiny.

"I've been wanting to congratulate you," he says. "Big, important job, huh?"

"Yes," I reply.

"I know Tom Heke well. He's a good man."

"Uh-huh."

"He was pretty pissed off when you got the job. He thought it was his, eh? Didn't think some sheila would pounce and take it from under his nose."

"Really? I'm surprised he told you that."

Nicholas's eyes flick sideways. "That's what I heard, anyway."

"Uh-huh."

"I used to be a boss, too, you know." Nicholas's eyes stare through me, before focusing on my face again. "I ran a property development company. We were worth millions."

I say nothing. Am I supposed to be impressed? I've met rich men before. Most of them are mean, like Robert.

"Yep," he says. "I was rich then, and guess what, I'm going to be rich again. Those bastards will be sorry they cut me down."

"Good for you."

Nicholas shoots a glance at me. Then he sidles closer and puts his hand on my leg. "I could do something good for you too," he says.

I flick his hand away. "Just fix the railing, Nicholas."

"I was wondering if you'd like to have a meal at the local Thai," he says. "And maybe take in a movie?"

"I'm not interested in going out with you."

"I'd be happy to just spend the night again."

"No, thank you."

"A quick fuck?"

"Fuck off, Nicholas."

"Come on, you know you liked it."

"Which part of fuck off do you not understand? Just fix the fucking railing."

His eyes narrow and his mouth tightens in anger. I grab my handbag and hurry down the stairs to the garage.

When I glance back at the house, I can see his silhouette etched against the sky, standing at the edge of the terrace, watching me as I leave. I have the measure of this man. A leech that preys upon others. Right now he is hunting high-earning women—like in days of old, when fortune-hunting cads would prey on heiresses.

I remember hazy images of that stupid drunken night, *fool,*

fool! Bile rises in my throat, and then I shake my head and push the memory away.

Deepak and I have been examining the figures and we are worried about Hera's business plan. Deepak doesn't think we have enough money on top of insufficient time to launch our services.

"Okay, we need to find a cheaper systems solution. Any ideas?"

Fred and Ian glance at Tom and say nothing.

"Fred," I say to our IT manager. "Tell me what you really think we should be buying."

Fred is one of the quiet ones who disappear into the woodwork if you don't watch them. He wears a bad suit and a diffident smile and nurses a sick wife at home. He came from Kiwicom, where they had passed him over for promotion because he was "too quiet" and their preferred leadership style was the confident egocentric type, the kind with a touch of the psychopath.

But I have learned that Fred is brave and smart and can be trusted to find innovative solutions to the toughest of problems. More fool Kiwicom; their loss, and very much our gain.

Right now Fred blinks rapidly.

"Fred," I say, pointedly, "I want to hear your views."

"I think we should get the best systems we can afford," he says. "This is a once-in-a-lifetime chance to get it right."

"I don't think we're going to be able to negotiate the prices down any farther with VNL," says Tom.

Fred takes off his spectacles and wipes them.

"Fred?" I ask again.

"I think we can reduce the costs," he finally says, without looking up. "We need customer order management, activation, usage collection, and the billing software. But we can buy just a couple of licenses for the network records software. And we don't need a network management system since we only have the one switch."

I nod.

"We could save a lot of money by building a basic data warehouse instead of buying the big one." Fred glances up. "We won't have anything much to analyze initially."

"We'll get a better deal if we commit to all the packages," Tom says.

"Possibly," I say. "But we can't afford the whole suite."

"VNL will charge more for each package if we don't."

Fred looks up again and smiles. "That's where we can make the biggest savings."

Later, I am alone in my office when Tom strides in, the warrior come to do battle.

"I'm not happy about Fred's ideas," he says. "I think he's oversimplifying the situation."

"He's clever," I reply. "And he has a wealth of experience. We should trust him."

I watch Tom's mouth turn down.

"I don't think you understand," he says.

"I believe I do understand."

"We can't afford to take any risks!" He paces around the room.

"We can't afford *not* to take some risks."

His eyes meet mine and he holds my gaze. In silence, I stare back.

Tom's mouth slowly relaxes and his eyes crease. "Why don't you trust *me*?"

Now he's trying on the charm.

I hold my face quite still. "I do trust you."

"I've called Scott in for an urgent meeting," he says, his eyes fixed on mine. He stares at me. I watch the thoughts move behind his eyes; watch him wondering what he can do to convince me.

"Good, I'm looking forward to it."

•   •   •

Later that day, I sack our consultants. Scott Peake stands before me, eyes glaring and lips snarling. For a moment he is silenced, unable to credit that I plan to survive without his high-priced advice.

"You can't be serious!" he barks.

Oh, can't I. "I'm afraid we need to cut back on costs."

"You won't find anyone better than us. We're the best this town has to offer when it comes to big projects."

More fool this town. "I'm sure you are."

"And you won't find anyone good who is cheaper. You get what you pay for. Pay peanuts and you'll get monkeys!"

Pay millions and get expensive monkeys. "We may not need the services of external consultants to manage our program at all."

"That's ridiculous! Everyone knows that organizations can't do this kind of work themselves. You've got to get in the experts."

We did and now we don't need you anymore. "Thank you for all your assistance, Scott."

"Tom won't stand for you losing us."

"It's not Tom's decision. It's mine."

He snarls. "You'll be very sorry you made this decision, Mere."

I open the door and wait for him to leave.

Fifteen minutes later Tom arrives in my office. "Lin! What on earth? Scott says you've terminated their contract!"

"Their share of the program budget is over five million for providing services we either don't need or can get at a quarter of their hourly rates. And we've spent over a million on them already with nothing to show for it."

"There was a huge amount of work analyzing our requirements and evaluating the options."

"But what was the point when the solutions they suggest are so far out of our budget we can't even negotiate? I've already told you I think their summary is a waste of time and money, Tom. And it's an area in which I am an expert. Are you questioning my judgment?"

The blood is pumping through my veins, but my face is calm, my Asian eyes still. Fire flares in Tom's eyes. After a few moments he looks down at his hands.

"You're the boss."

"Yes, Tom, I am."

When he has gone, I stand up and massage the back of my neck. I pace back and forth across the pale-gray carpet, before stopping by the window where the sea tosses beneath a turgid sky. No yachts today.

Fighting with Tom makes me feel edgy, unsettled. But my first duty has to be to Hera. I have to make the best decisions for us to meet that launch date with a viable business.

Of course there are risks. There are always risks.

Chapter 17

I watched a documentary once that talked about corporations behaving like psychopaths, in that every decision made by corporations will always be in their own best interest, with no thought given to the public good.

I haven't found business leaders to be quite so universally self-seeking. Sure, some people always aim for spending the least amount of money and making the most profit, but many will also consider the interests of the wider community when they make their decisions. In the longer term, organizations do better when they have a stronger staff and better relationships with their customers and suppliers. Ripping people off is bad for business.

The motives for corporate behavior can be confused, too, by whose money they spend. If it's not their own money, then you get even sillier decisions made, often decisions that reflect the imperative to avoid risk, avoid making a mistake, rather than a decision that may have some risk but has a better chance of a positive outcome. The Government flunkies in particular will favor that which avoids damage to their own reputation over frugality.

I am still trying to understand the motives of Hera's directors.

The directors have assembled in Wellington for the monthly Board meeting: Robert from Vegas, Dao from Hong Kong, Hobb from Sydney, Stanton from Auckland, and Pita from Christchurch.

"I thought those packages were too expensive," says Robert when I outline the systems solution Fred and I have established.

"We've managed to trim back what we need, and we've negotiated directly with the suppliers," I reply. "We propose to implement them without VNL and integrate them ourselves."

Mark Stanton is frowning. "That is a risk."

"We've mitigated the risk," I reply quickly. "The package vendors will help, and we've identified the extra expertise we need for anything we can't handle."

I flick to slides on the technical architecture and talk through the road map and then show a set of slides showing the respective work streams.

No one asks how we came up with the time frames for each task. If we had followed a normal waterfall approach, we would be struggling to show a plan that would have the systems ready in less than a year. So, instead, we worked backward from the given date and squashed the tasks until they fit.

But it will be very tight. Only Robert knows enough to understand what I'm talking about. The other directors say nothing.

Stanton has a blank look on his face. I think he wants to talk about risk again, but first he glances around at his fellow directors.

"The price is less than half that of the alternatives," I repeat the mantra. "And now it fits within the budget."

Robert smiles his small smile that shows his shiny teeth, and Pita Lane smiles his wider one. Hobb nods and Dao tips his head slightly. Stanton states that the systems suite and associated spend are approved. Helen records the minutes.

We are now up to the thorny issue of the agreement with the local lines company, Vecson, from whose poles we need to hang our cable.

Robert looks across at Stanton, the smile flickering across his lips. "I thought your crowd had sorted this," he says.

Stanton blinks and shuffles his papers. The seconds tick past.

Behind his glasses Pita Lane is looking serious. His eyes move from Robert to Stanton and back again. Quon Dao is sitting very still. Only Stewart Hobb looks the same; cool, calm, expressionless. He has plenty of power back at Ozcom. I guess he doesn't feel the need to get involved in this ego war.

Stanton swings around and snaps at me. "What happened?"

"Vecson is demanding an increase to the pole fees we agreed on, to cover future costs of the lines going underground, they say," I explain. "The contract isn't signed yet. We think they're trying it on, knowing we can't afford the delay of a court case."

"We'd win any case," he says flatly.

"They'll stonewall as long as possible."

The other Board members wait for Stanton to respond since the law firm handling the negotiations are his nominees, part of the privileged circle of Old Boys that make up the corporate legal fraternity in New Zealand.

Stanton scowls. I watch while his brain tosses around the situation, trying to find a way through the problem. His fists clench on the edge of the table.

"You should have made sure the contract was signed," he snarls at me.

Speed up a lawyer? I'm good, but I'm not a fricking magician.

"There is one option that might work," I say when it becomes clear he is thwarted. "We could hold aside the additional amount they're proposing but keep it under our control rather than paying it over."

"They're not likely to agree to that," he says dismissively.

"We won't tell them," I reply. "No need to spell it out. We'll just withhold that part of each invoice when they finally get round to billing us and we finally get round to paying. Which won't be until after we go live. And then we challenge it."

The other directors are leaning forward. Robert nods. I can see his eyes flicker as he thinks about how this will work.

"We would need to make sure the contract spells out that the reason for the fee being increased is to pay for future undergrounding costs," he says. "And we would need to be careful with the dispute and penalty clauses. Yeah. Okay. Might work."

Pita Lane looks alarmed. "I can't support this. It is dishonest."

Hobb glances at him. "Vecson started it."

Stanton, too, is shaking his head. "Hera's reputation would be damaged."

"Hera would survive to have a reputation," states Robert.

"We'll put it to the vote," says Stanton.

He and Pita Lane vote against, and the other three directors vote in favor.

Stanton clears his throat. "Record the decision that we've agreed to set aside funding for future undergrounding," he says. "But not that we don't plan to pay it over." He eyes me. "That will be your job.

"Next item on the agenda," he says. "Hmm."

"My shareholders think it better that we change the chair now, at this critical point leading up to the launch," says Hobb.

Stanton blinks. "You can leave us, Lin," he says.

At the end of the meeting, Robert comes into my office.

"Hobb won the chair," he says. "Which might be a problem."

"Why?" I ask.

Robert stands by the window and stares out. "He cares about Ozcom's interests and nothing else."

I tilt my head back and rub my neck. "So it depends on Ozcom's interests."

"Which are to protect their trans-Tasman business. They're not at all interested in the residential services. Much of what is planned is totally irrelevant to Ozcom."

I look at him in surprise. "What do you mean?"

"They might want to change the plan. Dramatically."

I stare into Robert's old, clever, artificially enhanced blue eyes. We know each other so well.

"That doesn't make any sense."

"It might make sense to Ozcom." Robert walks to the door and pauses.

"Take care, Lin," he says, and then saunters out.

Chapter 18

Tom and I have called a truce in our relationship. He is cautious about disagreeing with me, and in turn, I am letting him guide more of the decisions.

"Any progress on the planning permits?" I ask.

He shakes his head. "They're not budging."

The council are playing us like a fish—they let us run then they haul us back in. We are caught on the line, flapping ineffectually this way and that.

"Can the Government broadband people help?"

"I'll set up a meeting for next week."

Deepak walks in with a folder full of papers and a hangdog look on his face. "I'm worried about the figures, Lin. The salary costs are coming out higher than the figures I used in the model."

"Find out what has changed to increase the costs and then talk it through with Marion. Then tell me how you're going to get the costs back down again."

The damned budget was too tight in nearly every aspect.

Marion puts her silver head around the door. "Lin, do you have any time this afternoon?"

"Don't tell me. The union is demanding we change the contracts again?"

Marion smiles. "No, we've got the final agreement with the union. We said we were thinking of setting up our own separate union, which seemed to do the trick. I just wanted to ask if you could say hello to our new graduates."

Hera is giving four graduates their first job, the most important and the hardest to get. Old-timers sometimes complain that it's too much effort to teach them, but Marion says that passing on knowledge should be part of everyone's job.

"When do you need me?"

"Come and have afternoon tea with us. Three o'clock?"

"Helen, can I do a three p.m?"

"You can do three thirty but only for fifteen minutes."

I turn back to Marion. "Will that do?"

She smiles and pencils me in and I return to my desk, which looks increasingly like a rubbish dump. My office is no longer simple and uncluttered. The days seem to start in crisis and end in crisis.

"Do you want me to get you a sandwich?" asks Helen. But when she brings the sandwich, I take a couple of bites and leave the rest.

"Clevaco are downstairs," she says.

While she goes to collect them, I rise and rub my neck, then pace back and forth across the carpet, worrying about whether we can get the switch through customs and commissioned in time for the interconnect tests. While Hera will have its own network and its own customers on that network, you have to interconnect with the other telco networks in order for your customers to talk to everyone else, and that means a tense and formal agreement with Kiwicom, our competition.

On Saturday morning I wake abruptly from a vivid dream in which I was sitting with a bunch of hobbits and I'd forgotten to put on any clothes. The hobbits had enormous cocks sticking out of their breeches and they were arguing about systems integration—and then I woke up.

The sky is clear and the sun beats in. Indolence washes over me, that wonderful feeling of lassitude when you don't have to do anything in particular or be anywhere at a definite time. No one is expecting you to make a decision or do something for them, or put on a smile and act in the way they expect you to act.

I think it's called freedom, or maybe it's just called the weekend.

Ah, I say to myself as I stand by the window, gazing at the glistening harbor, and waiting for the coffee to finish gurgling its way into the little jug. *You can't beat Wellington on a good day.* And I decide not to go into the office today.

There is a knock at the door. For a mad moment my heart leaps in shock when I see a hobbit standing there, but then I realize it is a human child.

"Michael!"

He holds out a damp and soggy twist of white cardboard and brown paper. Inside are two battered chocolates.

"I am very sorry," he says. "This is all that's left."

"You don't have to share your chocolates with me," I say, handing them back.

"They're not mine, they're yours. Polly got them."

"Polly got them for me?"

He sighs. Definitely, a stupid adult. "Polly ripped the bag open and ate them. Sorry."

"Oh." We both stare at the two dark brown truffles. "Was there a card?"

He shuffles. "I'm not sure. Polly might have eaten it. But Mum said your name is on this bit," and he shows me a chewed piece of brown paper with the words "L Mere" and the house address, scrawled in black felt-tip pen.

"Someone sent me a congratulations present, I guess. Oh, well, never mind," I say and pat him on the head before closing the door.

But as I drop the remnants in the rubbish, I hear what sounds like something being murdered in the front yard and I hurry down the stairs.

Outside, Karim is sitting on a sheepskin rug that wriggles

beneath him. Not a rug, no, it is the truffle thief herself. Sally crouches beside Karim pouring something down the dog's throat. Polly struggles, but Sally holds her mouth closed and massages the dog's throat.

Sally looks up and sees me and frowns. "Release her," she says and Karim starts to rise.

Polly shoots out from under him, stops, vomits, and then vanishes down the path toward the back of the house. Another retching noise can be heard.

Sally and Karim smile at each other. "Mission accomplished," says Karim.

"You'd better wash your hands," Sally replies.

I am having a very stupid day. I don't understand what they were doing.

"Poison," she says.

"What! Polly's been poisoned?"

"She was hyperventilating. Dogs aren't allowed chocolate. It's poisonous for them," Sally says sternly, as if I had voluntarily chosen to stuff her mutt with truffles. "We've given her something to make her vomit it back up."

I look down at the pile of dog vomit and back at Sally.

"What?" she says. "God, you've got that inscrutable look on your face again! Haven't you seen dog puke before?"

"Sorry," I say and move my mouth into a smile. "Is that better?"

Sally snorts and rises to her feet and walks over to the hose.

"What's it like being a CEO?" asks Karim. "Is it exciting?"

"I don't know that I'd call it exciting. It's very busy."

"But you tell people what to do? And you get to do whatever you want?"

"It's a lot harder than you might think. And no, I don't get to do much of what I want."

He looks back at me and frowns. "So what's the point?"

"Well," I pause to remember, "there's an important job to be done. That's a large part of the satisfaction."

Michael dances out of the house and grabs his mother's hand.

"Honey, go with Karim and lay the table for breakfast," she tells him.

When they have entered the house, Sally looks searchingly at me. "I guess you don't approve of me."

I let the false smile fade. I have been avoiding Sally. "I enjoyed going out with you guys, but I am just so busy."

She bends down to turn on the hose and starts washing away the regurgitated truffle mess.

It isn't enough. "I can't afford to be drunk in public. Now I'm the chief executive, I have to be Caesar's wife as well as Caesar."

"Poor little you!"

"Poor little me."

Sally gives me a look, then returns inside the house and closes the door.

I try to ignore the feeling of loss and drive to the supermarket to replenish my wine supplies. I seem to be going through a lot of wine, late at night, by myself, where no one can see, and where there is no chance I'll do something stupid.

Later I pour myself a glass and climb to my rooftop terrace.

The wine is cold. The Jacuzzi is hot. There is a full moon tonight, but the clouds restlessly obscure its light. My body floats just beneath the surface. As the water gently caresses my skin, I can relax at last.

It would be nice to have someone with whom to share my triumph. Surely there'd be no harm in a little distraction?

I think of Luke's green eyes and handsome face. Out of bounds.

I think of Tom's tanned cheeks and perfect mouth. His strong brown hands. Doubly out of bounds.

Handy Nicholas?

I shudder. No and no and no.

• • •

Before I go to bed, I fish out the piece of wrapping paper that had contained the bag of chocolates. I turn it back and forth, but there are no sender's details and the corner with the stamp has gone.

I wonder whether I have an admirer. I smile, shake my head, and toss the fragment away.

If so, they'll need something more than chocolates to get my attention.

Chapter 19

"Hello my friend, long time, no see!" says Sally when I open the door.

Her hair is tied back in a ponytail and she is wearing knee-length orange pants and an embroidered white peasant blouse that emphasizes her splendid chest.

She waves a small yellow card in my face. "You told me to ask you again closer to the date. Get a life, Lin! Come to the wine festival with us!"

"What? Now?"

"You've got five minutes."

She seems to have forgiven my lack of care over our friendship. Her eyes are bright and her generous smile is as wide as her hips.

I look at her, I look at my watch, I look at the table covered in papers, and make a fast decision.

I *miss* Sally. I want her as my friend.

"What is the weather supposed to be like?" I ask, opening the wardrobe.

"Well it might be hot and it might be cold," she says from the living room. "You never know. Last year it rained and the year before it hailed. But that's okay. If it's too fine people get too smashed."

"So you aim to only get a little bit smashed?"

"I aim to get well and truly smashed, Lin, but not too fast. Take my advice," she says. "At the first couple of tents buy tasting plates and only buy tasting-size portions of wine."

I change quickly into jeans and a black top and then agonize before finally extracting an ice-blue linen jacket and changing my black top for a white shirt. I survey myself in the mirror. Yes. Then I clatter down the stairs behind Sally.

Polly realizes we are leaving and lies down inside the hallway.

"Out, out, damned dog," Sally cries as she pushes the dog out the door. Polly looks after us with an expression of dejection.

"She's as bad as John."

"I thought it was John's voice I heard last night."

"Yeah, he proposed."

"What? You mean marriage?"

"So old-fashioned of him."

"What did you say?"

"Told him I wasn't ready to settle down. Don't look at me like that! He's not quite right for me, Lin. He's not handsome, and he's definitely no longer well paid. I'll admit he is a very kind man and sometimes he's good company when he's not harping on about how he's been done wrong. But he doesn't measure up." She smiles. "Or maybe I'm still enjoying playing the field. Why settle for one man when you can have two?"

"I don't know how you do it. Dating your men and yet still being a good mother to Michael as well as your work at the hospital. You have it all: a career, lovers, family."

Sally pauses on the path and glances down at me.

"What you get is never quite as cut-and-dried as that. You make compromises and you make sacrifices, every day.

"My career? Being a pathologist was never what I wanted to do, it's what I ended up doing because, well, just because. Cutting up dead men to see what killed them is not, I repeat not, glamorous at all.

"Lovers? None of them are going to stay around as I get older and my skin starts to wrinkle and my belly absorbs my waist. Lovers are a young woman's game.

"Family? I have Michael, so yes, I'm lucky. But I've lost

people too. My brother died when I was twelve and it hurts every day. Dad, well, Dad left us when I was twenty, and my mother, hah! My mother is a piece of work. Don't mourn too much for the lack of family, Lin; they bring as much pain as gain. Sometimes a little bit of family is all you need."

She waves as a van appears outside the garage. It screeches to a halt, narrowly missing the letterbox. Karim is at the wheel, and John is sitting behind him, his eyes fixed on Sally. Two pretty young women I vaguely recognize from the Matterhorn are in the backseats.

"I thought you were happy," I say.

"I *am* happy. Aren't you?"

"I guess. Yes. Of course I'm happy."

This year the sun is shining and the skies are clear of clouds. I follow Sally's advice and sample the salt cod and the whitebait fritters and sip on Méthode Champenoise. Sally's eyes are bright under her satyrlike brows and she is swigging a full glass of red wine. She seems to have forgotten about the sensible half-glass measures.

"Fantastic Pinot!" she cries. "Have you tried it yet?"

I shake my head. "Can't stomach red wine before midday."

"John, get Lin something. What do you feel like, Lin?"

I scan the Board. "Pinot Blush," I reply. "I guess that's a rosé?"

"Two blushes!" directs Sally.

By the time we reach the fifth estate, the first casualties of the day lie collapsed in the trenches between the rows of vines, and even I am feeling lightened up and relaxed. I buy a full glass of Riesling and prepare to enjoy my day while the band plays "Cheryl Moana Marie," but as I gaze around the crowded courtyard, a figure I recognize as Hera's CFO waves at me from the far side.

I drop my hand and tip out the wine in my glass and refill it from my water bottle. Then I nudge Sally and nod to where Deepak is sitting.

"A guy from work. I'd better say hi."

She pats my arm and turns back to her men.

It is quieter where Deepak sits.

"I almost didn't recognize you without the glasses," he says. "The others have gone to get more wine. We've been up to Te Kairanga and now we're making our way back."

A shadow falls over me. When I turn, Scott Peake is behind me, swaying slightly, his face flushed, his eyes rimmed with red.

"That's my chair."

Deepak's earnest smile falters. "There are other chairs, Scott." He heads across the grass, foraging for chairs.

"That's *MY* chair!" Peake says again.

A couple of people sitting at nearby tables look over but turn away. I get up and give him the damned chair. He stands over it staring at me, and then splashes wine across the seat.

"You're a lezzy, aren't you? I don't want to feel the heat from your arse."

"What?" I say, thinking I can't have heard him correctly.

"You think you're so smart, don't you? Well you've got a surprise coming," he hisses, his face suffused in blotches of broken blood vessels. "You're going to get your comeuppance, lezzy bitch."

Deepak returns with a captured chair.

Peake swings around and smiles at him. "Thanks, dipshit, sorry, *Deepak!*"

I look at Peake's flushed face and at my glass. My hand rises toward him.

"Lin, I didn't know you'd be here." Tom arrives with Ian at his heels.

I lower the glass. They don't seem to have noticed Peake and I are about to cross glasses. Peake's red-rimmed eyes stare at me and his nose twitches, then his habitual smile emerges, and he slaps Tom on the back.

"Have you heard the one about the Bin Laden cell they've found in South Auckland? They've arrested Bin Drinkin', Bin

Fightin', and Bin Sleepin' but they still haven't found Bin Workin'."

He laughs and Tom smiles and shakes his head.

Ian lurches like a zombie marketeer. His thatch of hair sticks out in all directions and his eyes resemble poached eggs.

"I've tried all the winesh so far," he says. "What about you? Or you still tettle, teet, teetotal?"

I smile and toast him with my wine glass of water. "Water. I'm enjoying the food and the music."

Walking back to Sally, I take one last look at the group of my workmates and their friend. Peake is once again staring at me, and, as I watch, he sticks a finger in the air, waggles it, and smirks.

"Asshole."

"Who? Me?" says Sally.

"No, just some jerk I sacked," I reply.

John looks up and glares. "Sacked jerks have feelings too."

Suddenly, I feel sorry for him. To have so much and to lose it all, well, it can destroy you.

"You'll get back into the kind of job you're used to," I say.

John shakes his head.

"Do you have any children?" I ask him, desperate to find something positive in his life.

"Two stepdaughters. But their mother won't let me see them. She says I'm no relation, so why would they be interested in staying in touch?"

"Any other family?"

John shakes his head. "A sister in Auckland. But I haven't seen her for a while. She is embarrassed by me."

"Is that where you lived?"

"I used to live about an hour up the coast, in a big white house looking out across Kapiti to the west and the Tararuas to the east." John's eyes glow and he raises his hands and gesticulates. "Shaped like this, climbing up the hill, with a long, sloping roof partly made of glass panels. And a swimming pool and ten acres of good land for the ponies."

"It sounds beautiful."

But the smile ebbs away. "She's raised money against it, and now the bank is threatening to foreclose because I can't afford to pay off the huge mortgage she's racked up."

"Hopefully, you'll get something out of it when it sells."

He sighs. "It's worth a lot less since the market crashed."

Clouds are creeping slowly across the blue, and the air starts to chill. Sally staggers back holding cake and more wine. Her hair is slipping out of the tie, and loose wisps curl around her cheeks. Karim follows behind with coffee.

"Oo-er," Sally swallows her last crumbs of Madeira cake. "I think I'm done." She puts her hand on Karim's arm and he steadies her.

"Thanks, sweetie," she says and leans against him.

John stares at the pair of them. "Fuck this!" He scrambles awkwardly to his feet.

Sally looks up. "Be back at the car at five."

John scowls at her. "I'll make my own way home." He staggers away and vanishes into the crowd.

"It seems you can't have both after all," I say.

Sally stares at me, her eyes suddenly bright, then she blinks and her face relaxes into its habitual smile.

"Win some, lose some."

She made the van wait half an hour in case John turned up, but he never showed.

The trip back is quiet. Sally sleeps beside me, her head lolling as the van twists back and forth down the mountain. The other passengers are also silent. Halfway down we have to stop to let one of the nurses get out to be sick.

Sally wakes up, looks around, and then closes her eyes again.

I remember the tender light in John's eyes. Oh, Sally. I don't think he would leave you when you grow old.

Chapter 20

Every morning I wish I could walk down through the forest and through the pretty city streets, but every day is so full I take the fastest route, which means driving. When I step out of the car into the underground car park, I pull on my corporate persona before I catch the elevator up to my office. I hate being in that tiny confined space, but I do it anyway.

Every evening I wish I could walk home, but it is late by the time I leave and even in this safe little city I would not choose to walk alone through the dark parks at night.

When I open the door of my apartment, I kick off my heels, toss my jacket on the sofa, remove my spectacles, and fix myself a drink. My apartment is my refuge, where I can just be me and not the image I show to the world.

The end of the week arrives in a rush. I do not meet up again at the Matterhorn to play at doctors and nurses with Sally and her friends. Instead, I attend the ballet with Luke from LCNS and his cohorts. It is soothing to accept the attention of the smiling salesmen. My wish is their command. Luke bends his handsome head to listen to my every facile statement. Food and drink arrives without any effort on my part. I pick at the portion and sip on mineral water. Taxis appear to whisk me to the performance and will appear again at the end of the evening to whisk me home.

I don't take their polite ministrations seriously. It is the role they defer to, not the woman. When the ballet is over and we have met the ballerinas, forced to entertain us in return for sponsorship, I turn eagerly for home, craving my own quiet space and my cool empty bed like a drug.

There is an item in the network build report that doesn't make any sense. I stand up and rub the back of my neck. I want to walk somewhere, but there's never enough time. All I can do is take the stairs to the basement where Tom has his lair.

Tom is eating his morning snack. His mouth is full of sausage roll and he has tomato sauce smeared on his lip.

"Tom, what is this 'koha' entry for twenty thousand dollars?"

He swallows and picks up a serviette to wipe his mouth. Crumbs fall onto his desk and he carefully wipes them into his hand and throws them into his rubbish bin.

"Tom?"

"*Koha* is what we pay to the local *iwi* to bless our venture," he says. "And to remove any bad things from the path of our network."

"What do you mean, 'bad things'?"

Tom looks away from my face. "*Taniwha*," he replies.

"What?"

"*Taniwha*. Bad spirits."

"You're joking."

"This is the Maori way, Lin. We must pay *koha* and the elders will make sure that no *Taniwha* curse our network."

"So *koha* is what, a bribe?"

Tom's jaw tightens. "You don't understand our ways here in New Zealand. *Koha* is a sign of respect, a donation for the elders to distribute to their people."

I stare at him. He is right, I don't understand. But that doesn't mean I should reject what he is saying.

"It's your call, Tom. If this is customary, then I guess we pay."

Tom nods and his face relaxes.

"You don't really believe in bad spirits, do you, Tom?"

Tom flushes red. "Of course I bloody don't. But don't expect me to admit that in public."

"We'd better go through the rest of these figures," I say.

Tom pulls over a chair for me and we spend the rest of the day examining what we can cull or reduce to keep within our budget.

At nine o'clock I say, "Let's get something to eat."

It has started to drizzle. The streets of the business district are nearly empty at this hour; just the cleaners and a few other late workers like Tom and me walk the forlorn footpaths.

The drizzle turns into a downpour, the rain tossing water sideways at us like a hose. "The Arbitrageur is closest," Tom says and I follow him into a modern bar.

Suddenly the urge to relax and have a glass of wine overwhelms me.

Tom glances at me in surprise when I take up the wine list. "Coming off the wagon?"

"Just a glass. But it has to be good."

The barman climbs halfway up a ladder as if in a library. His hands reach out to find the bottle I have ordered. His head dips to check the label. I see him nod and climb back down. A moment later he stands at the table, whipping off the cork with a deft twist of his wrist. He smells the cork and places it on the table in front of us.

"Who will taste?" he asks and I hold out my glass. I swirl the small sample into a little whirlpool, the dark liquid releasing its secret aromas, and lift the glass to my lips.

I nod to the waiter and he fills our glasses.

"Salut!"

"Cheers," says Tom and keeps his eyes on mine while he sips the wine.

"I hear you know Nicholas Johnson," I say.

"Who?"

"Nick Johnson. He's a property agent. Used to be a developer, he tells me."

Tom's face looks blank. "Never heard of him. I use Exodus to manage my rental property," he says. "Matt Holmes in the Petone office."

"I must have misunderstood what he said."

"Someone you're seeing?"

"No way."

Tom laughs. "Sorry."

He leans in when I speak and watches my mouth while I suck the flesh from the dark olives and spit out the pits. The creamy softness of Kikorangi cheese oozes over my tongue while the blue edge hits the back of my throat. I swallow and turn my attention next to the flaccid stalks of oyster mushrooms that lie on a bed of creamed leeks.

Tom reaches out and touches my hand. "You look so tired."

"I am tired," I reply. "There is always something to worry about."

He pours the last of the wine into my glass. By now the warm feeling has made its way throughout my body, and I almost order another before I remember who I am.

Tom looks into my eyes. "You don't have to bear the burden all by yourself."

But I am not a Harlequin heroine. I have no urge to rest my head on his strong, manly shoulder. Instead, I sit back in my seat and put on my corporate smile, the one that never touches my eyes, and pick up the water glass.

"Where does your wife think you are tonight?"

"I told her I'd be late," he replies.

"You're lucky. Having the wife and children, and the *whanau*."

"Yes," Tom replies. "I am."

He looks at me again with his attractive smile. "What about

you, Lin? You've proven you're Wonder Woman when it comes to the career, but isn't it about time you had a family?"

I shrug. "I enjoy my job too much."

"Do you?" Tom says.

"Of course."

It is late by the time I get home, too late for a soak in the spa. All I seek is to get inside out of the rain, slip between my crisp sheets, close my eyes, and sleep.

There is something lying on the doorstep. A backpack. I wonder whose it is, and lean over to get to the door keypad. As the door opens, light falls on the discarded pack. It looks familiar.

I glance around, but there is no sign of the owner. As I step past, it falls onto the path and into the rain. I enter the house and close the door behind me.

Later, wide awake, I hear a couple of perfunctory woofs, as if Polly is letting whoever is moving outside know that the house is under guard and not to think they can get away with anything.

Then nothing more. I lie gazing into the darkness, listening to the rain hitting the tin roof. I roll over on my side with my knees tucked up against my chest and resolutely close my eyes. Still sleep fails to come. The pattering increases in tempo. It must be hosing down outside. I let out my breath and roll onto my back again.

It is no use. When I reach the bottom of the stairs. I turn on the outside light and open the door.

Light spills out over the porch, washing him with gold as he sits with his back against the dog box and his arms wrapped around his legs. As he looks up, a droplet of water slips down his cheek and splatters on his damp t-shirt.

"Fricking idiot!" I say. "You'd better come in out of the rain."

Chapter 21

"I'm not happy with the sensitivity analysis," says Board Chairman Hobb, flicking through the spreadsheets. "I can't see how we're going to get enough revenue coming in to cover the higher costs."

Dao has his arms folded. He glances at Hobb and then back at me. I can't read his face behind the reflective lenses. Pita Lane rubs his nose and turns some pages over. He doesn't meet my eyes.

"The financials are bloody poor!" says Hobb finally. "We're even more over budget than we were last month."

Why is he acting surprised? I had already warned him of the situation and told him the cupboard was bare.

Robert's face is serious and when his eyes meet mine, they slide away. *There must be something going on.*

"We're where we were expecting to be, Stewart," I say. "As I warned you, changing the build plans to focus on the commercial streets has slowed us down."

"Weren't you supposed to catch up?"

"We couldn't get permission from the council to work outside of the times they allow for work in the commercial streets," I say. "Once we get into the residential neighborhoods, the speed of the build will increase."

"That's what? February? Too late," says Stanton.

"We will have enough live, lit, fiber to launch the service. *That's* the critical outcome, isn't it?"

"But not hitting the build figure this month means we've broken the banking covenants. The bank doesn't have to keep funding the rollout. Which means we will have to fund the operation ourselves until we negotiate a new position," Hobb says.

"Deepak and I met with the bank on Monday. They're prepared to continue the line of credit, so long as we hit the launch date and incur no new costs above the figures we've given them."

"But they're charging us a penalty as well as increasing the interest rate!" Hobb snaps.

"Gupta was supposed to negotiate that down," says Mark Stanton.

"He hasn't had any success yet."

"He's too goddamn diffident," says Robert.

"That's just his style," I say, but the audience is not listening.

Hobb looks across at Stanton. "Didn't Gupta sign off the budget? He should have known better."

I pick my words carefully. "Building a new network and launching a telecommunication service is not an undertaking that happens very often. There are no blueprints, few guidelines, nothing on which to base a budget. So it's not surprising some aspects need to be adjusted."

"My group is not keen to put up any more money," Robert says and turns to Hobb. "What is Ozcom's position? You said Ozcom has other lines we might call on."

Hobb's eyes flicker. "I can look into some options. Let's talk further tomorrow," he says, and then faces me. His eyes are cool. "In the meantime, Lin, you need to tell us how you're going to get a better handle on the finances."

I stare back. "Deepak is—"

"Gupta has to go."

I look down briefly before raising my head again. "I don't think it would be fair to blame Deepak for Hera's situation."

"I don't think you're listening to me. I said Gupta has to go. We're agreed, I think." Hobb looks around the table at the other four Board members. One by one they nod their agreement.

"He doesn't have the experience we need going forward," says Stanton.

"He no longer has our trust," says Robert.

Dao and Lane merely nod. They are not putting their boots into the guy, but they're not speaking up for him either.

"You're aware there is a process to follow? We can't just sack the man."

"Just get it done, Lin. Use the budget blowouts. His fingerprints are all over them."

So, I think, but do not say, *are yours. The Board approved the budgets, too, and insisted on the changes to the rollout that has caused us the network build shortfall.*

"We should also congratulate Lin and the team on the excellent progress made," says Dao.

"Okay, minute our congratulations," Hobb says to Helen and she quickly types. "Don't minute anything about Gupta. Lin knows what she has to do."

Yeah, I know what I have to do. Sack someone who deserves no more of the blame than anyone else who was involved in the business plan.

It is not straightforward to get rid of an employee by New Zealand law. But if the Board loses confidence in the chief financial officer, his or her position becomes untenable. Deepak would understand the situation.

While I wait for him to arrive, I stand and gaze out the window at the yachts in the harbor. Deepak coughs, and I swing around with a fake smile that will not convince and gesture for him to sit at my table. I close the door.

I tell him how concerned the Board is about Hera's financial situation. He replies angrily that they've known all along we would need more funding. When I tell him he no longer has the Board's support, Deepak's lip quivers. He rises hastily and turns his back. I stop talking and wait for him to regain his composure. He drops his head and scuffs the carpet with his shoe, back and forth, back and forth.

"So what do they want?"

"I'm letting you know what the feeling is."

"They want me to go?"

"They're talking about performance failure over the handling of the budgets, the reporting, and how you've managed the relationship with the bank."

"They want me to go."

"I don't think I can persuade them to trust you again."

"How much?"

"Three months' salary, and I'll guarantee you the launch bonus. That's worth over two months' salary. And you deserve it, Deepak. You've done a terrific job for Hera."

Now he turns and can face me. "Not terrific enough, though, was it?"

"It's done," I tell the chairman.

"Good," he says. "Good. When does he go?"

"At the end of the week."

"Good."

"His number two is quite young, so I'll—"

"Scott Peake will take over," he says. "He's got the right background."

I look out the window to where the sea sparkles and a scattering of sails dance across the harbor. Lucky bastards, out on the water on a glorious day like today, one of Wellington's good ones.

Should I protest at being encumbered with a CFO I wouldn't have chosen? Someone whom I dislike and who dislikes me?

When I turn back, my face is carefully blank.

"I would prefer a different choice."

Hobb meets my eyes. His nostril quivers as if he is disgusted by something. Or someone.

"You don't get to choose."

I break our locked gaze and look down.

The chairman smiles and stands and stretches. "Get your girl to call me a taxi, will you?"

"Helen, a taxi for Mr. Hobb."

•   •   •

Something's going on, I can sense it. Robert replies to my urgent message and meets me for a drink that evening. I don't mind having a drink with Robert, he knows who I am.

"What the fuck was that all about?" I ask as soon as we sit down. "You guys must know that Deepak was only doing what he was told."

"Perhaps he shouldn't have done what he was told."

"Then you'd have dumped him and got someone else who would have."

"Or convinced us we were wrong and needed to put in more money. Then Hera might not exist at all. Or have different shareholders with different plans."

"I think it is unfair. Deepak has been a very good CFO. We wouldn't have got this far without his hard work and common sense."

Robert laughs. "What's fairness got to do with anything, Lin?"

"What options did Hobb propose?" I ask.

"Just make sure you hit that launch date, Lin," Robert says. "And keep those costs under control."

"And Scott Peake as my new CFO? I don't trust him."

Robert snorts. "Trust is a luxury in our world."

Driving home, I consider what Robert has said. Boards are there to set the company's objectives and give the management team guidance on how to achieve them. I would like to trust that they would give the best possible direction.

Then I wonder why neither the chairman nor Robert has shared with me any new plans being considered. How can I make the best decisions if I don't know what the options are? I hate not knowing. It makes my stomach churn.

Especially when I think about Scott Peake's smile.

Chapter 22

It is after nine when I park the car in the garage and walk up to my front door.

I wonder whether he will still be there. As I climb the stairs, the scent of something savory is wafting down the stairwell. I can hear the faint sound of music playing: Fado—Portuguese urban folk music. Songs of love, songs of loneliness, and songs of doom.

I push open my door. The music swirls around me, loudly now. The table is laid for two and decorated with hydrangea blossoms and vanilla-scented candles. My new Hoglund crystal carafe is filled with red wine.

The kitchen, however, looks like a bomb site of pots and pans and peelings. Amidst the debris a dish of lamb cutlets and a bowl of tossed salad sit waiting, a plate of cheeses beside them.

I drop my jacket and handbag on the bed and the folder of papers on the bedside table. I climb halfway up the steps to the roof terrace. The Jacuzzi cover is off. I can't see into the pool, but, as I watch, a hand emerges and takes up a can of beer.

Downstairs, I close the bedroom door, discard my clothes, shower, change into a black tunic and jeans, replace my spectacles with contacts, and return to the living room.

A glass of cold fizz sits on the table. I raise it to my lips and take a sip.

The door to the terrace opens and Ben comes down the steps, blue eyes guileless, and his mouth slowly curving into the smile I know so well. His brown hair is tied back in a short ponytail, although damp tendrils stick to the side of his face, glowing from the heat of the spa. He wears a pair of baggy khaki shorts and a white t-shirt from which tanned arms emerge, glistening with cooling perspiration.

We both stand still, each waiting for the other to make a move, but neither of us does so I pull out a chair and sit down, and Ben returns to the kitchen.

"Sorry I'm late," I say perfunctorily and take another sip of fizz.

The cold bubbly liquid hisses its way down my throat.

"Crisis at the office."

"No worries," he replies.

He's not annoyed. Damn.

"What are we having? Lamb chops?"

But he is taking a tray out of the icebox. "I brought you some bluff oysters," he says. "We'll start with a dozen of those."

He nods toward the deck. "I was thinking of eating out there, but she's a bit breezy."

"She's nearly always a bit breezy here," I say. "But you can't beat Wellington on a good day."

"I brought some things you left behind in the studio."

He passes me a plastic bag. Inside is a worn-down lipstick in Woodland Berry, a paua shell earring in the shape of a feather, a heavy filigree necklace of brightly colored beads, and a knee-high stocking.

There is something intimate about a discarded knee-high; that flaccid empty container, damp with the sweaty secretions of an absent foot. I push it aside with my finger and lift the necklace.

"I wondered where that got to," I say. "I missed it."

"I found it stuck down the back of a drawer."

He waits as if to hear me say I've missed him too, but I say nothing so he goes into the kitchen and returns with a dish of oysters.

I look down at the half shells of oyster. I can smell the salty juices and the sharp tang of lemon. I haven't eaten since the solitary scone with jam and cream in the warehouse this morning. My stomach rumbles. I tear a great fat juicy oyster from its shell and tip it into my mouth. Ben passes me a plate of thinly sliced brown bread to mop up the liquid.

The juices drip down my chin. He reaches over with a napkin and wipes them away. Our eyes meet. His hand stills.

Reality intervenes with the electronic jangle of my cell phone's ringtone.

"Hi, Tom. Yes, Hobb told me. No, I'm not happy. Whatever. No. You don't need to. Let's talk about it first thing. Right. Right." I hang up.

"So," I say, around a mouth filled with another plump morsel, "when are you planning to go to your sister's?"

He told me when I made up a bed on the sofa for him that he was on his way to visit his sister, Cheryl, in Picton, a little port town at the top of the South Island.

"Tomorrow," Ben replies. "Or the next day. Doesn't really matter."

I take the last oyster. "Tomorrow, Ben. I've got a function tomorrow night and a late meeting the next day."

He looks up and nods.

Ben seldom argues. It is one of the most annoying things about him. I wish he'd stick up for himself more. Although not, of course, when it's me who disagrees with him.

He goes and brings in the lamb from the barbecue, puts it on the sideboard to rest and adds a knob of butter to the pan. The potatoes have been baked in cream, and then cut into wedges. He slips them into the butter. The room fills with the glorious scent of fried potatoes.

I take out two red wine glasses. "My doctor friend Sally tells me butter and cream are okay so long as you drink red wine with the meal," I say. "But," and I eye the buttery, creamy potatoes. "We'll need the whole bottle to counteract this lot."

"You're looking a bit skinny, Lin. Thought I'd better fatten you up."

"Sometimes I'm so busy, I forget to eat."

I pour the red wine into the two goblets, and Ben brings in two plates of lamb, potatoes, and salad.

He lifts his glass and clicks it against mine. "Cheers."

"Salut."

We sit at the table eating together as we have done countless times before. The silence is edgy. I glance at Ben's profile as he scoops up a forkful of fries then return my gaze to my own plate. He looks at me, swallows, and puts down his fork.

"Is the job going well?"

"Well enough. Very political."

"Who's the problem?"

"More a question of who isn't than who is. First off, there's the Government who have an Old Boy network all of their own. They don't mind the Brits, but they really don't much like any other nationality. Especially not Americans, although they like our money.

"And then there's the local council. They don't like any big business at all. It seems there is always a reason to say no and never a reason to help us out."

I spear some salad. "The power lines company is trying to rip us off, and Kiwicom wants us to miss the launch date and thereby remain a healthy dwarf. Bastards."

The lamb chops are moist and succulent beneath their crusting of herbs. The potatoes are to die for.

"How is business?"

Ben's furniture made him a modest living. A very modest living. It used to constantly annoy me how little he cared about money.

"Slow. Cheryl rang up, worried about something or other that she hasn't got round to telling me about. I'd just finished a table for a rich prick up in Queenstown, but his wife keeps changing her mind about the chairs, so I thought I'd come and see what's wrong."

"How is she? Is she still with—what was his name?"

Ben is eating his lamb chop with his fingers, tearing the flesh off the bone with his teeth. He puts down the bone and wipes his hands on one of my new napkins.

"Bruce. No, they split. Now she's with some guy called Joe. He has a houseful of children apparently, so she's stepmum and stepaunt and even stepgrandmother to the youngest."

"That must make her very happy."

Cheryl was one of the pretty girls who were effortlessly adroit at capturing a tall, handsome, well-paid man. Bruce gave her everything she asked for but the one thing she really wanted—a baby. He had refused to adopt. When Cheryl called Ben, distraught, he'd dropped everything to comfort her.

Including me. Which was okay. Ben knew he didn't have to look out for me. I didn't mind when he canceled the trip I'd paid for. I didn't need to be coddled like Cheryl. I could look after myself. I was used to it.

"What about your sisters? Since you're here for a while, I figured you'd try to track them down."

"I found them. They live on a farm in Hawke's Bay."

"Have you met?"

"I tried, but they weren't home."

"You should try again."

"When I get the time. How is Emmy?"

His eyes crinkle and his mouth stretches into a fond smile. "She's doing very well."

"Still splitting her time between your house and her mother's?"

"Yes, although Fay is on sabbatical in South Africa next year, so Emmy will be living with me full time."

Finally, Ben reaches out and touches my wrist. We haven't yet talked about what has happened between us. I think he wants to, but doesn't know how. He takes my hand in his and holds it and looks at me. His eyes are serious, sad, questioning.

"Lin," he says. "Lin?"

But I shake my head and withdraw my hand. "I've got some

reading to do," I say. "If you need any more blankets, they're in the cupboard."

And I get up and leave him and close the door firmly behind me.

The contract seems even dryer than usual. I read the same numbered paragraph for a third time and press my fingers against the back of my neck, rubbing where it aches. There is a faint murmur of television noise coming through the wall. Half an hour passes before I reach the last page and know that the final version is complete and needs no change.

All is now quiet. I undress, pull on my nightdress, slip into bed, and lie with my eyes open, gazing at the dark ceiling.

I roll onto my stomach and bury my head in the pillow and close my eyes. I roll over onto my back again and open my eyes. I can't risk being distracted from my fabulous job, I know that, and yet—

Being at the top is worth all the sacrifices.

Isn't it?

Chapter 23

When I leave the house, he is still asleep, and when I get home that evening, he has gone. I put the sofa back into position and replace the cushions. A faint scent of his aftershave lotion seems to linger, but perhaps it is only my imagination.

My apartment is a haven of tranquility—no people to please, no decisions to make. Empty of distractions.

Perhaps too empty of distractions.

I reheat the leftover buttery potatoes, open a bottle of wine, and sit by the window to eat my meal. As the sun sets, the rose-tinted clouds lie against the eastern hills like fire-lit nudes.

I pour another glass, light a cigarillo, go up to the terrace, and slip into the Jacuzzi. My body floats in the warm water.

What do I want?

I have these feelings; tingling, edgy little feelings, of something more out there. When I close my eyes, I can picture Ben's face, Ben's body. Not a shadow, but rather a bright presence; warm, solid, and near, as if I should open my eyes and turn my head and he would be there.

I sigh, stub out my cigarillo, and return indoors.

The next night when I get home, early, at eight o'clock, Nicholas is downstairs in the hallway, wrenching the front off the massive wooden dresser that is built into the back wall of the hallway. There is a vague smell of something rotten in the air.

He looks up as I pause in the doorway and stares at me with small cold eyes, but I decide to smile politely. Best if we both forget our little contretemps.

"You look busy."

His eyes flicker. "Gotta get at the drains," he says. "Looks like they run underneath this thing."

"Uh-huh," I answer and start up the stairs.

"You wouldn't believe the rubbish stuck behind these drawers," he gestures at a pile of assorted papers and pens and bits of fluff. "There was a returned letter of yours somewhere."

I step back into the hall and examine the pile.

"Here it is," he says, and hands over a stained and torn envelope.

"Thank you." I take the envelope upstairs.

Nicholas's eyes follow me up.

I can't read the stained front of the envelope, but on the back is the address for this house, and—it is not my writing. I tilt the light to examine the name. It is not an "L Mere" but an "R Mere."

Richard Mere. My father.

I look on the front of an envelope again and I can just decipher the words: "Insufficient postage."

Oh, Dad. So fricking typical of you. I get a sharp knife and slit open the envelope. Inside is a handwritten letter to an address in Macau.

> *My dearest Li,*
> *Forgive me. You know it didn't mean anything.*
> *I have to stay here, you must realize that. This is where my work is.*
> *I miss you terribly, and so does little Linnet.*
> *Please come home.*
> > *Richard.*
> *P.S. I never said it, but I LOVE YOU*

Oh God, he sent a letter and it never got to her. I rest my face in my hands. My skin feels hot and moist against my palms. And he betrayed my mother, too, with his screwing around.

When I look up again, the sky has grown dark. They are both dead. It is too late to fix their mistakes.

At my PC I bring up the directory listings and find the telephone numbers of Marchmount, C. and V., and Repati, A. and W.

Finally, I lift my phone and make the call.

A woman's voice, cultured, as if she has had elocution lessons, answers with a voice mail greeting. "Hello, this is the residence of Christopher, Vivienne, and Maximilian. Unfortunately, we can't take your call right now. But do please leave us a message after the tone."

The beep sounds, but I press the off button without speaking.

The letter sits on the table like a prophet of doom. I take up my phone again and punch in the numbers.

This time a man's voice comes on. "Yeah, g'day, this is Ali and Wal Repati's house. Leave a message."

"Hello? This is Lin Mere calling. I'm living in New Zealand now and I was hoping we could meet. My number is—" and I leave my phone number.

When I put down the phone, my hands are shaking. The die is cast.

When the telephone rings, I look at it, take a deep breath, and slowly reach out my hand to answer.

"Hello?"

"It's me."

"Ben! How are you? How is your sister?"

He lets out a sigh. "She's okay, but she wants me to go."

"It normally takes three days for guests and fish to stink. It's only been two."

Ben laughs. "Well, I thumped her boyfriend, so she's panicking and wants me out of the house before he wakes up."

"Good Lord, what for?"

"He beats her up. I wanted to make sure he knows how it

feels. Anyway, would you mind if I stay for a couple of days? My flight home isn't until Monday."

I feel something warm spreading through my body. I sense something bright hovering at the edge of my mind.

"Sure," I reply. "I'll leave the key under the pot."

"Okay. I'll see you tomorrow, then."

"Tomorrow."

I put down the phone, roll onto my side, and close my eyes. *Forgive me. You know it didn't mean anything.*

Chapter 24

When I get home the following evening, Ben is nowhere to be found, not even outside in the Jacuzzi. His pack is in the corner of the living room, and his toiletries are strewn across the bathroom vanity, but the man is not there.

"Hiya!" comes Sally's voice, followed by Sally herself. "Ben's dragging Polly's kennel round the back of the house," she says. "I've been wanting it moved, and he was happy to oblige."

"Ah," I reply.

"Ah, indeed. What a lovely man, Lin. Can I have him?"

"Hands off. I haven't finished with him yet."

Ben returns in a flurry of child chatter and dog bounce. I watch him come up the stairs toward me, smiling—*shit*. He's got a black eye.

"Send him down to me and I'll see what I can do about the swelling," Sally says as she leaves.

"Are you okay?" I ask, examining his face. The eye is the most noticeable mark of his battle, but he also has a scrape on his forehead.

"I'm fine," he says crossly. "That Joe bloke is a big bastard."

"Sally says she might be able to do something about the swelling."

He opens the freezer. "I'll use these."

He throws himself down on the couch with a bag of frozen peas across his face.

The telephone rings and I reach across the table to retrieve the handset.

"Hello, this is Lin."

"Lin? It's Alison Repati."

At last!

I clear my throat. "You got my message."

"Yes, dear, it was lovely to hear from you."

Ben draws near, his eyes questioning. "My sister," I whisper.

"I don't know if you knew I was in New Zealand."

"Yes," came the response. "We knew as soon as you got here, well almost. I was hoping you'd call. But I guess you're very busy."

"I have been busy," I say, wondering why neither of them called me. Perhaps they did and we kept missing each other? Whatever. We were talking now.

"Why don't you pop up to see us some time? If you're not too busy, that is. It doesn't matter if it's not convenient."

"Tomorrow," whispers Ben.

"I would love to. Uh, I have a friend visiting and we were thinking of driving up to Napier this weekend. Perhaps we could stop in?"

"Oh. Um. Would you, um," she says, hesitantly. "Would you like to come for a meal? Or is this too short notice?"

"A meal would be nice."

"Right. Have you got a pen? The easiest road to take is to come up Highway 2, and then—" and she gives me detailed instructions how to get to their farm.

"We'll see you around six," I say.

"I look forward to it," she says.

We are both silent for a moment.

"Okay, see you then."

"See you."

"Fuck," I say when I hang up. And then again, "Fuck."

"So they knew you were here all along?"

"Apparently so. She said she was hoping I'd call."

I get up and start tidying the newspaper, placing the sheets together and folding them up. "Fuck."

Ben stands behind me and puts his hands on my shoulders. "Lin. They've invited you to visit. That's great."

I feel too edgy to stand still under his hands, so I step sideways and pace across the room to the window.

"I wonder why they never tried to call me?"

"Ask them."

"I don't want to."

I pace to the door, and then I go upstairs and outside on the roof terrace. Again I look north.

Would they really accept me? Or would they turn away?

In front of the mirror, I survey my image, in a white linen dress shorter than I normally wear, and a closer fit around my body than I normally show. I have offset the plainness of the dress with the filigree bead necklace that Ben returned to me. And I leave off the spectacles, slipping my lenses onto my eyes instead.

When I emerge, Ben is sitting up and has returned his pea pack to the freezer.

He runs his eyes over me. "Very nice," he says approvingly, and for the first time in a long while I feel like an attractive woman rather than a public image.

Ben has never wooed me with beautiful words so "very nice" is as good as it gets. Ben is not the romantic type. He was more likely to prepare a beautiful meal, or fix something broken, or make me a CD of music he likes. I remember him picking me a handful of wildflowers once. Those fast-wilting flowers were more special than a dozen of the florist's best red roses.

When I felt romantic, I would run my hand up his back, feeling the firmness and the warmth of his flesh, the intimacy of the touch you can only give a lover. When I wanted to show how I felt, I bought him things he couldn't afford; clothes, expensive restaurant meals, good wine, airfares. When I spend money, I feel in control.

I don't know why I could never tell him that I loved him.

"I could cook," he says.

"No," I say. "Let's go out to dinner."

I take him to Floraditas, my favorite restaurant on Cuba Street.

"Expensive," he says. His eyes flicker and the tiny crease in his forehead deepens.

"I'm paying," I say.

"Hmmm," he replies, noncommittal.

Ben can be so irritating. I can far more easily afford to pay for the meal than he can, he knows that. Why doesn't he just shut up and enjoy it?

We eat fried stuffed zucchini flowers and risotto balls, and then I have the fish and Ben the steak. I order a second bottle of wine.

Conversation is ragged. I ask questions, trying to keep the talking going, but Ben is quiet tonight. His brow keeps slipping back into that furrow. I don't know if he's worried about money or about his sister.

"Is Cheryl going to leave this guy who is hitting her?"

"She won't leave the children."

I would have liked a child, but, well, you keep putting it off, thinking there'll be time and then suddenly you're looking down the barrel of middle age and it's too late. I don't have a mate, I certainly don't have any spare energy, and I don't have anyone to help me raise a child properly. Better to leave it to the experts.

"Can't she take the children with her? I thought there were safe homes for battered families."

"They're not her kids. She won't be allowed to keep them."

I snort. "God, she could still try, couldn't she?"

"Cheryl's not like you."

I'm sick of hearing about how tough I am, compared to poor little Cheryl and dear little Emmy. Everyone could be tough if they tried.

"How come you're leaving Emmy for a whole week? That's not like you."

"Her mother wanted extra time since she's going to be in South Africa for the next six months."

"What's she doing over there?"

"A sabbatical or something. Anyway, it means I'll have Emmy to myself."

Ben didn't have quite the same problems as me regarding family and career. He had his beloved daughter with him at least half the time, almost joined at the hip, and his mother nearby, and cousins in Invercargill, old school friends all about. He had his clientele in Queenstown and the wealthy farm areas around the Lake District.

He didn't have to cross the world like I had to, looking for someone to love me.

I stop talking and finish the creamy Parmesan polenta. Ben chomps on the last of his steak.

"Dessert?" I ask.

"Not for me."

"There's still wine left."

"Not for me."

Outside the streets are busy with people coming and going and talking and laughing. Ben walks silently beside me to the taxi stand. He's pleased because he can afford the fare. I watch him counting out the coins and wish he would just let me pay, but men have to do the macho breadwinner thing one way or another.

When we get inside, I walk around the living room, rearranging the cushions, putting away the towel Ben has left sprawled over the floor, putting the dishes he has left out into the dishwasher.

Ben is silent. He has already made up his bed on the sofa. His pack lies in front of the bedding like a barricade.

I glance at him standing by the window, looking out over the city. The wine has me in its urgent grasp. I want to go and hold him, bring him to my bed, have my way with him. I step toward him.

He ducks around me and sits on the sofa to pull off his shoes. "Good night, Lin."

I lie in my bed and wonder what the hell I should do. Well, there's always tomorrow night, although I guess he may want separate rooms. Damn.

And then I let myself finally think about meeting my sisters. Oh, God, it's nearly happening. Tomorrow is going to be the big day.

Chapter 25

When I wake in the morning, the sun is shining in through the crack in the curtain, but all is silent. So I close my eyes again and snooze until I can hear him moving about in the kitchen.

I pull on my robe and pad out into the living room where Ben has laid out the coffee and the newspaper. He is reading the World section. I take up the Business pages.

When the knock sounds, I assume it must be Sally, come to check Ben out again. But it is not Sally.

"These are for you," says Nicholas, thrusting a bunch of tired mauve chrysanthemums in my face. "Women like flowers, eh?"

I put one hand to the wrap over of my robe to make sure the material covers me, and I push the flowers away with the other.

"No thanks, Nicholas."

His eyes slither over my shoulder. Ben is standing behind me. Nicholas stares at Ben's black eye and then at the strong forearms that rest lightly by his side. There is a moment's silence while some kind of thought process goes on behind his squinting eyes. Then he turns away without saying another word and goes back down the stairs.

At the front door I see him stop, then step over to Sally's door. I turn back into the penthouse and close my door.

"Who was that?"

"The property agent."

"Bearing flowers?"

"He's ever hopeful."

"I suppose you get a good few men chasing you, huh?"

I pause with my back to him, and then I smile and turn.

"A few."

An hour later I am downloading some of the week's reports, but there is a problem with the Internet and I can't get the last three.

"I'll take the bags," says Ben. "Have you got the keys?"

"The garage door remote is on the dresser. The car's not locked. I'll be down in a minute."

Ben frowns when he sees my laptop bag. "Do you have to take your computer, Lin? Can't you take the weekend off?"

"I need to pull together a report for the Board." Hobb has asked for a more formal suite of reports as per the Ozcom project office standard.

"Can't you write it up when we get back? You're about to meet your family for the first time and you want to sit at your computer instead."

"I guess I can do it tomorrow night."

Sally emerges as we pass. Her sharp eyes scan our faces.

"Going somewhere?"

Ben gives her a wide grin. "We're visiting Lin's sisters in Hawke's Bay."

Sally's eyebrows rise. "Sisters?"

"I'll tell you about it another time," I say.

"You'd better," she says and watches us go down the path.

"She's a character," says Ben. "She asked me if I wanted to audition for something. I wasn't sure what she meant."

"Huh."

"Did you tell her I played guitar?"

"Can't remember."

"That'll be it, then."

"Yeah, right."

Today, the sun shines and New Zealand does indeed look very beautiful. I let Ben drive. Driving is a man thing—they like to do it and I don't mind. It means I can see the countryside properly instead of focusing on the road.

Will they look like me? Not very like, of course that's not possible with my Chinese blood. Will they like me? How will they explain their rejection of past attempts to contact them? Was their mother's hatred so strong that they couldn't—wouldn't—think about me in a kindly way?

Eventually I put on a CD and try to drown out the questions.

"This car is a dog," Ben says when we reach the zigzag hill and the car chokes and gasps as we climb the first zig.

"I think it's pretty. And a beautiful shade of orange, don't you think?"

"I thought you preferred yellow?"

"That was last year."

"The oil light is on. Have you checked the oil?"

"Not recently." *Not ever.*

"You can ruin the engine if you don't."

"Mm."

"And it's a junk heap! Don't you ever clean out the rubbish?"

"If I get home in the daylight, I do. We're getting close. Keep an eye out for a very large mailbox on the left-hand side."

The weather is warmer and the skies are brighter than when I drove this way two months before. It feels natural to be sitting in a car beside Ben. I glance sideways at his face. His eyes are focused on the road and his mouth is curved into that familiar half smile. I remember how I used to kiss that mouth. I let my eyes slide down his neck and shoulder to his sinewy tanned arm and his long-fingered hand. I remember what he can do with his hands.

He glances across at me and I look away quickly. I keep my head still and move my eyes to the right so I can see his tanned thigh emerging from the khaki shorts. I can remember embracing his thighs with mine. My eyes slide up, but his groin, of course, is hidden behind the folds of cloth.

I remember what lies within the khaki.

"Do you want to go down?"

"What?"

"Isn't this the driveway?"

We have reached the turnoff with the sheep-size mailbox.

"This is it."

"Ready?"

My heart increases its beat. I can stand in front of an audience of hundreds with far less trepidation than sitting here now in the car, about to meet my father's first family.

The hot sun of Hawke's Bay heats the back of my head. I close my eyes for a moment, and breathe in the scent of grass and of livestock, with a hint of some blossom, perhaps honeysuckle, perhaps wild rose. I hear the faint baa of a lamb seeking its mother and birds twittering amongst high-up branches. When I open my eyes, the image of the entrance to Ngatirua etches itself on my brain. Grass dancing on the hillside, blue sky above, an avenue of tall trees pointing us toward the farm.

I smile my careful smile. "Of course."

Ben turns into Alison's driveway and parks behind the SUV. The dogs start barking. I get out of the car.

The door opens and a woman comes out, wiping her hands on the legs of her jeans, and shushing the dogs. She is taller and wider than me, and her hair is short and sandy colored. But you can see the family resemblance in the shape of the cheekbones and the tilt of her chin. Her eyes are hazel like our father's.

Her face breaks into a smile like the sun, and she holds out her hand.

Chapter 26

"Come in and meet the family!" Alison says, even her voice sounding a little like mine, but with a Kiwi accent not mid-Atlantic.

We enter a living room where a thickset man greets us with a wide white smile.

"This is my husband, Walter," she says.

He envelops me in a bearlike hug. "Look at you, just like your sister!"

"My friend, Ben," I say.

He leans over to Ben and grabs his hand, shaking it. "Nice eye you've got there."

"Wal," says my sister, "leave the poor man alone."

Ben explains he got the black eye protecting his sister from her drunken partner.

Wal nods approvingly. "Good on you, mate."

I'm not used to this. I'm not quite sure how to act. I look around the living room in my sister's house. Papers are scattered over most surfaces and books bulge from the shelves lining one wall.

Alison looks at me and smiles again. She turns to the open doorway and calls, "Jess!"

A teenaged girl with a full-lipped mouth, dark hair, and brown eyes like her father's, emerges from the house's other wing.

"Your aunt Lin," says Alison.

"Hi," the girl says.

Jess has the archetypal teenage expression in her eyes—annoyance that she has been interrupted, embarrassment that these clumsy beings are her parents, tepid interest in any visitors over the age of twenty-five.

I take a step forward to hug her. With a look of alarm, she takes a step back.

I figure I should take my cues from my family. "Cool dress," I say. She is wearing a caramel-colored shift draped in loose black netting, with clusters of beads and feathers decorating the bodice.

"She designed it herself," says my sister proudly.

A golden-haired young man walks in the door behind us. Wal lays an arm across the boy's shoulder and pulls him forward.

"This is our nephew, Max. Your aunt Lin and her friend Ben."

He offers me his hand and a shy half smile. "Mum says she'll be along later."

Max has clear blue eyes, a halo of gold curls, and the kind of fair skin that flushes readily into pink, especially when embarrassed as he is now.

I glance at Alison and see her smile fade. There is a brief silence. Wal opens the French doors to the terrace and tells us to take a seat outside while he brings us a drink. Alison returns to the kitchen. I am given a Chardonnay and Ben and Max are handed cans of cold beer.

"Jess?" asks Wal and offers her a bottle of ginger beer.

Her mouth turns down, but she takes it. My sister carries out a platter of olives, sun-dried tomatoes, and pâté. She catches my eye and smiles, then carefully places the tray on the table. I keep staring at her, looking for the traces of my own face in hers.

"Sit down, Ali," her husband tells her. She gives him a brusque dismissive grimace and returns to the kitchen.

Wal turns back to Ben and me. "How do you like Wellington?"

"It's very beautiful," I say.

"You'll find it hotter up here," Wal replies.

"Has the weather been good?" I ask him.

"Nah," he replies. "Not enough rain." He laughs. "You city folk think it's good when the sun shines and it's dry, but we farmers need the rain to grow grass to feed the lambs. We don't do too badly here; we're higher up so we get more rain, and the land is limestone so it holds the moisture in the ground."

Max smiles, his face flushing. "We're biodynamic. We farm without chemicals. Uncle Wal pioneered our methods," he adds. "I'm just the apprentice."

"Dunno for how much longer we can keep it up. Organic certification is a nightmare," Wal says. "The bureaucrats justify their existence by finding something wrong. You have to pay to fix whatever they demand and then pay for them to recheck everything. It's got to the point the cost of compliance is more than any premium you get for organic beef and lamb."

"Maybe one day nonorganic producers will be the ones who have to pay the extra costs and fees instead," Ben says.

"Fat chance in my lifetime," says Wal.

"What about you, Jess?" I ask. "Are you planning to work on the farm too?"

"Not bloody likely," she says.

"She wants to go to university and study fashion design," says Wal. "But her mother's not keen on her going so far away."

"What am I not keen on?" Alison joins us and hands her wine glass to her husband. "Chardonnay, Wal. Oh, Jess going to university? Of course, she can. But to the local institute, not the one down in Wellington."

She gestures to Wal to refill my glass. "Do you like the wine, Lin? It's local. Clearview."

"It is very good," I tell her.

"Hawke's Bay makes the best Chardonnay in New Zealand," she says with satisfaction.

She moves the platter and passes out the plates and forks and napkins that Wal had forgotten to distribute. She looks at me and catches me staring at her and smiles again. It's okay for her, she is used to seeing a sister's face; she's been seeing Vivienne's ever since they were born. But I am not used to this sudden familiarity. I turn and look at Jess's profile, hoping to see something I recognize in her. But Jess has her father's features. *Perhaps something about our chins?*

Wal keeps the conversation going while Alison ducks in and out of the kitchen. He laughs a lot. Max is quiet, but smiles and replies when Wal brings him into the conversation. My niece looks bored and soon makes an excuse to return to her room. She vanishes across the terrace with her hands before her, clicking away at her cell phone.

Ben watches her go with a smile. "Very like Emmy," he says. "They're always on those bloody cell phones, aren't they?"

Alison calls Max into the dining room. "Can you chase up your mother, dear?" she asks in a loud whisper. "Dinner will spoil if we wait any longer."

Max leaves the house. Wal opens more wine, and Alison takes her seat with us.

"Does Vivienne have a problem meeting me?" I ask.

She looks down at the table and straightens the food, moving the plate nearer to Ben.

"Vivienne is always late," she says. "What do you think of the bread? I get it from Havelock North. Good, isn't it? Ben, have some more olives. Finish them, there's plenty left in the jar."

She rises abruptly and takes the empty bowl into the kitchen to refill.

Ben reaches across and pats my leg. "Okay?" His blue eyes look into mine and he smiles encouragingly.

"Okay," I reply. I put my left hand over his, briefly.

A cold draft blows across the back of my neck as a door opens behind me. The scent of something sweet, spicy, and exotic catches my nostrils. When I turn, she is standing there.

My other sister, Vivienne.

Chapter 27

Vivienne's hazel eyes are large and her cheekbones high, her nose is straight and her mouth curved and generous. She has our father's auburn hair, coiffured in sculpted waves to her shoulders. Her elegant body, a slimmer version of Alison's, is encased in a ruffled black dress and her long, shapely legs end in high-heeled shoes.

She stares at me, taking me in just as I am her. No one says a word. Then Vivienne's face relaxes into a small, polite smile and she pats my arm with red-nail-tipped fingers.

"Lovely to meet you," she says, and turns to Ben, ignoring his eye. "How do you do?"

Ben puts out his hand, and she touches it briefly.

"My husband, Christopher," she says, gesturing at her two silent menfolk. "And my son, Maximilian."

Christopher reaches out his hand.

"We've already met," I say, taking it in mine, realizing that while he cannot recognize my face, my voice with its accent is unmistakable.

"What?" says Vivienne, her eyes widening.

"The lady who came to the door," Christopher replies. "I forgot to tell you someone was asking for you."

"I didn't give my name."

"Dinner's on the table," says Alison. "Come inside. Don't worry about your glasses. I've got fresh ones. Wal, haven't you opened the red wine yet?

"Lin, you sit there on Wal's right. Ben, you sit here next to me. Viv, put Christopher next to me and then you and Max.

Jess, over there next to your father. Oh, Jess, not those napkins. Go and get the black-and-red ones."

Dinner is a large filet of beef, accompanied by roasted root vegetables, mashed potatoes, and a dish of green beans, broccoli, zucchini, and peas.

"So, what is it you do?" Vivienne asks.

"Wal, the wine."

Wal pours red wine from a decanter into each glass.

"It's Stonecroft," says Alison. "The best Syrah in New Zealand."

I am describing my working day. "And then the Government told us we must—"

"Darling, would you like yams?" Vivienne says to Christopher. He nods and she serves him two perfectly pink grub-shaped objects.

"Oh, dash, I've forgotten the—" and Alison leaps up and returns to the kitchen.

"Baked tomatoes," she says and wedges the final serving tray on the table.

"Terrific spread, Alison," says Ben.

"Yes, lovely," I say.

Alison beams, her gift of food acknowledged.

I stop talking about what I do. No one is remotely interested in Chief Executive Lin Mere. It is curiously cathartic to be just me for a change.

"And what do you do, Ben?" asks Vivienne.

"I make furniture," he replies. "One-offs mainly, on commission."

"Oh, you must come up to the house," she says. "I have some fine pieces."

"Vivienne has excellent taste," says Christopher and reaches out to touch Vivienne's arm. "She's made the house a showcase."

Vivienne smiles and puts her hand over his.

"Where are you guys staying?" asks Wal.

Ben glances at me before replying. "We were planning to drive into Hastings to find a motel."

"Oh, no, you mustn't do that," cries Alison. "We have plenty of beds here. And you won't want to be driving these roads so late at night."

Alison pauses and glances at Vivienne, whose face has stiffened.

"You guys stay with us, okay?" says Wal. "Plenty of room."

I look at Alison's face and can see only kindness in her eyes. "If you're sure it's not an imposition?"

She smiles at me. "No, no, not at all."

Ben asks Wal about organic farming practices, and the conversation rushes around the table like a Mexican wave.

For a moment I detach myself from the strands and let the voices wash over me. I look around the table at my newfound family. At Alison's kind face and comfortable body. She has welcomed me into her home and her family. She doesn't treat me like an alien. She doesn't treat me like a chief executive. She treats me like a sister. It is an odd feeling.

Vivienne is harder to fathom. She seems devoted to her blind husband. I glance across at her son, Max. A nice boy, looks nothing like either of them. Seems closer to his uncle Wal than to Vivienne or Christopher. I catch his eye, and he smiles automatically. Good-looking and doesn't know it.

And Jess? Scowling silently into her meal. I'll bet she's going to be a handful when she finally cuts loose from her parents.

"What have you made for pud, Ali?" asks Wal as she clears the plates away.

"Jess! Help!" she says to her daughter.

I stand up, but she shakes her head. "No, no, it's Jess's job. I've made prune cake," she says in reply to Wal's question. "Figure they won't have had that before."

"Never heard of it," says Ben. "But it sounds terrific."

I take another sip of wine, rest my elbows on Alison's white tablecloth, and let my body relax from its habitual stiff poise.

•   •   •

Later, after we have eaten Alison's cake, Vivienne and Christopher prepare to leave.

"Pop in tomorrow before you head off, if you want," she says, with tepid enthusiasm. "Max, are you ready?" and they climb into their car to drive up the hill home.

"She's pretty black out here," says Wal. "No streetlights so when the clouds cover the moon and stars, it's easier to drive between the houses."

It must be cloudy tonight because as I look around I can see nothing apart from the taillights of Vivienne's car. You forget how very dark it can be without the city lights.

"Mind you, Christopher can walk the farm pretty easy, day or night. But we don't want Vivienne falling off those shoes of hers and into the roses, do we?" Wal laughs and shuts the door.

Back inside Alison is tidying the kitchen and refuses my offer of help. I return to the living room and Wal tops up my glass. The two men are having one of those male things, some kind of ritual of bonding. They talk about the cricket and then about the rugby, and match each other as they drink their beer, glass for glass.

Suddenly a rifle shot crashes into the silence of the night. I start and spill my wine.

"Max must be shooting possums," Wal says. "You shine a flashlight up the tree and when you see their eyes shine back, wham!"

He sees my expression. "They're vermin, city girl! You have to get rid of the vermin. Max is a good kid. Don't know what I'd do without him. Christopher's not much use around the farm, of course."

"Has he always been blind?" I ask.

"He was in a bad car accident when he was in his twenties. Went through the windshield. He used to have a little sight in one eye but, apparently, it's gone now."

"Must have been hard for Vivienne and Max."

"Christopher isn't Max's father. Viv was married to Fergus McDonald, but he walked out on her. Not that I blame him, Viv can be bloody hard going."

"What's that, Wal?" calls Alison from the kitchen.

"Nothing, dear."

There is an awkward silence as Alison reenters the room. She is frowning.

"Vivienne and Christopher met in hospital," says Alison. "Viv had a breakdown when Fergus walked out. We still worry about her."

She returns to the kitchen. There is another awkward silence.

"Another glass, Ben? Since you don't have to drive," says Wal. "That's some ugly car you're driving."

"It's gutless, too," says Ben.

"But it's in very good condition," I excuse myself. "I don't have to maintain it or anything."

"Just as well," says Ben. "You barely know where the oil goes."

"That's not quite right, Ben," I say.

"No?"

"I don't even remotely know where the oil goes."

Wal laughs. "Typical sheila," he says. "And they never bother filling the car with petrol either, do they? Run it on empty until muggins here fills it."

"What's that, Wal?" asks Alison as she comes back into the room carrying towels.

"Just telling Ben how much cheaper petrol is up here in the Bay."

"Everything is cheaper here than in Wellington," says Alison with satisfaction.

"Now, I've put you two in here." She shows me a pretty double room.

I don't tell her we're not a couple. What could I say? That we loved each other once and now we're what? Just friends?

Ben pulls off his sneakers and his shorts and scrambles under the covers in his t-shirt and boxers. I take my time washing my face and cleaning my teeth. When I return to the room, he has rolled over to face away from me. I turn out the light, slip under the covers, and lie on my back. It is very, very dark.

"Well, I've finally met them."

There is a rustle as Ben rolls onto his back.

"They're a nice family, Lin."

"Alison is very kind. And Wal is a character, isn't he?"

"Witty repartee."

"Yeah."

"I'm not sure about your other sister."

"She is beautiful. Far better looking than me."

Ben makes one of those noncommittal grunts men make when they don't wish to either agree with you or contradict you.

I lie in darkness beside a man I have loved for two years now and feel the whisper of a cold wind against my cheek. I find myself thinking about growing old, which I've never thought about before. I've always expected everything to only get better. But next year I turn forty. A good age to be a chief executive, yes, but a bad one to be a single woman.

I know I must try to force out the words.

"Ben," I say, quietly, feeling the word break free from my lips, feeling my tongue finish his name against my teeth. "Ben, Ben, Ben."

He doesn't reply.

"I would do anything to undo what happened with Robert. But I can't. Can you forgive me?"

It is like a cork emerging from the bottle; the wine is ready and must now be poured.

"And, Ben? I love you."

There; it is said, but Ben says nothing in response.

I wait, but he is silent and I realize I have left it too late, that he no longer loves me.

I wallow for a moment in self-denigration, then I think, bastard, and I turn to him and say, "And I forgive you, too, for being such a fricking jerk!"

"Wha?" he says, blurrily. "What did you say? Sorry, I was asleep."

"Nothing important. Go back to sleep."

Ben's breathing slows, but I stay awake. Ben doesn't leave again until Monday.

There is still Sunday.

Chapter 28

Alison comes in with a bright smile and a tray of tea and toast and we sit up and prop ourselves against the pillows and pretend it is the most natural thing in the world. By the time I use the bathroom, Ben has dressed and gone.

"Gidday!" says Wal when I emerge into the kitchen. "Ali's out collecting the papers. Thought I'd take Ben for a drive 'round the farm. You coming?"

I shake my head. "I'll wait for Alison."

The men climb into one of those SUVs that real farmers drive, not just suburban housewives, and I hover awkwardly, waiting for my sister.

Alison smiles when she comes in, and passes me one of the newspapers. "The other's for Viv. I'll go up later." She glances at me. "Or perhaps you'd like to take it to her?"

So I walk up to the main house and knock at the door. This morning she is wearing cream linen slacks and a gray silk blouse. Our hair coloring is very similar. I even own a shirt in an identical shade.

"Thank you." She takes the newspaper with a perfunctory smile. "Do come in. I'll make coffee."

Max and Christopher are in the kitchen, a square, white room with a lot of white tiles and a large white granite-topped island in the middle of the room. Max is at the sink rinsing out an elaborate juicer and Christopher sits at the island drinking the freshly squeezed juice. A farming program plays on the radio.

"Max, can you make Lin some coffee?"

My nephew gives me his perfect smile and makes a perfect cappuccino on Vivienne's expensive machine.

"Tch!" says Vivienne, looking at the newspaper, her face suddenly in flames.

She mutters something about foreigners and farms and turns to her husband. "It's a crying shame about those Asians buying up the Simpson farms."

"They've got approval?" asks Christopher. "Bloody sissy Government."

Vivienne continues to read.

Max's smile fades. He glances across at me, embarrassed. "I'll show you the house if you like, Auntie."

Vivienne snorts. "I don't think she expects you to call her Aunt."

"He can call me Aunt if he likes," I reply. "Do you have other aunts besides Alison and me?"

Max's face goes blank, and his eyes dart at his mother's face and away again.

"He has no other family," Vivienne says. "His father deserted him years ago. He's never bothered to return any of Max's calls."

Ah, poor kid. I know how he feels. When anyone eyed Mom's face and then mine, there would always be questions. She'd say my Chinese mother deserted me when I was a baby. I know she didn't mean it to hurt.

Vivienne flicks the newspaper back into an even set of folds and stands up. "I'll show her around."

She walks ahead of me down the long, wide hallway with its beautiful waxed wooden floors and artwork carefully placed on the walls. At one side is the guest bedroom with antique furniture and its own bathroom and sitting room. At the far end is the formal living room. She opens the curtains and the sun floods into the room. Here, too, the walls and the shelves are covered with original art and sculpture.

I ask about a piece of ceramic, and she picks it up and caresses the surface and tells me about the artist before returning it to its carefully chosen position. She shows me the formal dining room, the family sitting room, and then the main bedroom wing. Max's bedroom is up in the eaves. His room is unusually tidy for a young man. Vivienne repositions his silver hairbrush on the dresser.

I have seen and admired the whole house except for the suite at the far end, beyond the main entrance. I guess it to be hers and Christopher's.

Then she takes me to the front entrance and holds the door open.

"You're welcome to use the pool," she says. "It's unlocked."

I step outside and Vivienne closes the door behind me. I walk past the tennis court and turn to look back at the house, sparkling in the fierce morning sunshine. Birds swoop in and out of the tall trees that line the path. The air smells sweet; of grass and flowers and fresh clean air.

I return to Alison's house, change into my swimsuit, and walk through the rose garden to the swimming pool, encased in blue anodized steel and glass. The noise from the filtering system and the lapping of the water reverberates against the glass with a distorted echo. I dive in and breaststroke to the far end, then turn and thrust myself through the water again, emerging gasping. The water is tepid, with a cool edge as it touches my skin. An air mattress floats enticingly on the surface of the pool. I climb aboard and lie with my sun hat on my face, toasting in the sun, and think about the last twenty-four hours.

This is the magic place my father talked of, his eyes gazing into the distance. I think I, too, could grow to love it here, and my newfound family. Kind Alison and prickly, elegant Vivienne. Bluff Wal and cool Christopher. Pretty Jess and gorgeous, sweet Max.

I am part of a family, a proper part, connected by blood. I belong here.

And maybe, just maybe, Ben and I can work something out. As a smile stretches my mouth, I suddenly feel a bump beneath me and then I'm tipped off the air mattress and into the water, falling against a hard body.

Huh! He thinks he can dunk me and get away with it! I slip downward and grab his Speedos and pull them down.

Speedos?

I kick away to the edge of the pool, looking back at the thrashing shape of my sister's husband Christopher. I have just groped a blind man.

"I thought you were Ben."

Christopher's face turns toward me. The sun glints off the droplets of water on the dark glasses that have managed to stay on his face. He says nothing, but scrambles out of the pool.

"I guess you thought I was Vivienne. When you bumped me off the air bed."

His jaw is set. "I didn't realize anyone was in the pool at all."

I appraise him openly. After all, he can't see me looking. He has a splendid body, unscarred by whatever happened to him in the car crash.

Then I shake my head, ashamed. "Do come back in. The water's lovely."

"I think I've had enough for today." Christopher stalks out of the pool room.

God, that was embarrassing. I swim a few more lengths before I, too, leave the pool. I meet Vivienne on the path.

"Have you seen Christopher?" she asks.

"I think he went back to the house." Thank goodness she didn't come down any earlier.

"You look flushed, Lin."

"It's very hot," I reply. "I've had a little too much sun."

She reaches out and touches my shoulder. "I'm glad you came after all," she says. "I'm sure it will work out."

I smile, searching her beautiful face for her thoughts. "I hope so."

She nods and walks past me to the pool.

When I arrive back at Alison's house, she takes me by the arm.

"I thought I'd show you the studio," she says in a half whisper. "Come along."

We climb the hill in the direction Christopher had led me on my first visit. I wasn't stupid enough to only bring high-heeled shoes to a farm, like the archetypal New York city slicker, but my sandals aren't quite up to the dangers of the paddock. I manage to avoid the crunchy round disks of cow pie only to fall victim to the squishy pellets the sheep have dropped.

"That sheep is walking on only three legs," I tell Alison.

"This is the dog tucker paddock. Any animals that get injured are put in here. If they don't get better Wal kills them and feeds them to the dogs."

"Oh."

"Unless they're diseased, in which case he buries them in the offal pits."

Ugh. "I guess there's a less pretty side to farming."

"Pretty?" Alison gives a snort. "It's a business, Lin. We do what we do for money. Like you and your—whatever you do."

I have to smile because I don't think what I do is remotely like anything here.

Amongst the trees is a small hut crouching on the very edge of the cliff. Alison fishes the key out from under the doormat and opens the door.

I walk into a room with a large window and a spectacular view out over the valley. The studio has everything you'd need to make yourself comfortable: a television, an old stereo with a stack of CDs, a bookshelf full of classics, a guitar, and a big divan covered in cushions. To one side are a small kitchen bench, sink, and pantry. A steep staircase rises to a mezzanine.

"He built it himself," Alison says, in that same half whisper.

"Dad?"

She nods. "After he left, Mum used to come here and paint. When she died, Gran let Viv and me have it as our playhouse. Now we just use it for extra guests."

I open the door by the pantry to see a small shower room and a hand basin.

"The toilet is outside. A long drop over a long drop." Alison giggles.

"Do you remember him at all?" I ask.

"Of course we remember him, dear, but we don't talk about him. Mum couldn't bear him being mentioned, and Gran would always tell us off. So I guess we just got out of the habit."

Alison gives a small sigh, and then opens the door and holds it for me to leave the studio. After she relocks the door, we walk back on the path between the trees to the field.

I glance at my sister's broad face and ever-present smile. I want to know why they never tried to make contact, but I'm afraid to ask.

Now that I've found them, I don't want to run any risk of losing them again.

Chapter 29

"The brakes feel jerky."

"For God's sake, Ben, stop beating up on the car!" I say. "It's perfectly all right."

At the turn of the bend, I look back and can just glimpse Vivienne's house behind the trees. Sometimes you see something that is so beautiful that it makes you feel small because you know you could never create anything quite as perfect no matter how much time or money you have.

"Magical."

"The house?" Ben asks.

"Every room is perfect and every piece of furniture perfectly chosen. The floorboards are some lovely old wood waxed to a perfect shine. In the living room, the walls and the ceiling are paneled, and she'd lime washed the wood."

"Wal puts lime on the driveway. Did you know they have an old limestone quarry?"

"And she's filled the rooms with a mix of old antiques and modern pieces of furniture. Everything either coordinated or completely contrasted. You should have come. You would have loved what she's done."

"Wal was keen to show me the farm. Did you know there's a special bug that eats thistles?"

"And the art and the sculpture. She has originals all over the house. The colors were just right. When I came last time, I only saw what was hanging in the hallway. But she has gorgeous pieces everywhere, from some of New Zealand's best artists, I'd say."

"Wal makes his fertilizer from fish heads he buys on the

wharf in Napier. Brews them up in a big iron vat until he gets this stinky black rotten mush. Then he sprays it on the paddocks with this twin-armed thing—"

"Vivienne has a bronze twin-armed fertility goddess in the garden."

"I bet her garden smells better than Wal's paddocks."

"I have never seen such a beautiful place."

"It seems funny she goes to so much effort to make the house beautiful for a blind man to live in."

"I never saw their bedroom. Perhaps she doesn't bother putting any art in there."

"Was she any friendlier?"

"Not to start with." I give a sigh. "She didn't look at me. Rushed me round the house. Ignored my compliments. So I walked back to Alison's, but when I went back for a swim she seemed a little friendlier."

I stare out the window, searching the green hills. "Alison showed me our father's old studio. It's several paddocks back, on the edge of the same cliff as the zigzag road. He built it himself, she said." I turn in my seat. "I think it must be just over there, to our right. The road takes a long loop north before cutting back to the ridge. The farm isn't far away from here as the crow flies."

We reach the top of the ridge and start the descent.

"I didn't see the spectacular view when I came the first time, the weather was too shitty. But you keep your eyes on the road, Ben."

"You're beginning to sound like Alison."

"Tha—"

We're going too fast, heading toward the bend in the road and the cliff face beyond. Ben stamps his foot on the brake, but nothing happens.

"Ben?"

Ben fumbles with the handbrake, but it is not enough, the car is still accelerating.

"Ben!"

He slams the gearbox into reverse and the car shudders and then skids into the fence line on the edge of the road, twanging against the wire.

The car teeters on the edge, the front end over the edge, held by three slim strands of barbed wire. In front is a long drop onto the final twist of the road below.

I can hear the fence posts creak and creak again as the heavy weight of the car's clumsy metal body pushes against the wire.

"Undo your belt and climb out! Carefully."

I press the belt release, but nothing happens. Ben leans down and presses it for me and holds the belt away as it slips loose.

"Won't me moving make it worse?"

"Please, Lin, get out. I want you to be safe!"

The handbrake is creaking, and I can almost feel it shudder.

"If the car starts to slip, I can jump," I say. "But I'm not moving until you do."

The sun shines down oblivious to our plight. Birds fly across the sky in front of us, their calls disappearing with the wind. Animals graze in the pastures just beyond us, the safe side of the pasture, where the land is steep but not perpendicular as it is here beneath our car's wheels.

The brake is still holding.

"Let's both get out slowly."

I open the door and edge my way across the seat, trying to keep my weight balanced, avoiding any sudden lurches. I look back and Ben is doing the same.

"Count of three, okay?"

"Okay."

"Ready? Three, two, one, jump!"

I roll free and immediately turn to make sure he is out.

Ben is safe. He is standing beyond the car, which is rocking but hasn't slipped off the edge.

My pulse slows.

Ben drags a broken fencepost over, shoving it under the car, in front of the back wheels. I push a stone over, wedging it in front of the post.

"I think it will hold."

I take my cell phone out of my handbag. "I'll call Wal."

"Yeah. But give it to me."

Jess answers the phone and Ben asks if her father is around.

"Wal? I've managed to put this dumb shit of a car into the ditch. Any chance of getting a tow?"

"Sure, mate! Where are you?"

"On the zigzag. You won't be able to miss us."

"I'll be there in two shakes of a lamb's tail."

When Wal arrives in the Land Rover, he gazes at the orange car in silence. "How the bloody hell did you manage that?"

"The brakes failed."

He ties the towrope to the bumper and pulls the car away from the edge of the cliff. The men settle it on flat ground.

"Let's have a look," Wal says and crawls in on his hands and knees.

He jiggles the pedal and then backs out of the car with something in the palm of his hand.

"Looks like this might have got stuck under the foot brake and maybe slipped sideways, jamming the pedal up," he says, holding it out.

"A spring?"

Ben climbs into the car, presses the brake that now falls flat to the floor, and turns on the ignition. The brake holds firm. He puts the car into gear and drives slowly down the zag, testing the brake all the way.

"She's okay now."

I climb into the passenger's seat.

Wal rubs his chin. "I won't tell the girls what a close shave you've had. Vivienne gets anxious about car accidents."

We wave good-bye and head on down the road.

"Phew," says Ben. "That was close."

"It wasn't my lack of maintenance anyway," I reply.

"In future, remember not to let junk roll round in the car," he says. "Any idea where it came from?"

"Nothing that springs to mind," and I giggle.

Ben smiles and pats my knee. I reach out and run my hand up and down his warm, strong back and let my head rest briefly on his shoulder.

When we get home, I set out some Stilton and crackers and open a bottle of wine.

"Alison asked if I want to join them for Christmas," I tell him.

"I bet she'll put on a great feast."

"Yep."

"And Christmas is the time you're supposed to be with your family."

We finish eating in companionable silence.

"Another glass of wine?" He holds up the bottle and smiles.

I look across the table at the man I chose to give up when they offered me the job. I still haven't written the report.

The wolves are calling me to rejoin the fray, but their calls have grown faint. Instead I hear the sound of the birds' distant cries as we teetered at the edge of the cliff, wondering whether we would live or die.

"Why not."

We take the bottle up to the roof. The sky is dark now, and the ever-present breeze nips at my skin. Below us the lights of the city twinkle, like the stars above us.

"Ahhh!" Ben gasps as he lowers himself into the warm depths of the Jacuzzi.

"Do you enjoy *this*?" I say, reaching out.

I float across his body. "And *this*?"

Chapter 30

Ben is still asleep when I wake, just before the alarm on my cell phone is due to sound. I lean across to switch it off so it won't disturb him. His face looks peaceful in the gentle light that intrudes through the crack in the curtains. Jaw relaxed, eyes shut, brown hair coiling over the white pillowcase.

I should get up. Yet still I lie, warm in the depths of my bed, my lover beside me. He sighs and rolls over. I snuggle against his back and reach my arm over him. His hand catches mine against his chest and he rolls toward me, and we make love again.

When I finally slip out of bed, it is nearly nine o'clock and Helen will be wondering where I am. I send an e-mail to tell her I will be late. Can she get Tom to summarize the figures and write the report for Stewart Hobb?

Ben is lying on his back propped up on the pillows. We haven't talked about when we will meet again.

He smiles as I hand him his coffee and climb back into bed. "Aren't you going to be late?"

"It's okay. I've got Tom to write up my report. Paper?"

"Thanks." He takes the World section and I open the Business pages.

I finish my coffee and we swap sections.

"Have you decided to join them for Christmas?"

I glance over at him, but he is looking down at the newspaper again. "I want to. It's important I build some kind of relationship with my sisters. And, if I turn them down, they may not ask again."

I don't want to lose them.

I don't want to lose Ben either. "When can you come back?"

He drops the paper on the floor and picks up the advertisement insert. "Perhaps you could come and visit Em and me?"

For a moment, I feel warmed by his invitation. But it's not really feasible. Getting there takes hours. I don't know when I'll be able to spare the time.

"It's easier if you come here."

"It's pretty bloody expensive, Lin. I can't afford it."

"I don't mind paying."

"Well, I do. Besides, with Fay going away it will be hard for me to leave."

"How old is Em now? Seventeen? Surely she could spend a weekend on her own."

Ben frowns. "She's still only a kid. She gets afraid when she's alone in the house."

"Perhaps she could have a friend over to stay? In America we did that all the time. Well, not me, but some kids did."

He is shaking his head. "Parents don't like to leave teenagers to fend for themselves. You never know what might happen."

"Oh, come on, this is New Zealand! The safest little country in the world."

I can see by the way his face has set that he has no intention of leaving his little girl alone in his house, even with a friend to stay, whatever I say.

Reality crashes back down on me. Why did I think Ben and I could have any kind of relationship? We'd never managed to meld our lives together before. And even though I'd come to the same goddamn country, we were still a long long way apart.

Same old impossible situation. Today he will leave like he always leaves me, with no promise of any return.

I flick to the end of the section, put it down, and get out of bed. "I'd better get ready."

When I emerge from the bathroom, Ben is in the kitchen making toast. I get dressed quickly and sit in front of the mirror.

I hold my face between the palms of my hands and feel the heat of my skin, still flushed with anger. Then I paint on my corporate face, stroke by stroke, tint by tint.

He carries in a plate of buttered toast dabbed with Marmite and places it beside me.

"I don't have time to eat that."

Ben stands behind me holding the plate. In the mirror I watch his smile slowly fade.

"Right," and he turns away and goes back to the living room.

"I'll be off then," I say, taking up my laptop case. "Can you leave the key under the pot when you go?"

Ben looks at me and I look back at him. I don't move. Then he walks over, puts his arms around me and kisses me. I hold myself rigid.

"Good-bye, Lin," he says, and his hands slip away from my shoulders to let me walk out the door.

And I walk down the path, get in my car, and drive to work.

I don't think about him. There's no point. No point at all.

Helen brings me my schedule for the day. My schedule is always full. I wonder for a moment if there is anything I can get Tom to do instead of me. He seemed happy to write the final summary for the Board. I shouldn't have to do everything myself.

"Did you have a nice weekend?" she asks.

I glance at her and see nothing but friendly interest in her gaze. But I'm sure she's probing, wondering why her workaholic boss got in late for once.

"An old friend was visiting," I reply. "We took a trip up to Hawke's Bay."

"Oh, yes?" she says. "What did you think of Napier? All the Art Deco buildings are marvelous, don't you think?"

"We didn't make it that far. But I'm spending Christmas there, so I'll make sure to visit Napier."

She nods, relieved that I won't miss out on some of the wonders of New Zealand.

"It's great you're getting to see more of New Zealand, Lin. And that you're taking a bit of time off. You know what they say about all work and no play?"

"But I am a dull girl, Helen."

"Nah! You're so clever and so energetic, no one would think of you as dull. And you're always dressed in nice colors, and your hair is lovely."

I smile back at her and she nods again and leaves. I follow her out and go into my bathroom to check that my lipstick is still perfect.

In the mirror the immaculate image fades under my gaze. Instead, I see the dull-brown little girl growing up in Mom's house, the grind who always did well at school but was never invited to parties. Never got the cool guy as the boyfriend.

When my cell phone rings, I see my home telephone number displayed. Even though I know there's no point, my pulse starts racing.

"Ben?"

"Lin, I—" but the phone goes dead. Damn. Forgot to connect it to the charger last night.

My anger has ebbed away, leaving me feeling foolish and anxious and regretful. I hurry back up to my office.

Helen looks up from the phone and says, "I've got Mr. Smith on the line for you, Lin."

I point two fingers in the air and vanish inside, closing the door behind me, and call home from my desk.

But the call switches to voice mail. "This is Lin Mere. I can't answer your call right now so please leave a message after the tone. Beeeep."

Helen puts her head in the door. "He's been on hold for a couple of minutes, and I think he's getting annoyed."

"Give me a minute."

But when I call again the telephone rings and there is no answer.

I sit at my desk and let out a long sigh, and then I pick up the phone again.

"Okay, Helen, you can put Robert through now."

When I hang up the phone after being yelled at by Robert, the breath of the wolves tickles the back of my neck. I had promised I would give Hera my complete commitment and I had failed. I reach up and try to rub the coldness away. I had relaxed and spent a weekend without any thought for the job.

And now I had to pay the price.

Chapter 31

"Tom," I say calmly when he answers, my voice under control. "Why did you put all those red flags in the Board summary?"

There is silence on the line. "Scott helped me write it. We've got a lot of issues, Lin."

"Issues, yes, but nothing we can't solve. And I always provide the solutions as well as any problems in the report."

"But we don't have any solutions."

"There are always solutions. Let's have a meeting with the team and see what we can flush out."

I am still fuming when Helen puts her head around the door. "It's the chairman," she says.

"Linnette," Stewart Hobb says, "we are extremely concerned about the number of red flags in the report this month. And why was Heke writing the report?"

"I asked Tom to prepare the summary. Obviously, I should have reviewed it before he sent the report out."

"If there's a major problem with quality, then it's important the Board gets to know about it."

"There isn't a major problem with quality."

"That's not an answer, and you know it. I am not happy about this, and I'm not happy that you are misleading us."

I hold the phone and curse silently. "I am sorry you feel that way, Stewart," I say in a clipped voice. "I can assure you that we have practical work-arounds for all the issues listed in the report. On the up side, we've managed to get the council to agree to let us work on the esplanade between the hours of midnight and five a.m."

"That will cost more."

"Inevitably, but it is the best we're likely to get. Unfortunately, we haven't been able to get the Government to budge on the launch date."

Hobb snorts. "I told you not to bother trying."

"We had to give it one last shot," I reply.

He hangs up. I sigh and then I start going through the issues for which we need to find solutions. My temper is very short today. The thin veneer is wearing through.

Tom introduces the first issue on the list.

"The customer-care package doesn't match the sales process the consultants defined," he says. "So it looks like there will be more modifications, which will push out the time frames and hit the budget."

"Why don't we model the processes around what the packages can support?" I suggest.

"But those won't be the *best* processes."

"*Best* is a luxury we can't afford."

Tom's lips thin and he looks down at his papers.

"Next?"

Peake introduces the next issue. "Ian wants the customer operations staff to start in the New Year. We didn't budget those costs until March."

"But March is when we're supposed to go live," says Ian.

"So that's when we need salespeople."

"They need to be trained first."

"How long does it take to train people?"

"More than a couple of days for God's sake!"

"Surely, less than a couple of months!"

"Ian," I say. "We can't take on any new staff until February. And we can only take on half the number you're asking for."

"We can't give our customers the best possible service unless we have the full team and spend the full eight weeks on training them on all the processes."

"We can't afford the extra staff and training to give our customers the *best* possible service. We can only afford a core team, enough for *very good* service, which we'll get by training them to think about the customer and use their initiative to solve problems, rather than be trained in every possible scenario."

"We wanted the best!"

Get real! "Sometimes very good is good enough."

The next issue is the testing of our billing processes.

Peake gives another smile. "We don't have time to run the full suite of tests," he says. "We need to call in some assistance."

Fred is looking at his hands again. I know by now this means he disagrees but doesn't want to say so. He is such a very *nice* man.

"Fred?"

"It's not the lack of people working on the system, it's the sheer amount of testing we should do. It's like pregnancy—you can make two women pregnant, but it will still take nine months to get a baby. More people will just get in the way."

Peake casts a cool eye at Fred, who flushes and looks down.

"We would run the risk of sending out incorrect bills," says Tom, his face darkening and his mouth tightening as it does when he is angry and frustrated.

"So what? Why would it be so bad if we don't send out any bills for the first month? It's not as if we will have many customers to bill to start with. We could calculate them and type them up by hand, for God's sake."

"You can't do that." Tom says.

"It's what they did in the old days," I reply.

Fred assures Tom he expects the bills will be correct. "Manual methods will be our fallback if there are any major problems with the bill run," he says.

"But—" says Tom.

"But nothing," I reply. "These are the tests we must complete before launch and these are the ones we complete if we can. We launch even if we don't finish those tests."

•   •   •

After the other managers leave, Peake says he wants a quick word. He smiles widely as he stretches out his legs under my desk.

"We can't go on like this," he says. "I've organized a review."

"A review of what exactly?"

How can anyone review anything at all at the moment when everything is moving so fast that we have been giving verbal updates instead of written reports?

"I thought an assessment of Hera's maturity."

I'm angry with him, but I don't show it, yet. We're flat out launching a smart new business in the record-breaking time of six months, but we're going to be measured on how well documented our processes are and how consistently we follow them?

"Hera is a very new company," I say. "It's too early to expect us to be mature."

He flashes another smile. "Never too early to start improving," he replies. "We don't want to be considered immature."

"The opposite of mature isn't necessarily immature. We need to be young, fresh, agile, innovative."

"I've cleared it with Stewart."

"Cancel it," I say, my composure cracking.

Peake's face stills.

"I'm not suffering another infestation of consultants. The distraction could be fatal. We're too busy right now."

His smile returns. "I'll tell Stewart you're refusing to accept a review."

I paste my inscrutable face back together. "I will reconsider your proposal after the launch."

After he is gone, I stand up and rub my neck and gaze out the window. Wellington's waterfront glistens in the sun. White sails scud across the water and pink bodies lie in the park by the lagoon at the edge of the sea. I wish I were out there.

The job no longer makes me feel as thrilled as the night when Robert told me it was mine. The challenges keep mounting, and I don't get to feel proud when I find solutions to tough problems. There's no one to say, "Well done, Lin." The Board couldn't give a rap about how their chief executive *feels*. I'm not supposed to have feelings, just objectives and measurements and an eye to my bonus.

But I do have feelings.

The days pass and Ben doesn't call.

Chapter 32

It's eight o'clock in the evening and I am still in the office reviewing every last cost line when my cell phone rings.

"Lin? It's me."

"Sally. What's up?"

"You've got a visitor."

My heart leaps in hope. "Ben?"

"His sister, apparently. She's been beaten up. I've patched her face, but she really should go to Accident & Emergency for a proper check. And she should be talking to the police too. But she refuses to budge."

"I'll be home in fifteen minutes."

Cheryl's face is a mess. I would not have recognized the pretty woman I met several years before. She has the same large, soulful blue eyes as Ben, but now one eye is swollen shut and her lip is split. Her beautiful chestnut hair is greasy, tied back into a rough ponytail, and she is dressed in a shapeless, gray pullover and tracksuit pants.

"No police," Cheryl pleads. "And you mustn't tell Ben."

"What are you going to do?"

"I have to go back," she says. "The kids will be missing me. And Joe will be sorry he hit me. He always is."

"Next time he might kill you."

She shakes her head and then winces. "I have to go back. I have to take care of the kids."

I gaze at her in frustration. "They aren't your kids, Cheryl."

"You don't understand! If I'm not there he might, that is, he gets so angry! I can't just walk away!"

"Angry?"

She looks away and her mouth trembles. "The kids aren't safe."

"Ben could sort Joe out, like he did last time."

"Noooo!" she cries and dissolves into tears. "Joe and his mates are tough guys. They won't stand for Ben coming and beating one of them. They won't! Make him stay away, Lin, please!"

"Have you thought of taking lessons in self-defense?" I ask.

Her eyes go round. "No."

"Although, he is a big bastard, isn't he?"

She looks at me blankly for a moment and then nods her head. She's a wimpy little thing. Even if she had a gun, she'd be too gentle to use it.

"Can't you call Social Services about the children?"

Cheryl shakes her head again and then buries her face in her hands and sobs despairingly. "I can't do that to them. And Social Services would give them back again anyway, because there isn't any proof. I just, I just—" and she chokes and gulps and won't say what she knows.

"And you can't take them away yourself?"

She shakes her head. "They would never let me."

"What about the children's family, can you talk to any of them?"

"His sister won't listen to me. She thinks if Joe hits me it's my fault for being a nag. She won't believe Joe would ever hurt his kids."

"What about grandparents?"

Cheryl wipes her face dry with her sleeve. "Lola? She hates me."

"But would she take good care of the kids?"

Cheryl sniffs. "Probably. But she lives in the North Island and the children are in the South Island. I don't think she has a car or anything. I don't think she'd be able to get them, even if Joe was prepared to let them go."

"You have to call Ben."

"No! I don't want him to know! Lin, you mustn't tell him, promise?"

She starts weeping in great gusty sobs, so I call Sally.

"Cheryl keeps crying. Is there anything you can give her?"

"Do you have any lint?"

"Lint? You want me to give her a bandage for her broken heart?"

"No dummy, *Lindt*!"

I investigate the pantry. "I'm out of Lindt. There's a block of Whittaker's, will that do?"

"That will do fine. And get her a glass of something to wash it down with. Not gin, mind. Sauvignon Blanc would be best."

"You can't drink Sauvignon Blanc with chocolate!"

"Chill out, Lin. Most women can drink Sauvignon with anything. Next, a Georgette Heyer novel or, failing that, a chick flick. I don't suppose you've got much of a DVD selection?"

"I can get something from the local video store. Um, *Pretty Woman*?"

"Nothing starring a brooding sultry hunk. That would just remind her of her bloke."

"*The Notebook*?"

"Too sad. Try to find something with Hugh Grant. He's about as opposite as you can get from a sultry and brooding hunk."

"Okay."

I pour Cheryl a glass of wine, open the wrapping on the chocolate, and take them to her. Listlessly, she holds out her hand for the wine. Her head turns as she catches the scent of the chocolate, and her other hand reaches out and takes the packet.

"Thanks."

"Tomorrow I'm going to take you shopping."

"I don't have any money."

"I want to buy you an early Christmas present. And something for last year too, and the year before that. Come on, please let me, it will be fun."

Finally, a watery smile moves across her face. She swallows her mouthful of chocolate and chases it down with the wine. "I haven't had anything new for a long time."

An hour later, fortified by wine and chocolate, corn chips and guacamole, and a wedge of Camembert and crackers, we settle in front of the television to watch *Music and Lyrics*.

"Aww," she says. "Isn't he lovely? I wish I could meet a nice bloke like that."

"I'm sure you will."

"Ben's a nice bloke, Lin. Are you guys going to get back together?"

"I...hope so."

When Cheryl has gone to bed, I lie on the sofa, trying to work out what to do. I analyze several alternatives before coming to the solution I think has the best chance of success.

There would be risks, especially to my reputation. I gaze at the wall. I couldn't let Cheryl go back to be beaten again and again and again. I gaze at the other wall. We couldn't desert those children to be beaten either. I gaze at the ceiling. So, I would do it. But not alone.

She begged me not to call him, but everything was heading in the one direction my own heart wanted to take me. I select the number.

"Lin!" he says. "You rang. I am so glad. How are you?"

"I'm fine, but Cheryl's not. Joe beat her up again and she came to me."

"Is she all right?"

"A black eye and bruises, but no broken bones. But she's worried something might happen to the children if she's not there to protect them, so she's talking about going back."

"She mustn't go back! We'll have to call Social Services—"

"She refuses to call them, she says it's a waste of time. She thinks they'll do nothing until someone actually hurts the kids, and she won't stay away and wait for that to happen. I've told her to call the grandmother up in Hawke's Bay, but she says Lola won't believe her."

"I could go and see him, threaten him or something, if he touches her again or the kids."

"She doesn't want you to. She's worried about Joe's mates as well as Joe."

"I'm not afraid of them."

"Well, she is. And she won't forgive herself if you get hurt. Besides, I don't think he'll stop even if you threaten him. She says he's violent when he's drugged or drunk. He'll hit first without thinking."

"We can't just do nothing about the children. And I'm not letting her go back to that bastard!"

"Can you get away for a few days?"

"To help Cheryl? When she's been hurt? Of course."

So I explain what I've been thinking, and he agrees it might work.

"I'll make the bookings," I tell him.

"Okay. Well, I'll see you soon."

"Yes, soon."

I hold the phone against my chest and feel my heart beating fast, adrenaline surging in anticipation.

Of course there are risks. There are always risks.

Chapter 33

Tom and I sit on one side of a table in a giant fishbowl in Auckland, waiting for the delegates from Kiwicom to join us.

A couple of chirrups break the silence. Tom puts his hand in his jacket pocket, and I reach down and take my phone from my handbag.

WE'VE REACHED PICTON, says the text message from Ben.

I place the handset on top of my folder so it can't make that annoying buzz on the surface of the table.

"They're on their way," says Tom, and places his phone on the table beside his papers.

The door opens and two men and two women come in and lay down their papers. I haven't met these people before. Kiwicom likes to restructure every six months, so this lot are new to their roles.

They introduce themselves, shake our hands, and sit down. In unison everyone switches their cell phones to silent and places them on the table as if they are weapons. It is like a meeting of opposing drug cartels.

As the meeting moves through the opening phases of politeness, where teeth are bared in smiles while eyes scrutinize for reaction, I keep a surreptitious watch on my phone. Half an hour later the phone quivers. I reach down and take a look.

SHE'S GOING IN NOW.

"We can't guarantee we can meet the time frame you're insisting on unless we get these test plan forms completed," says the dark-haired woman.

"We completed the forms and sent them to you last week."
"This is a different set."
Tom examines the forms. "I haven't seen these before."
"You didn't ask for them."
"We didn't know about them."
"You should have asked."
"We—"
I touch Tom's arm. "We'll get them to you tomorrow."
The woman smiles. "Next item on the agenda."

An hour passes. It is now three o'clock, and I haven't heard from
Ben whether Cheryl has made it out with the children.
"Shall we take a five-minute break?" I suggest.
Everyone picks up their phones and checks their messages.
I text Ben. IS SHE THERE YET?
SHE'S JUST COME OUT, he texts. SHE HAS THE BABY IN THE PRAM
AND THE TWO LITTLE BOYS, BUT THE TEEN NEPHEW IS WITH THEM.
CAN'T YOU TAKE HIM TOO?
NO, HE'S UNCLE'S PET, HE'D TELL JOE.
"Coffee?"
I look up. "Flat white. This is taking longer than I hoped.
Can we skip the next three items? I don't need to be involved in
those discussions. You and Tom can sort out the arrangements."
THEY'RE AT THE SCHOOL GATE.
The fatter of the two men from Kiwicom looks up from his
phone, his thumbs still flicking over the surface. "Joanne needs
to join us for the next agenda item."
CHERYL'S IN A PANIC. NEED TO THINK OF SOMETHING.
"How are you enjoying New Zealand?" asks one of the jun-
iors as she hands me the next stack of papers.
"It's a beautiful country," I reply automatically, my fingers
moving busily.
SEND THE BOY A TEXT TO MEET AT THE HOUSE IN FIVE MINS.
WHY WOULD HE MEET ME?

DON'T SAY WHO IT IS.

A tall woman arrives and is greeted with deference by the other Kiwicom staff.

"Shall we get going?" she suggests.

The fat man looks around. "Where's the coffee?"

HE'S JOGGING BACK TO THE HOUSE. WE'RE GOOD TO GO!

"We're good to go," says the dark woman as the coffee arrives and is handed carefully out.

The final agenda item is the process for requesting changes to the interconnect tests. We are given a twenty-page pack containing diagrams and footnotes and a set of new forms.

By six o'clock I still haven't heard again from Ben. I pick up my phone.

"Sorry," I say. "I've got to chase up an important deadline."

"Are you on board yet?"

The phone switches to Ben's voice mail message, so I return my attention to the swim lane that describes the process for requesting changes.

"What!" Tom looks up. "Are you saying we haven't given you enough notice?"

The tall woman smiles. "Well, technically, you have missed the boat."

My phone dances, but when I look it is not Ben's cell phone number, so I ignore the message.

"We have your e-mails and those of your predecessors," I say. "And so do the lawyers and Dr. Grey. Their opinion is that we followed the process that was published at the time and therefore we have provided the requisite information in the requisite time frame."

The fat man and the tall woman exchange glances.

"As I was about to say, we're prepared to cut Hera some slack on this point, but please don't expect us to allow you to fast-track the process again," Joanne says.

This was the final issue to resolve. Tom and I rise to leave.

Hands are shaken again and phones turned back on, and Tom calls a cab to take us to the airport.

I read my message.

BEN BATTERY FLAT WE ON FERRY SAFE NOW, CHERYL.

"What was the urgent deadline you had to chase up?" Tom asks in the taxi on the way to Auckland airport.

Your chief executive has been helping kidnap some kids.

"It's a family thing," I say.

He nods, satisfied, and turns away.

I am vacuuming the apartment when I get Cheryl's text to say they're off the ferry and are on the road north.

I text back and ask her to let me know when they reach Lola's, finish cleaning the kitchen, and go to bed, where I lie awake worrying about what could go wrong at the last minute. What if Lola refuses to take the children? What if she calls the police? What if she calls Joe? Cheryl says Joe's far too lazy to do anything about her once she's away from Picton, but who knows what an angry man might do?

Then I start worrying about whether it was really necessary. Was I sure Cheryl's fears were justified? Or would Joe behave differently to his children than he did to her? Have I just deprived another set of children of their father?

My eyes close and I drift off to sleep and jerk awake only when the text comes through that they have safely delivered the kidnapped children to Lola's.

I call Cheryl's mobile. She is weeping uncontrollably, and I get no sense from her.

"Can you put Ben on?"

"The grandmother says she will keep them safe," Ben's voice says. "But she is an old cow. She made it clear Cheryl was no longer part of the family and had better stay away."

"No visits with the children?"

"None. Anyway, we're almost at Alison's. I'll see you tomorrow."

"Ben?"

"Yeah?"

"It was the right thing to do, wasn't it?"

"Probably. Only time will tell."

When I put down the phone, I drop my head into my hands and run my fingers through my hair. The children are safe, but they've lost their father as well as Cheryl. Cheryl is safe but she has lost the children.

Was it the right choice?

Chapter 34

When I get home from the office, Ben is there.

"Hey," he says, getting up from the sofa and taking a step toward me before halting in the middle of the room.

He's wearing blue jeans and a t-shirt with "It's Willamette, Dammit" emblazoned across the front in bright yellow. I bought him that t-shirt in Portland a year ago.

He starts to hold out his hand, but then his arm drops as if he waits for me to give him a signal.

Maybe I'm waiting too. "Hey."

He clears his throat. "So how was your day?"

"Just the usual," I reply.

Cheryl rises from the sofa. The bruises have faded. Her hair is clean and she is wearing a dress I bought for her since she'd packed so few clothes.

"Thanks for loaning us the car and everything," she says.

"I'm trying to persuade Cheryl to come back with me to Dipton," says Ben.

Cheryl's eyes start to fill. "I hate Dipton," she says, her mouth quivering. "I want to get a job. There aren't any jobs in Dipton."

The thought of coming home to Cheryl is not remotely appealing. It's not that I don't like her, but we have nothing to say to each other. And she makes one hell of a mess.

But she is Ben's sister. Family.

"You can stay here as long as you want, Cheryl."

She gives me a tremulous smile. "Are you sure? I don't want to be a nuisance, and I know you're busy."

"I insist."

I put away the opened loaf of bread and the dish of butter that has melted and coagulated again, put the dirty plates in the dishwasher and the banana skins and sheets of newspaper in the rubbish, and take a quick shower. When I emerge Cheryl is planted in front of the television, but Ben is up on the terrace with the barbecue. I join him.

"How was the trip back?"

"Joe called Cheryl's cell phone on our way home today. I threw the phone out the car window without answering."

I smile. *Looks like we're in the clear.* "How was Alison?"

"She insisted on feeding us a cooked breakfast. I like your sister. Sure, she's a bit of a fusspot but she is a bloody good cook."

I stand next to him and turn the kebabs. Ben turns the steak.

"Alison asked if I would like to join you all for Christmas," he says, flicking a sidelong glance at me. "I told her I normally share Emmy with her mother over Christmas. But it turns out Fay wants Emmy in Cape Town for two weeks. The old boy has offered to cough up the fare."

"Yes?"

"So I guess I could."

He is frowning at the steak.

"Look done."

"So are these." I add the kebabs to the platter.

"I could come for a couple of weeks," Ben says. "What do you think?"

As I look up and examine his face, I see the feet of the crow at the edges of his eyes, and the tendrils of hair at his temples fading to silver. *Tempus fugit.*

"I think that would be a great idea."

I touch Ben's hand and he reaches his arm around me and pulls me close. I lean my head on his shoulder and let him hold me.

•   •   •

Later, when Cheryl has gone to bed, we take out the sheets and the blankets and make the two sofas ready for the night. In the bathroom, I change and emerge, nonchalant, in a gold silken nightdress that starts low on my chest and finishes high on my thighs. The fabric molds to the curves of my body and glistens in the pale light. As I bend over the sink the silk slithers across my hips and stretches around my bottom.

When I turn back, Ben's eyes are on his book. Which is up-side down.

"Water?" I ask.

"What? Oh, yes, thank you."

"Is that pillow comfortable?" I ask, reaching across to plump out the pillow behind his head.

My breast hovers an inch from his face. His hand rises to caress my back. I slip my leg over him, grasp his shoulders, and kiss him until we run out of breath. We fall together and twist and turn as silently as we can so his sister won't hear and then fall asleep in a tangle of limbs.

My father blew it, but we have another chance, Ben and I.

The following morning, Ben catches a taxi to the airport, and I get ready for work. As I sit in front of the pots and tubes facing myself in the mirror, I smooth the expensive elixir around my eyes and touch the hair at the side of my face. Time for another tint.

Tempus fugit.

When I get home that evening, there is no sign of Cheryl. The bedroom door is closed. I knock and call her name, but there is no answer. I push open the door.

The room is dark and I don't see her immediately. She is on the floor beside the bed, clutching a green dress too slinky for my chief executive image. Her head leans against the side of the bed and her swollen eyes stare straight ahead.

My heart leaps in shock. "Cheryl!"

But then she moves, turning her face toward me. The light from the living room catches the tears on her cheeks.

"He didn't love me at all."

"Joe?"

She buries her face in the silk dress and sobs. I reach out and pat her shoulder, feeling ineffectual.

She lifts her head and stares blankly across the room. "There were clothes lying on the floor by the bed. Our bed!"

"Clothes?"

"A green dress a bit like this," she says. "Black underwear. They weren't mine."

"Oh."

"No one was looking after Ro properly. Her poor little bottom was raw with diaper rash and the twins were locked in the shed when I got there. I knew I had to leave him and take the kids. But now I'll never see them again."

Her face resumes its blank stare as if she looks into a future that holds nothing of joy ever again.

I retreat to the kitchen and pour a glass of wine and break open more chocolate. She takes them listlessly.

"I'll get another DVD," I say. "And Thai take-out. Okay?"

She nods, sniffing and wiping her cheeks with her hands.

When I arrive at the Thai restaurant to collect our order, it isn't ready. The young girl apologizes and says the roti bread will take five minutes.

While I wait, I examine the wall. There is a photograph of a young man who looks like my nephew, sitting with two other people whose backs are to the camera. A woman and a man. The woman is wearing a maroon jacket I have seen before.

I look closer, but there is no mistake. Vivienne eats in my local restaurant.

Chapter 35

As I open the gate, I hear a shout and a cry from above, and the deep baying of Polly's best bark from the back of the house where she is tied to her kennel. The front door stands wide open. Halfway up the staircase is a large and angry man, built like a bull. Muscled arms bulge from the sleeveless leather vest which strains across his chest. *Joe?*

"Bitch!" he calls to the closed door at the top of the stairs. "I'm coming for you!"

As I stare up, Jiro cautiously opens the door to his and Dirk's apartment and gapes as the man surges past him up the stairs. "Just a minute," he says and closes his door firmly.

Joe hammers on the penthouse door with his fist while I pause below. *Damn, I've left my cell phone upstairs. I can't call the police.* I knock on Sally's door. Joe hears and starts back down.

Angry eyes narrow and nostrils flare. "You must be the chink bitch."

I stand holding the boxes of Thai take-out and consider my options. As I place the boxes on the hall table—no need to ruin our dinner—Sally's door opens and she comes out.

"What the?" Then she sees Joe coming down the stairs. "Just a minute!" she says and ducks back into her place.

I am about to follow her when the door to the middle apartment bursts open and Jiro emerges wearing one of those white martial arts outfits. He smiles, adjusts his headband, and makes a few sample kicks in the air, landing like a cat.

Joe pauses to glance at him. His body tenses. He's not backing off for some fancy-assed judo expert. Behind me Sally appears again, but now she is wearing thin latex gloves and holds a very large hypodermic needle. She points it in the air, checking the contents, and then stands beside me, smiling.

Joe stares at the needle. His eyes widen. Then his eyes narrow again, his nostrils flare, and he comes down the stairs toward us, his hands clenching into fists.

A thump shakes the house and then another thump. The sound is like some great *Taniwha* is trying to get in, or like the mother of all earthquakes. The house trembles with each blow. Thump, thump, thump.

For once in his wild and violent life, discretion overcomes Joe's valor; his jaw drops, his eyes widen, then he runs past us and disappears out the gate.

Whump! Goes Polly's kennel against the side of the house again, as she drags it behind her, desperate to defend her home against the invader.

"Good dog!" I call.

Sally peers down the road as a Mark IV Zephyr drives away with a squeal of tires. "Bugger!" she says. "I was looking forward to stabbing him."

Jiro joins us, looking disappointed. "Has he gone? Damn, I was looking forward to a good workout."

"I'd better go up and reassure Cheryl."

When I open the door there is a smell of pee and Cheryl is cowering in the corner whimpering.

"It's okay," I tell her, bending down beside her and holding her tightly. "He's gone."

But still she cries, until Sally gives her a sedative and we tuck her to sleep in my bed and return downstairs to Sally's.

"Cheryl is still refusing to talk to the cops. She still seems to care about the bastard."

"But he threatened you, too, Lin. You can report him."

"I don't want any publicity, Sal. He's just a buffoon. I'm not afraid of him."

I would have to explain to the police why Joe is so angry with us. I can't afford the risk.

"Cheryl is in danger."

"Yeah. She can't stay here." I fork up some cold green curry that looks like something Polly regurgitated.

"Tomorrow I'll take her to my sister's. He won't know anything about Ngatirua. She'll be safe there."

Cheryl shivers beside me in the car as we drive north to Hawke's Bay. Eventually, she closes her eyes and sleeps, and I can concentrate on my thoughts. Why would Vivienne be in my local restaurant? Stupidly, I hadn't checked the date. Was it before or after I moved in? If after, why didn't she try to see me?

My thoughts go around and around and make no progress and after another hour I arrive at the turnoff, climb the hill slowly, and arrive at Ngatirua.

Alison emerges from the house as I turn the car into their driveway.

"You poor thing," Alison says, grasping Cheryl's hands. "Wal! Take Cheryl's bag to the studio," she directs, and then ushers us into the house for a nice cup of tea.

I drink my tea seated on the comfortable sofa while Alison brings out cake, and a stack of magazines for Cheryl, and packs up a box of provisions to take to the studio.

It is curiously relaxing in my sister's house. Here I am just a somewhat feckless younger sister who needs to be taken care of. I lie with my head tilted back on the headrest, my eyelids drooping closed, listening to the silence, broken only by the faint sound of sheep calling out in the paddocks.

"You look worn out," says Alison. "Do you have to drive back straight away?"

I nod my head. "The staff Christmas party is tonight and

they expect me to make an appearance. But I'll be back on Christmas Eve."

Half an hour later, I drag myself to my feet and prepare to leave. Wal puts a cooler on the backseat of my car.

"A leg of lamb," he says. "It's still frozen, and I've slapped in some freezer pads so you should be all right."

Alison gives me a bag of vegetables from their garden and a basket of fresh eggs. "These should keep you going until you come up for Christmas."

As I get into my car, bowed down under their gifts, I remember what I need to ask.

"Alison, do any of you get to Wellington at all? I think I saw a photo of Vivienne, Max, and Christopher on the wall of our local Thai restaurant."

Alison looks into the space beyond my left shoulder. "We use the penthouse ourselves when it's not being rented."

"The penthouse?"

"I told Nick to send you flowers when you moved in, didn't you get them?"

"There were flowers, yes, but they were from a company called Alienne."

"That's us. Alison and Vivienne. Oh, dear. I just took for granted he'd put our names on the card. I wondered why you didn't reply."

"You own the penthouse?"

"We own the whole house. I thought you knew that. Anyway, we'll see you next weekend. Bye, dear!" and Alison shuts the car door and waves.

I drive away in a daze, coming to terms with the knowledge that Alison and Vivienne own the house in which I live. They are my landlords.

Chapter 36

As I reenter the house after spending the requisite hour at the staff Christmas party, Sally opens her door.

"Oh, it's you. I thought it was Nick."

"I thought you were out with your friends from the hospital."

She shakes her head. "Karim has found himself a new young sweetie, and I can't stomach listening to him cooing at her. And I don't want—that is, I'm not, oh, I don't know. I just didn't want to go down to the 'horn tonight."

"Nick?"

She flushes. "I taunted him about something, I can't even remember, and so he decided to take his revenge."

"Sally?" I ask.

"I don't want to talk about it."

As I look into the strained green eyes, I remember this is my friend, and you don't leave your friends alone when their faces are looking like Sally's.

"I have a bottle of Bollinger I was going to drink in the Jacuzzi."

Sally's eyes light up. "Is it hot?"

"What? Oh, the Jacuzzi? I turned it on this morning. And I do believe there's chocolate in the gift basket I scored."

"Are you taking care of me, Lin?"

"Do you have a problem with that?"

Sally ducks into her apartment and returns with a small plastic box with an aerial poking out of it.

"Baby monitor."

We climb into the steaming water and lounge on the molded seats, sipping champagne and chewing chocolate caramels.

It is a calm night, one of the good ones in Wellington. Above us the stars twinkle in the dark sky, and below us the lights of the city glitter against the dark office towers. There is a distant, faint noise of people talking and music playing through opened windows.

"What has Nick done?" I ask.

Sally shakes her head and pulls on a smile. "Nothing important." She throws her head back against the headrest. "I saw John at the Christmas party this week."

"Uh-huh?"

"Uh-huh nothing. At least he's not glaring balefully at me any longer."

"Uh-huh."

"He was with one of the admin staffers."

"Uh-huh?"

"A nice enough girl. Woman. Ten years younger than me."

Her voice is sad. She is looking up at the stars, but I don't think she sees anything.

"How is the lovely Ben? Are you properly back together?"

"We'll be together for the holidays. I don't think about the future."

"The daughter will eventually leave home. How old is she?"

"Seventeen. She'll be at high school for another year, and then at university in Dunedin. Ben wants to stay close by."

"So, no happy-ever-after story."

"Happy for a couple of weeks is good enough for now." I reach into the little box for my cigarillos. "Let's wish for a better year next year."

"A better year and better men. Oops. I suppose Ben counts as a good enough man." Sally sighs. "We're brainwashed that relationships are based on pure romantic love, but I think success is as much about the practicalities, the conveniences of being together, than some amorphous feeling."

"It wouldn't be very *convenient* for me to live in Dipton."

"For whom? You or Ben?"

"Between being the chief executive of an exciting new venture and a housewife in Dipton, there isn't much of a choice is there?"

"The Dipton scenario is a bit of a challenge, I will admit. God!" she says. "What is that?"

"A girly cigar. Would you like one?"

"Don't mind if I do."

She puffs on her cigarillo, blowing the smoke out like she's blowing a last retreat. "I didn't know you smoked."

"One of the things I keep to myself."

"Like the fact you have a family in New Zealand." Sally takes a few more puffs. "How did you lose touch in the first place? Surely, your father would have made sure his children met each other."

"He tried. They refused all of his overtures, my stepmother said. And then he died when I was twelve."

"I would have thought the lawyers settling his estate would have chased up the children from his first marriage."

"Mom told me he left nothing but debts. I think she did get the authorities involved so at least they would know their father had died, but she was never given any contact information."

"A detective could have tracked them down."

"I wanted to do it myself, in person. And I did."

"What about your mother? Did you ever find her?"

I don't want to talk about the mother who left me. "Nope. She died before Dad did, apparently."

"How did you end up living in the same house as your father?"

"That was a bit of blind luck. When I Googled the address from his papers, the advertisement for the penthouse came up. There I was, trying to work out whether to stay or go and trying to work out where to start looking for my sisters. How could I turn down the opportunity?

"But, Sally, here's the odd thing." I tap out the ashy end of my cigarillo. "My sisters still own the house. They knew I was coming as soon as Nicholas told them my name."

"Your sisters are the Alienne people?" She whistles. "I think I've met one of them. An elegant redheaded woman. She stayed a few days just before you moved in."

"Leave me alone!"

Sally holds up her hand and turns her head toward the sound.

"Get back!" says the voice.

She leaps out of the Jacuzzi with alacrity unexpected in so large a woman and hurtles, dripping, down the steps, through the penthouse, and out the door. I can hear her feet running down the stairs.

I get out of the Jacuzzi and wrap my towel around my body. *My God, what is happening?*

"You stupid dog, stop licking me!" comes Michael's sleepy voice.

"Polly, get down! You know you're not supposed to be up there!" says Sally's voice over the monitor.

I let myself smile, turn off the Jacuzzi, and put the cover back on, collect up our glasses and the bottle and the ashtray and return indoors to my bed.

But although it is very late and I am physically spent, my mind churns and I can't sleep.

Why didn't my sisters ask why I didn't respond to the flowers? It seems odd they didn't comment on the fact I'm living in their house.

And what has Nicholas done to hurt Sally?

Chapter 37

The week before Christmas flashes by in a blur and finally it is the morning of Christmas Eve. I glance up from my PC to the painting that adorns my office wall, the picture I bought over the Internet as my Christmas gift to myself. If anyone looks closely, they will see the artist bears the same surname as me.

At midday Helen carries in a plate of fruit mince pies, and Ian follows bearing a bottle of bubbly.

"Time to knock off, Lin!" says Ian. "Where are Tom and Fred? And Marion? Call them, Helen, tell them we're in Lin's office."

When we're all there, Ian opens the bottle. The cork hits the ceiling, and the wine bursts forth. He tips the bottle toward our waiting glasses.

"Merry Christmas!" "Cheers!" "Bums up!" "Cheers!"

"Salut!" I say, and we sit together drinking our wine and nibbling the pies.

There is an empty chair on the far side of the table, where Deepak should have been. Scott Peake was invited, but he hasn't come. He follows his own path and doesn't inform me what he is doing.

Tom explains he will be traveling up to stay at the family bach in Lake Waikaremoana.

"Bach?"

"That's what Kiwis call our holiday homes. It's short for bachelor pad, because typically they're small, rustic, and shabby," Marion explains.

She is having Christmas in Wellington and then going to her

bach on Flat Point beach. Ian hasn't got a bach yet, but his girlfriend's parents have a holiday home in the Marlborough Sounds so they're going down for New Year's. Fred's wife is not well so they're having a quiet Christmas at home.

Me? I am staying at my sister's farm, I tell them. Yes, I have a sister. Actually, I have two sisters. They live in Hawke's Bay. Yes, it's a lovely part of New Zealand. See my new picture? That zigzag road is the road to Ngatirua farm.

Tom walks over to the wall and examines the painting and says he knows the area well. Then we finish the wine and sweep away the crumbs and head off for our Christmas break.

Sally and Michael are packing their Prius when I get home. Polly is padding back and forth with her brow furrowed, hoping she gets to go too. Sally is not smiling her beautiful wide smile today.

"Don't try and carry all that, Michael!"

Too late. He has dropped the bag, and Sally's makeup splatters across the path. Her face contorts, and for one awful moment, I think she's going to cry—Sally the brave, the never serious, the always sanguine. But she pastes her face back together, and her lips stretch into the semblance of a smile.

"You're looking happy," she says. "When does he get here?"

"I'm collecting him from the airport in an hour."

"I'm so glad you caught us. I have a gift for you somewhere. Michael, where did we put—oh no, don't put it there!"

"It doesn't matter. Give it to me when you find it."

But she raises a hand to her temple and rubs it, sighs, and leans down to the box at her feet. "Ah." She straightens and hands me a round shape wrapped in fluorescent green. "Be careful, it's fragile."

A lime-green glass perfume bottle flecked with tiny crimson and white swirls emerges from the wrapping.

"I know how much you like colored things."

"It's beautiful. Thank you."

I give Michael an envelope of money—a boring present, but

all I had time for, and hand his mother a bottle of '73 Madeira. "Your birth year," I say.

"Yeah, right."

"Are you okay, Sally?"

"I'm fine. Just been doing some thinking about the future, you know?" she replies. "Suddenly, someone makes you feel you're not invincible."

"You are invincible."

"Okay, I am invincible." She smiles a real smile this time, and I reach out and hug her, my friend Sally.

"Have a good Christmas," I say.

"And you."

I drive the back way to the airport, along the ridge and down through the valley to the south coast. I love this drive. The wild seas crash against the rocks as I meander along the road, dodging mad cyclists who think the road belongs to them. When I turn the last corner, Lyall Bay stretches before me.

Today there are surfers riding the waves to the shore. Beyond them the airport straddles the peninsula, the runway bordered by roads and sea at either end. A Boeing is on final approach. I think of Ben on board and my heart leaps and I feel that warm feeling of anticipation. My man is arriving, and we will have two weeks together.

Traffic is jammed up on the road through the airport. I beat my fingers against the wheel and check my watch. *Move, you bastards, move!* I crawl up the ramp in first gear and flick my eyes across the concourse. At the far end is a familiar shape, dressed in shorts with his pack by his side. I veer over to where he stands and park the car crookedly. As I climb out, he catches me up in his arms and squeezes the breath out of me.

"You mustn't stop!" says the official in the bright-green jacket.

"Okay, we won't," I reply, and hug Ben back. "Although it's busy and you probably need the parking space."

The official scowls at me so I open the back door, and Ben throws in his pack and puts out his hand for the key.

"We'll be sleeping at Vivienne's tonight," I tell him as he drives us through the heavy traffic out of Wellington and onto State Highway 2. "You'll get a chance to see inside her beautiful house."

"I suppose they must be quite rich," he replies thoughtfully.

"I'm not sure. Alison and Wal live quite modestly, but Vivienne and Christopher seem to have the best of everything. But perhaps that's from Christopher's side of the family."

"Did you have any idea they owned the house in Wellington?"

"None whatsoever."

"Funny none of them mentioned it when we stayed last month."

"They didn't talk about Wellington at all, just Hawke's Bay. Thinking back, Alison only talked about Dad when we were alone and she showed me the studio."

"How long are we going to stay with them?"

I run my finger up his tanned arm. "Four nights and then back to Wellington, by ourselves."

Ben's mouth curls into a smile and he pats my thigh.

The roads are crowded with holiday traffic and it is a slow trip. The highway only has one lane in each direction and the passing lanes are few.

"These roads are terrible. You'd think they'd build a decent motorway for God's sake!"

"It's that socialist ethic of ours. We're embarrassed by good infrastructure; feel it smacks of capitalism or something. Then we blame drivers for the road toll when really it's the pathetic quality of the roads."

"I suppose the train trip would be better."

"They canned the line a couple of years ago. No investment in the tracks."

"Huh. So what do they invest in?"

He points out a farm as we pass. "Dairy farms and dairy production. Agriculture, horticulture, forestry. Offshore oil."

"Oil!"

"Yeah, New Zealand's fourth largest export is oil. Bet you didn't know that."

"When Americans think of New Zealand, which isn't often, it's to wonder where it is."

Ben snorts. "The Europeans know us better."

"The only thing the French know about New Zealand is the All Blacks team."

"And the Brits?"

"Land of milk and honey."

"There you go."

We reach the turnoff and drive carefully up the zigzag hill, although Ben cleaned the rubbish out of the car when we stopped for gas so we should be safe this time.

My heart lifts. Away from city life, away from the cares of corporate life, I feel I am coming home.

Chapter 38

Vivienne opens the door slowly to let us in. Her eyes drop as we walk inside. "Do you mind?" she says.

Ben looks uncertainly at her and then glances down to see two sets of shoes placed carefully by the door. We kneel to remove our sandals and Vivienne smiles. I should have warned him about her floors. His feet are not very clean.

"I've put you in the west suite."

She shows us into an elegant room with a double bed, a bathroom, and its own small sitting room. The walls are cream, the floor is made of wide, polished boards of some native red wood, and the quilt is embroidered silk in charcoal and lilac. Ben puts our suitcases beside the dainty walnut dressing table.

"I'll leave you to freshen up," Vivienne says. "Supper will be served in the front room in, shall we say, half an hour?"

"Strewth," says Ben when she closes the door behind her. "I'd better go wash my feet." He vanishes into the bathroom. "I wonder if she's got a bid-thingie? Yes, she has. Good."

He likes to wash his feet in the bidet. I can't seem to train him out of it.

In the front room, opera plays softly on a Bang & Olufsen music system. The high ceilings are painted a rich deep cream, and the walls are paneled in pale lime-washed wood. At one end, a massive fireplace contains a bowl of roses in every shade of white; at the other, French windows look out over the tennis court. A fine old piano in some exotic wood sits in one corner; in another, a collection of tall vase shapes; in the third, an antique dollhouse. On the walls hang original modern art works, and the mantelpiece holds a collection of sculptures: some ceramic, some metal, some glass, one made of feathers. Tall flutes of pale glass, ringed in black, provide light. Three very large modern sofas, two in cinnamon-colored leather and one in cream, sit facing each other in the center of the room. A coffee table in ebony, edged with a lighter wood, holds a silver tray of glasses. Three wine bottles swathed in white linen napkins stand opened beside the tray. The room smells of leather.

"Strewth," mutters Ben again.

Christopher lounges on the cream sofa with his back to the door and his dog at his feet. As we enter, he turns. As usual his blind eyes are hidden behind dark lenses.

"Hello," he says. "Grab a seat." He gestures in the direction of the other two sofas. "Would you mind helping yourself to the wine? She worries about me spilling it."

We sink into the sofa opposite him, and Ben reaches over to pour Gewürztraminer into two crystal goblets.

Max carries in a platter of antipasti: little smoked mussels, sun-dried tomatoes, balls of smoked fish, cold meats, tiny stuffed bell peppers, marinated artichoke hearts, three varieties of olives, two different pâtés. Vivienne follows with a plate of French bread and four different crackers.

"Do help yourselves," she says and sits next to her husband, patting his knee lightly. "What shall I get you, darling?" she asks.

Christopher's handsome jaw moves into a smile. He touches her silk skirt over her thigh. "Whatever you think I'll like."

He turns his face in my direction. "I guess you Yanks eat turkey for Christmas?"

"I haven't had Christmas in America for years," I reply. "But Mom always used to cook a turkey, yes."

"Yours are those massive grain-fed things, aren't they?"

"They are quite large."

"Everything's big in America, eh?"

"It's a big country," I reply.

We silently fill our plates with food. I glance at Vivienne's immaculate face. I want to get my questions over with.

"I didn't realize that you and Alison still owned the house in Wellington."

Vivienne's face stiffens. "Gran took over the mortgage when your father deserted us."

There is a sudden chilly silence.

"What a beautiful room," Ben says.

"Thank you," Vivienne smiles at him.

"I like the red picture," I say pointing out a large canvas depicting the wine country in shades of red, or at least I think that's what it is.

"Mm," replies Vivienne.

"These mussels are delicious," says Ben.

"Thank you." She bestows another gracious smile on Ben.

"I didn't know New Zealand grew Gewurtz," I try.

"There isn't much grown," she replies. "Where's this one from, Max?"

Max flashes his brilliant smile. "A few valleys over," he replies. "Instead of turning at the ridge, you keep going."

"Max wants to be a winemaker," she says.

Max's face flushes pink. "I'm happy being a farmer," he says, and turns his attention to his plate.

"I would so love a vineyard," she says and goes to stand by the bay window that looks across the fields. "Over there."

Max glances down, saying nothing.

"Is the land suitable?" I ask. "You're quite high up."

"We get frosts," says Christopher. "And the soil in this part of the farm is too rich."

"Oh, you are a spoilsport, Christopher!"

"And it would cost a fortune," he adds.

"Which I'm afraid we don't have," Vivienne turns to me. "I imagine you get paid very well as a chief executive?"

"I do okay."

She holds the bottle out to Ben. "A top-up? Or would you

prefer the Syrah? It's to go with the cheese, but you could have a glass now, if you'd like."

Max rises to clear the plates and takes them to the kitchen. He returns with an impressive plate of cheeses.

Vivienne points out the varieties. "Gorgonzola, Camembert—real Camembert, Manchego, Gouda, Wensleydale, and some local goat cheese. I couldn't find any decent imported stuff. And I couldn't find any American cheese."

"Do Americans make cheese?" asks Christopher. "Or do they create it out of plastic or something?"

"Yes, but nothing you'd bother importing."

"I suppose once they remove all the dairy as well as all the fat there's nothing left." He laughs at his small joke and reaches out his empty glass for Vivienne to refill.

"Naughty," she says, smiling, and taps his wrist.

Christopher wants to talk about nuclear power next.

"You Yanks are pretty pissed off about New Zealand's nuclear ban, aren't you?"

"Frankly, I don't think America gives a damn about New Zealand's nuclear ban."

His hand pauses on its way to his mouth. The cheese drops off the cracker and lands on his belly. He doesn't notice and puts the cracker in his mouth, startled when it enters empty.

"We don't need nuclear power. We've got hydropower and geothermal power."

Max gets up again and pours me some red wine.

"Do you play any sport, Max?" asks Ben.

Max flushes. "I used to play soccer, but I stopped when I left school." He glances at Christopher.

"A sissy's game," says Christopher. "Rugby is the real Kiwi sport." He looks toward Ben and smiles. "I used to play rugby."

"What position?" Ben asks.

"Wing, mainly, though I've played fullback as well."

"Christopher was a star," Vivienne says. "He was selected for the All Blacks."

Ben looks up and his eyes narrow. "I think I remember seeing you play. Yeah, Chris Marchmount. I remember you. You were bloody good. That try from the five-meter line!"

Christopher smiles again. "Those were the days."

He and Ben share memories of rugby tests past until Vivienne decides it's time for us all to go to bed.

"I guess the accident must have wrecked his life," I say to Ben as we lie on crisp linen sheets under luxurious covers.

"He was the embodiment of every boy's dream: handsome, talented, popular, big rugby contract just about to be signed. As I recall, there was a huge outcry because he was driving drunk, went off the road, and killed his girlfriend and his best friend. They threw the book at him. So, yes, I'd say it destroyed his life."

"Although he seems happy here with Vivienne."

"It's a nice lifestyle, but your sister is hard going. I couldn't hack living with her."

"It is the most beautiful house I think I've ever seen."

"But he can't see it."

"Vivienne's an artist. She can't help but create a beautiful living place. It's who she is."

"He's a good-looking chap. I guess he goes with her décor."

"She dotes on him. Wouldn't you like me to dote on you like that? Ben, darling, let me get you some more Manchego?"

"I like you just the way you are, Lin. Don't go all darling on me, please!"

"Anything you say, dear."

"Not that either! I like your family, Lin."

"I do too. I am so glad we found them."

"They don't want to talk about the house in Wellington, do they?"

"I'm best off asking Alison. And I'll ask her why they didn't try to contact me."

"Tomorrow?"

"Maybe. Or the day after."

"You're procrastinating."

"I know. But it's Christmas. A family Christmas. I haven't had one of those for a long, long time. I don't want anything to spoil it."

Chapter 39

For Christmas I give Ben a new leather jacket. He smiles and thanks me, but puts the jacket to one side. Maybe he'd rather keep wearing the tatty old thing he's had for years, but I've already stolen it and consigned it to the dustbin, so he'll have to wear the smart new one I've given him.

He hands me a tiny package wrapped in a wisp of blue tissue, tied with a thin gold thread. Inside is a blue stone with swirls of gold and speckles of red. As it rolls around my palm, the gold glistens.

"I got paid with an opal for a piece I made for an Aussie miner," he says.

"It's beautiful."

"You can have it made into a—well—anything you want."

"But you shouldn't have. I mean, you should have sold it. I know you need the money."

Ben rewraps the stone in the tissue paper and folds my hand around it. "I wanted to give you something special, something valuable."

I smile at him and have to blink because suddenly my eyes water. I had forgotten what it was like to be given a special, valuable gift. No one has for a long time.

We escape after being fed an elegant breakfast of fresh fruit and expensive muesli. As we walk through the pasture, I warn Ben to watch his feet so he doesn't tread in cow pie—*pats, they're called cow pats, Lin, Alison had corrected me.*

•   •   •

Cheryl is lying on the divan downstairs watching morning television but bounces up to hug her brother. The bruises have faded
and she is looking her pretty self again.

"Merry Christmas, sis," he says and gives her a wrapped
parcel.

She's like a child in her enthusiasm to open her present. "Oh!
Thank you, Ben, it's lovely!" He has given her a wooden picture
frame he has made himself. The photograph it frames is of the
four children, playing in the children's area on the ferry.

"Not the best-quality photo," he apologizes. "But it was all
my cell could take."

Her lip starts to tremble, so I hastily hand her my gift.

"Oh, Lin! An iPhone! Just what I always wanted."

"I got you the white model. More interesting than black,
don't you think?"

Ben and I wait outside for Cheryl to get dressed.

"When I said she could do with a new cell phone, I didn't
mean you to buy the most expensive on the market."

"I can afford it, Ben. And she liked it, didn't she?"

"You're as bad as Vivienne."

Alison's house is buzzing with energy and family. Wal's mother,
Flo, sits in state in front of the television. Wal's sister, Magda, a
very large girl with a very wide smile full of very white teeth, is
in the kitchen while her husband, Murray, helps Wal move tables and chairs to make enough seating for all of us to eat together. Murray keeps stopping to tell Wal about the deals he's
just made. Ben steps up to take the end of a table from him and
moves it where it needs to go.

"Bloody Asians are pushing up the prices for land," Murray
says.

"Steady on, mate," Ben says. "Anyone's got a right to buy
land."

"Foreigners shouldn't be allowed to, particularly the slant

eyes," grunts Murray, without even a glance in my direction. "Bloody Government needs to do something about it!"

Jess is in the corner ignoring everyone, her fingers busily texting. Four children ranging in age, to my untrained eye, from about five to ten race around the yard and in and out of the house, playing with the water pistols they received from Santa this morning. I stand very still while two of them duck around me shrieking with laughter.

"Outside!" yells Magda.

The room is dominated by a huge Christmas tree decorated with a rainbow of balls and toys and streamers, and colored lights that blink on and off. A pile of discarded wrapping paper is strewn around the base of the tree.

"Jess!" calls Alison. "If I've asked you once, I've asked you a dozen times to get a box and tidy away that paper."

Jess stalks past us to the tree and picks up an armful of paper and stalks out to the back of the house. Today she is wearing a pale-lemon-colored dress and a flower behind her ear. A pink ribbon, a gold tinsel bow, a scrap of red crepe, and a twist of multicolored Christmas paper fall from her grasp along the way.

"Wal! Wal! Get Ben and Lin a drink. Oh, don't put it there! Put it there!" and Alison gesticulates until everything is just so, then bustles back into the kitchen to tell Magda how to boil the eggs.

I follow Jess, picking up the scraps that fall.

"Which bloody rubbish bin do I put the wrapping paper in, Mum?"

"The paper bin, Jess. The paper bin. Not that one, the other one. And don't you swear at me, young lady!"

Jess drops her armful of paper and rolls her eyes. I shake my head at her and am rewarded with a small smile.

"She's doing my head in."

"Nice dress," I tell her. "You have a real gift."

Her eyes fix on mine, and I get a wider smile this time.

"Do you think so, Auntie Lin? You've got beautiful clothes, I can tell they're from overseas."

"France and Italy, mainly."

"What's it like in Italy? I'd love to go to Milan."

I smile at her. "Someday you'll have to come traveling with me."

Her eyes are very bright and she is about to say something more, but her mother calls her into the kitchen.

Vivienne and Christopher arrive, dressed to kill. Vivienne wears pale-pink Trelise Cooper, a Kiwi designer with a nice line in color and fabric. Christopher wears a crisp, white linen shirt and fawn jeans. I can see why my sister is clutching his arm so adoringly. He really is a very handsome man. They navigate the room to avoid the aged granny and the children and settle themselves at the most comfortable seats.

Eventually, order is brought to all proceedings, and we are all squeezed around the tables ready for the feast. Alison brings out a tureen and starts ladling a dark-red soup into bowls and passing them down the table.

"Chilled spiced cherry soup," she announces.

Just then a car screams up in a shower of gravel, and she pauses and looks out the window.

"It's your brother," she says. "Get another couple of chairs."

A younger version of Wal struts in with a German shepherd at his side.

"Yo, bro!" he says, slapping Wal on the shoulder. "Hey, Ali," kissing my sister's cheek. "Ma," another smack for old Flo.

He nods at Magda and Murray and offers his hand to Ben and then to me.

Cheryl gets her own kiss. "Good to see you again, gorgeous!"

Nicholas walks in the door behind him. My blood slows.

"Met Nick down the road and told him he should tag along," says the dark young man.

"Lovely to see you!" Alison says.

Vivienne sees my frown.

"Nick is our property agent, but you know that, don't you, Lin?"

Chapter 40

"Tie your dog up, Matiu," says Wal. "I don't want him amongst the sheep."

"He wouldn't harm a fly."

"We don't want him to be tempted. Remember the mutt you brought here last year?"

"It wasn't his fault."

Wal sees me staring and assumes it's the conversation that is worrying me. "Once they get a taste for killing, they don't stop. We had to shoot the brute."

Matiu ties the dog up on the back porch, and Alison lays another two settings. We all shuffle together a little more to make room.

Across the table, Nicholas smirks at me. Does my family know about him and me? *Oh, God, I can't let Ben know about it!*

"What happened to Taihape?" asks Wal.

"Still there last I heard, Witi."

"And wotshername? Or did she get a better offer?"

"I got the better offer, bro," his brother replies and his black eyes move around the table, flashing a smile at Cheryl. "Didn't want to miss Ali's cooking."

Alison smiles in satisfaction. "Jess, clear the bowls. The beef will be ready in a tick."

Wal brings out the roast filet of beef and carves it at the table. Alison carries in a bowl of new potatoes and a bowl of ratatouille. Magda follows with the salads.

"Give Ben a bigger piece, Wal. A bigger piece!"

"Hey, did you hear the joke about the Kiwi, the South African, and the Aussie?" asks Nicholas. "They were touring Dubai and got caught drinking, so they get hauled up in front of the big Pooh-Bah, and he sentences them to twenty lashes each. But as it's Christmas, he tells them they can have a wish before they get the lash.

"Well, the South African says, 'Okay I wish for a pillow!' And he straps it to his back. But it only lasts five strokes before it's in ribbons, and then he's screaming like a woman. So the Aussie guy, he says, 'I'll have two pillows, thanks, mate,' but his pillows only last for ten strokes and then he's screaming like a girl.

"The Pooh-Bah turns to the Kiwi, and says, 'Well, I know New Zealand is a very beautiful country, so I'm going to give you two wishes before your lashes.' The Kiwi guy says, 'Thanks, mate, because you're a man of taste and discrimination my first wish is to get one hundred lashes instead of just twenty.'

"What a man! thinks the Pooh-Bah. 'And so what is your second wish to be?'"

"Tie the Australian to my back."

The whole table erupts in laughter. Murray howls so much he falls backward off his chair.

"There isn't much racism in New Zealand," says Alison, apologetically, to me. "Only against Australians and that doesn't count."

I smile, but she doesn't notice.

"More beef, Ben?" she asks. "Matt?"

"Witi, pass me the gravy," Matt/Matiu replies.

"Is Witi the Maori equivalent of Walter?" I ask.

Wal laughs. "More like Walter is the Pakeha equivalent of Witi. Actually, my name is John but everyone calls me Witi or Wal. It's because of my surname being Repati. Witty repartee, geddit?"

Eventually Alison brings out the trifle, made with red wine, damson plums, homemade butter spongecake, white chocolate custard made with a dozen egg yolks, and a lot of cream and butter. If you are what you eat, then Kiwis are cream-colored and soft and melt in the sun.

"Do you remember Billy T's joke about the handbag?" asks Matt and the family is away, telling joke after joke after joke. They've probably heard them all before, but it doesn't matter. I guess that's what families do. It's a shared history, something they do when they get together.

And then a warm feeling slips over me, from head to toe.

I am part of a family now. This is my whanau. Nicholas can't spoil this for me.

"Why don't you all go for a walk around the block while I clear up," says Alison. "You too, Lin. Jess can help me."

Jess scowls at her mother. Max gets up and goes into the kitchen. "I'll help you, Auntie," he says.

"Where the hell's the block?" asks Ben.

"She means out past the studio to the ridge and then back up the road. It takes about forty-five minutes to walk. Burn off some of those calories, eh, Cheryl?" says Matt. Cheryl giggles and follows him as he struts outside to put on his boots.

"We'll leave you now," says Vivienne. "The house will be unlocked."

She and Christopher saunter arm in arm back up the driveway to the house at the top of the hill. Nicholas joins Cheryl and Matt ahead of us and Wal falls into step with Ben and me.

The dogs start barking as we reach the first paddock.

"Siddown, you bastards!" yells Wal. "Siddown, I say!" And the barks trail away to spasmodic woofs.

The wind catches us as we walk up the first hill, lifting my hair. I can smell something rotten in the air.

"Poo! What's that stench?"

"The offal pits are up there," says Wal. "Where we dump any waste we can't burn." He turns and smiles at me. "No rubbish collection around here, city girl."

The wind drops again and the smell dissipates.

As we near the studio, Wal points out other features of the farm. "Up there is our main spring," he says, pointing toward a stand of trees above the studio. "We have a system of pipes and pumps to get the water to the troughs in each of the paddocks."

"*Jean de Florette*," I say, musing about the understated importance of water to agriculture.

"Eh?" says Wal.

"A movie about a man who tries to set up a rabbit farm, but he needs to grow feed for the rabbits and to grow the feed crop he needs water. He checks the weather records for the region going back for decades and he predicts there will be enough rain, but that summer there's a once-in-fifty-years drought. So he borrows his neighbor's donkey to carry water from the village well, but the neighbor stops letting him use the donkey because he's secretly in league with the man's enemy who wants him to fail. So then his crop dies and he has to let his rabbits go. But he tries again. He tries to dynamite a well for himself, but the rocks fall on his head instead and he's killed."

"Nice story," says Wal.

"Oh, it's a lot better than I've told you. And, of course, there's a twist at the end."

"There's always a twist at the end."

"It's my favorite movie, *Jean de Florette*," I reply. "Because it's a story about commerce, about an entrepreneur trying to build something from scratch. It's not a love story."

"Don't you like love stories, Lin?" Wal asks.

"We all like love stories. But life's about more than love."

"Talking of love, has your brother been—seeing—my sister?" Ben asks Wal.

Wal flicks him a sidelong glance. "I don't think there's any talk of love there, Ben. He seems to have cheered her up though."

Ben grunts.

We stop at the edge of the farm, at the top of the cliff above the zigzag road, and look out across the broad valley. You can see for miles, all the way to the sea. The wind tears at my clothes and chills me to the skin. I shiver.

"Be careful," says Wal. "It's a long way down."

We step back from the brink and join the others on the road home.

Later in the day, I decide to get rid of some vermin.

I find him at the pool, lying on an air mattress in the water, his skinny body clad in tartan swimming trunks, his finger waving in the air to the beat of whatever he is listening to on his headphones. Matt snoozes on the second air mattress, tanned body glistening in the last rays of the sun, a scruffy khaki hat pulled over his face.

"Matt," I toss a tennis ball at his stomach to get his attention.

He sits up with a start and promptly falls into the water.

Nicholas opens his eyes and takes off his headphones. "The lovely Lin," he drawls. "What can we do for you?"

"How long are you guys staying?"

"Oh, I don't know. The food is pretty good here, eh, Matt?"

Matt pulls himself back onto the air bed. "Bit slow, though."

"Ali has a set of cousins arriving tomorrow," I reply. "She is too polite to say."

Nicholas flicks water at me. "There's plenty of room up at the big house."

I shake my head. "Sorry, but Ben and I are using the guest suite and Vivienne's redecorating the other two bedrooms."

Matt sits up. "Thinking of heading back anyway," he says. "My dog is sick of being tied up on the porch."

Nicholas scowls at me, but there is nothing he can do. I head back to Vivienne's house, treading carefully over her immaculate floor to the guest bedroom. I sit on the bed and close my eyes and wonder whether my father had slept in this room and left his clothes in the walnut dresser. And for a minute or two it seems I can sense his presence, here in the house where he would have stayed with his wife and family, on holiday from his job in Wellington.

It feels right that I, too, am here at Ngatirua with my family and Ben, on holiday from my job in Wellington.

Chapter 41

The flames have died down into glowing embers. Ben takes a sip of beer and carefully places the lamb chops on the grill, sideways so they don't slip into the fire. As the fat sizzles and melts and crisps in the heat, the meat darkens into sweet caramelized brown.

Vivienne was an uncomfortable hostess. She kept tidying up the things Ben kept leaving around and wincing whenever she heard me speak. So the following day, once Nicholas and Matt had left for Havelock North, Ben and I escaped to stay at the studio with Cheryl.

It is a slice of heaven—the warmth of the sun on your neck, the tang of a cold Sauvignan Blanc in your throat, the smell of barbecuing meat in your nostrils, your man beside you doing the cooking. I felt my father here too.

"The chops will be ready in two!" Ben calls.

Cheryl seems content, relaxed, and at peace, not scared any more. I guess that brother of Wal's has been good for her.

"Are you sure you won't come with us?" I ask her a second time.

"Matt's asked me to a party on New Year's Eve," Cheryl replies.

"Not anywhere near Joe's family in Haumoana, I hope."

"Nah. Up in Wairoa."

Later, Cheryl returns inside to watch television, and Ben and I sit watching the sun set like fire behind the hills. Ben has extracted the old guitar from the cupboard and is tuning it.

"You still have to talk with Alison."

"I know, I know. Just not until I have to."

"What are you afraid of?" Ben asks.

"Nothing. I just don't want to spoil being here with my family."

"It's your call."

"So I need to go back to work for three days and then we're free after that," I say. "Do you want to go south? Or north?"

In the dark, I can just make out his smile. "Why don't we just play it by ear," he says. "Go with the flow and all those other clichés."

Then he starts playing "Alhambra" and I lie with my head tilted back listening as the beautiful notes trickle into the night air.

Cheryl is asleep on the divan by the time Ben and I quietly climb the stairs to the loft. Although the bed is old and lumpy, it suits us to fall together into the dip in the middle. Ben puts his arms around me and we kiss like we kissed last summer, before it all fell apart, and then we move together like we used to, and all is well with the world.

A sound like glass breaking wakes me. In the moonlight I can make out Ben's sleeping shape. I clamber out of the bed and tread softly over to the ladder and look down. Below, all is still. Nothing has fallen. Perhaps it was the wind in the trees.

Ears straining, I think I can hear a soft footfall, but then all is silent. Perhaps it is a sheep moving outside. Ben reaches over and sleepily pulls me back into bed, snuggling against my back. I try to lie still and go back to sleep, but my body is still tense. I need to check the house, I decide.

When I climb downstairs and pick my way across the room, the scent of smoke wafts lightly across my nostrils. I am sure we dowsed the barbecue coals, but perhaps something slipped out and is still burning somewhere? I go to open the door, but it is stuck, the handle won't move. Now the smell of smoke is stronger.

"Ben!" I yell. "Get up! Cheryl, wake up!"

I push the door again and again, but it doesn't budge. Ben is climbing down the ladder.

"What's wrong?" he asks.

"There's a fire burning outside, and I can't open the door."

Cheryl climbs off the divan and comes to stand beside me. "It's Joe!" she shrieks suddenly. "He must have come for me!"

Ben charges and kicks at the door, but there is no effect. I can hear the crackle of flames, and now we can see the dancing of the fire's light under the door. It seems to have something wedged in front of it.

Ben goes to the window and breaks the glass. Fresh air pours in and so does the strong smell of smoke.

"We can't get out there!" I cry. "It's a sheer drop!"

I turn to the bathroom, where a small louver is open, letting in some air. Too small to fit through.

"Start filling pots with water," Ben says. "We'll keep the flames down until I can break us out of here."

The fire is taking hold of the wall beside the door. We might be able to escape once it has burned through.

"Each of you grab a blanket and get it soaking wet," he says. "And put something on your feet."

Cheryl is gulping in fear, but she stands in the bathroom running water on a blanket while I do the same in the kitchen.

The smoke is thick so I smash more of the window to let in air. Ben rummages through the cupboards trying to find something he can beat on the panels with, hard enough to break us out of this death trap. He takes up the vacuum cleaner pole and uses it to hit the panels next to the door, the ones half burned through from the fire outside. He smashes through and starts on the next. I grab a mop and hit the wall too. Not very effectively. I hit Ben instead.

"Leave it, Lin, I'll do it."

Then he picks up the television and smashes it against the hole we have made. Cheryl wails loudly. "Noooo, not the television!"

Somehow I'm laughing and then Ben grabs a wet blanket and pushes his way through the hole, hopping as the fire on the ground licks at his feet and throws the blanket on the ground. I follow behind tugging at Cheryl, but she pulls out of my grasp.

"Cheryl!" yells Ben and heads back inside. There is a shriek and Cheryl comes tumbling through just as the roof collapses.

"Ben!" I call, but the hole is now covered in flaming planks.

I can see the barbecue tilted against the door. I take up my wet blanket, covering my hands and drag the barbecue free. Ben crashes through the door, and we stagger back out of the way of the flames and fall down into the grass.

Ben is holding the guitar. "It's a beauty. I had to rescue it."

The fire has taken hold of the front of the house, but the thick wood is slowing it.

"Soak your blanket in the trough by the gate," I tell Cheryl. Ben whacks the flames with the blankets again and again. A methylated spirits bottle, the head broken, rolls out from under the ashes.

And then Wal arrives with Murray, and they have fire extinguishers, and we quickly put the fire out.

Wal looks at the burnt studio. "What the hell happened?"

"Did you leave coals burning, mate?" asks Murray.

"Get the girls back to the house, Muz," Wal tells him. "We'll be along soon."

I wrap Cheryl in a blanket and send her away with Murray and rejoin the men.

"The door was jammed shut," Ben says. "Looked like the barbecue was propped against it. And we found this." Ben kicks the meth's bottle towards Wal. "I didn't use meth's to start the fire, and I don't remember seeing the bottle."

Wal bends to see it. "Did you hear anything?"

"I thought I heard something, but I wasn't sure," I say. "But it meant I was awake and noticed the smoke in time."

Wal looks at us with a somber expression. "This is serious. You could have all been killed."

We enter the studio and pick through the debris.

"Sorry about the television, Wal."

He laughs. "Vivienne has a few spares."

Ben and Wal climb the ladder and rescue our possessions. Wal fills Cheryl's bag with her clothes.

"We'll get anything we missed tomorrow."

Back at the farmhouse, Alison is in control. Cheryl emerges from the bathroom dressed in a robe two sizes too large for her. Her face is drawn.

"She has a couple of nasty burns," says Alison. "Let's have a look at yours."

She gets to work with her salves and bandages. "Wal will take you up to Vivienne's to sleep."

My burns are okay, manageable, and Alison's salve helps. The cuts on Ben's hands are bleeding. Ben protests when Alison insists on bandaging them entirely. But I tell him we don't want to get any blood on Vivienne's precious sheets, do we? That shuts him up.

I look at Cheryl who sits rocking herself in the corner. "How do you think he found her?"

Wal is standing by the fireplace, a frown on his face. "I suppose word got around we had a visitor staying."

Cheryl shakes her head. "Why did he try to hurt me? Doesn't he care about me?"

"We have to report this," Ben says.

"Was there any proof it was Joe?" I say.

He shakes his head. "I don't think so."

"Or even proof it was arson?"

"I know I put out the fire in the barbecue and I know we didn't leave it so close to the door that it could have fallen and jammed the door shut. But I can't prove it."

"So there's no proof." I look down. "I'm not too keen on reporting this, Ben. I'm the chief executive of Hera. I can't afford that kind of publicity."

"It's dangerous, Lin."

"I can't take the risk."

Ben lets out a long sigh. "All right, we won't take it to the police. But, Cheryl, you'll have to leave now he's found you."

Ben, Cheryl, and I drive back to Wellington. It is a quiet trip. We don't get there until late.

Ben and I lie in my bed. We lie apart. It hurts to touch anything with my hands.

"I am sorry," he says. "I have to go with her. She's lost everything—her home, the man she loved, and the children she will always love. All she has left is Emmy and me."

"I know."

"And I've got to be there to protect her in case Joe finds her again."

"I know."

"You're so strong, Lin," he says. "And Cheryl isn't."

"I know."

Early in the morning their taxi arrives.

I kiss Ben.

"Safe journey," I say and turn to hug Cheryl. "Take care."

"You take care too," she says, and hugs me back.

"I'm not the one with a psycho ex-lover," I mutter under my breath.

Then I stand watching as he carries their bags to the taxi and leaves me, again.

Part III

Knock the Bastard Off

Chapter 42

By late January, the FP X68 is planted in the heart of the concrete bunker, and bundles of fiber extend themselves like roots along the walls, through the carefully constructed openings, and down the corridors until they reach the street. There the roots stretch beneath the streets, forking when they meet an intersection and sending smaller bundles twisting and turning in their trenches down the Esplanade, across Cuba, down Jackson, and out into the suburbs. Here the roots emerge into daylight, climb the poles and become branches, stretching from pole to pole, tied off and ready for that last spurt of cabling that will reach into each property to meet its final destiny in an outlet with a wireless modem somewhere on the inside wall of your house.

The master bundle of roots will continue down the Esplanade, alongside the railway tracks and into the city, where they will intertwine with the roots of other great trees, older but not necessarily thicker, and certainly not as smart. One spur will end in our offices on the quay, snaking in through the basement where they are captured and fixed into the network boards. From there the captured cables will sedately twirl around each room and up through the walls to the next floor and the one above until finally they arrive in Hera's boardroom where I now sit, ready to present to the Board.

"Gentlemen," I say. "We are on target to launch on the first of March.

"The switch has been commissioned and the interconnect tests between our network and Kiwicom's are going well," I tell them. Their faces don't move. "We expect to complete within two weeks."

"Interconnect tests take months," states Chairman Hobb. "How can you be sure you're going to get the sign-off from Kiwicom?"

I look down and let my lips form a small, satisfied smile. "They haven't been able to fault us. The customer, mediation, and billing packages have been configured for our products and processes."

They are still looking stern. "Did you make the changes we suggested?" asks Hobb.

"We made the high priority changes."

"We expect all the changes we asked for to be made."

I look down. This time I don't smile. "We will add the others in the first post-launch release."

Hobb glances at Stanton, sighs, and shuffles his papers.

"We're waiting on the interfaces before starting the tests of the end-to-end processes."

"You haven't completed the integration?" asks Robert.

"We've completed the high-volume transactional interfaces. We'll handle the low-volume interfaces manually until we have time to automate them. We're making good progress on the operational and management reports," I say with pride, because we have been working long hours on the systems and we're very nearly there.

Tom has been our steadiest rock during the last few weeks of pulling together the operation. When Fred became anxious over test results, Tom made the decisions on what was important and must be fixed, and what was less important and could be handled manually. Marion walked the floors and listened to all the complaints and the fears and the last-minute panicking over what was too late to fix, and Ian laughed and cracked jokes and kept us sane.

Peake? Peake smiled and said little.

But still the directors frown.

"The call center is up and running and we will have our customer operations staff in place by the end of the week. We start customer service training next week and process training in two weeks' time."

"Why not now?" snaps Stanton.

"We're still working on the processes to handle the exceptions. As you know, at the beginning of a new service, exceptions are generally the rule."

But the Board is not amused.

"The warehouse is stocked with three-months' supply of residential cable and modems." I look around the table and every bastard's face still looks stern. "We have taken on our first team of salespeople. The sales material will be available in two weeks' time."

"Why the delay?"

"The lawyers have only just finalized the terms and conditions. There were some changes they wanted made to the fees for breaking contracts.

"As agreed, we're launching quietly in order to reduce the calls into the call center and so we can best manage customer expectations over installation lead times."

Dammit, their faces are still sour.

Hobb speaks, "We want to review the business plan. We're considering making some changes to the network rollout, and I want to know the impact."

"Changes?" I say. "It's late to be changing the build plans. I don't think we—"

"Peake says he can start this weekend. Get the rest of the management team together to work on it on Saturday."

My lips part and then close again. No point telling the chairman I had made other plans.

"What did they say? Were they pleased?" asks Ian, his face breaking into a wide grin.

"Did they approve the approach for testing?" asks Fred, with an anxious frown.

"Will they let us appoint a customer champion?" Marion asks, her face its normal placid state.

Tom says nothing. His eyes gaze at me then he turns to stare out the window at the yachts that dance across the water of the harbor.

Peake has not come to my office for a debrief. He chairs the audit and finance committee and is still discussing details of the latest figures with Stanton and Hobb.

"They're not unhappy," I say. "I didn't talk about the testing issue, Fred. The time wasn't right."

I glance at Marion. Her eyes watch mine. "Nor was it the right time to suggest a customer champion."

"Is there anything we need to know?" Tom asks.

I stare into his face, his jaw now set in a grim line. "No."

That night I open a very good bottle of wine and fill my glass, but it tastes like soap. The excitement I had been feeling about the successful progress has evaporated.

Up on the roof the Jacuzzi waits, cool and passive, forgotten about for weeks. When I look at my watch, I realize, no; no time to heat the water, I'll be asleep before it's even tepid, let alone hot. I sip the wine and look out on the lights of Wellington. The yachts have gone from the water. Back to their berths, I guess, with their crews in the bars by the marina, talking of wind shifts and the time it takes to raise the spinnaker and which boats did what and to whom.

Tonight I had been expecting to feel like Caesar: conqueror, and a winner, admired and respected.

I sip the wine again. I had been saving this bottle. I hadn't expected to open it tonight. I'd expected to be down there in the city, drinking with the Board, toasting the fact that Hera has reached the point where we would make that launch date unless something very unexpected happens. Instead, I shiver as the ever-present breeze nudges my back.

With a last glance, I turn away and go back down into the apartment. I have one last task to complete.

There is no answer. "Ben," I say to his voice mail system. "I won't be able to make it this weekend. I'm sorry. Crisis at work." I pause, wondering what to tell him, but there isn't anything else to say.

"I'll call you," and I hang up.

Chapter 43

When I get home, late again, and eat cheese and a few crackers because I'm not hungry, I tell myself that tomorrow I'll do something different, find some way of relaxing so I can sleep, but each night follows the same pattern.

I go to bed exhausted yet night after night I jerk awake in the early morning and don't seem to be able to fall back to sleep. There are so many things that could go wrong, and we have so little time to fix anything. In the darkest hour, the one before dawn, I feel a sense of unease. I tell myself it's just the effect of blood sugar levels being low and I turn and face the other way hoping to get more comfortable. But when I do manage to fall asleep, it seems only minutes pass before I wake groggily from deep unconsciousness to the sound of my cell phone's alarm and I crawl out of bed to once again face the day's trials.

And so the days pass until the weekend arrives, and each Friday night I tell myself I'll sleep in tomorrow, but every Saturday I wake at five and stay awake, mulling over the week's problems and wondering if I should have made different decisions.

I tidy the house and do the laundry and pay the bills and shop for groceries I won't eat, then fall asleep trying to read the latest Kate Atkinson. I wake early and toss until it's light outside then spend Sunday preparing for Monday and telling myself I'll catch up with friends the following weekend and so it goes on.

Four weeks out from the launch date, I have to cancel my trip to see Ben again because the Board is in town and they want an update. When I arrive home that Friday night, I step in the door and trip over a pack. Ben? Ben! But no, I don't recognize this pack.

Someone has hung a gauzy green dress on my bookcase. Someone has been sitting in my chair at the table, which is pulled out and has a jacket thrown over the back, and someone has been drinking from my favorite orange-and-black mug, which sits on the kitchen counter.

A slip of paper is lying on the table. "Hey Auntie Lin, Max and I got tickets to the rugby. Hope it's okay if we stay? Jess. ☺"

It is the weekend of Wellington's premier sporting event—the International Rugby Sevens contest—when all the spectators dress up and parade the streets. I'd been offered tickets, but I had expected to be in Queenstown with Ben, now canceled, so instead I watch a sad movie and drink a bottle of wine and fall into bed shortly before they stumble home, giggling, young, life all before them, not yet disillusioned when all their dreams come true and they find it wasn't what they wanted after all.

"Shh, shh," they whisper, the giggles stop, and we go to sleep, me in my big double bed, them on their separate sofas.

In the morning, I emerge when I hear Max making coffee. Max's face breaks into that beautiful, wide smile, and Jess manages a small, restrained smirk, and they seem happy to see me, happy to claim me as their aunt.

These kids are my family, my *whanau*.

The cloud lifts a little, and I smile and pull open the fridge and make the traditional gifts that aunts make: food, followed by spending money.

When Max heads downtown to buy something they need, ear extensions I think he said, Jess curls up on the sofa and lets me cook breakfast for her.

"Mum's driving me round the bend!" she says. "She's like, that's a nice dress, Jess, but don't you think you should wear a sweater with it? And Dad is so embarrassing. He made some really stupid comments on my Facebook page about how cute I was. I was *so* embarrassed and my friends were saying, 'like what's with the dude? Is he into you or what?' "

I laugh. "Parents should keep off their kids' Facebook pages."

"Yeah!" she says. "I had to defriend him. You know what I mean? And I get the hard nag from Mum on helping around the house. Not that I do anything right. I had to get Max to bring me here to get away from her."

"Have you decided what you're going to do now you've finished school?"

Jess looks down at her eggs. She pushes a fragment back and forth across the plate and then forks it and puts it in her mouth. Her eyes flick toward me and away again.

"Spit it out. And I don't mean the egg."

"I want to study fashion design, Auntie Lin. In Wellington."

"And your parents aren't keen?"

"Mum wants me to go to the tech in Hastings. But Wellington's program is the best in New Zealand." She plays with her egg again. "I submitted my portfolio in October, and they've offered me a place."

Jess reminds me so much of myself at the same age. Mom wanted me to go to the local college, but I applied to schools far, far away and eventually took up a scholarship in England.

"If it's what you want, then you should go for it. Go for the best you can."

She looks up with a shy smile. "You really think so? I mean, I can get a student loan and all that, so I can afford to leave home. Of course, I'll go back from time to time."

I never did go back.

"What about Max? Does he want to leave too?"

"Not Max. Ngatirua is all he's ever wanted. And he won't leave his mother to look after the place by herself, nor Wal without help on the farm."

"Your parents seem to love him."

"Yeah, more than me."

"Rubbish, Jess."

"I suppose so. I don't mind that they love him so much. It means I'm free to leave because he'll be there for all of them."

"Poor Max!"

"No, it's lucky Max. Lucky it makes him happy to be needed."

I doze in the sun and dream I am trapped in a dark place, but then Sally arrives to rescue me. Sally is wearing scrubs, and slung over her front is a large playing card depicting the Queen of Hearts.

"You too?" I ask.

"We're determined to win this year," she replies.

Soon we're in the city sitting at a table watching groups of revelers in fancy dress on their way to the International Rugby Sevens tournament.

"Here comes the rest of the pack." I wave to the crowd.

A gaggle of medics wearing cards, talking and laughing and jostling for position, sweep up to our viewpoint on the side of the road.

John is amongst them. As I watch, he looks at Sally, and she looks back at him. John's face relaxes into a tentative smile. He stops.

Sally doesn't move. The pageant seems to flicker around us, and everything seems to narrow to Sally and I sitting in a café, while a man waits for her to make a decision.

"Go on," I tell her. "Go for it."

Sally's face breaks suddenly into her gay smile and she rises and leaves me sitting there, watching, as she takes John's arm and the pack carries on down the road and vanishes in the distance.

A group of hobbits caper up the street, brown jerkins pulled tight with ropes around their middles, and purple hoods on their heads. When they see me, they cheer and wave and I wave back. Tom is leading them, Marion is in the middle, and I think I can see Helen arm in arm with Fred. "Come with us," they call, but I shake my head and raise my glass to toast them. Ian and Deepak bring up the rear. Ian waves at me, a smile lighting up his freckled face, but Deepak turns away.

I heave a sigh and look down at my empty glass. A half-empty bottle sits on the table so I refill my glass and look back out at the street.

A motley collection of reptiles is chasing the hobbits, I think they're supposed to be dragons, or maybe *Taniwha*? I recognize the one with the large bottom and the long, white tail. Sure enough he angles his serpent head toward me and it is Scott Peake.

"I can't tell if you're a snake or a leech," I say, but I don't think he hears me. He turns away and slithers on down the road.

A breakfast wanders past—eggs, bacon, sausage, and something red. The man in red looks a bit like Nicholas. Perhaps he is supposed to be stewed tomato or maybe a red herring.

Finally, I watch a small group of Chinese men walk past. They are dressed as Chinese businessmen. Quon Dao sees me and comes over to where I sit.

"Lin," he says with a smile, "you're not going?"

"I was supposed to be somewhere else," I reply.

"Everyone is wearing fancy dress. We don't know what to do about our clothes," he gestures at their plain gray garb.

"I'll help you." I cross the street to a tourist shop and beckon Dao and his three assistants inside. "Hawaiian shirts!" I tell them, "Pick out the color you like and throw them on over your clothes." Then I grab four leis from the stack hanging on the rack. "And wear these around your necks."

The Chinese are now all smiles as they, too, head on down the road.

•   •   •

When the elf king and the elf queen arrive back, I am dozing on the sofa.

"How was it?" I ask.

"Brilliant!" says Max. "Especially the final."

"Fantastic!" says Jess. "Especially the parade. Next year we're going to get a bigger group together," she adds excitedly. "Next year I'll have my own retinue of elves."

"So who won?"

"New Zealand," says Max.

"The pack of cards," says Jess, like many of the attendees: more interested in the fancy dress than the game.

I get up and go to the kitchen. "Tea? Or, something stronger?"

"I drink herbal tea, Auntie, do you have any of that?"

"Call me Lin. Auntie is so aging."

"Sure, Auntie Lin. And I'm hungry. Do you have anything to eat?"

"Omelet?"

"I had eggs this morning."

"Sorry. Um, foie gras?"

"What?"

"Pâté."

They settle for foie gras on toast followed by Stilton and crackers.

Max tidies up and puts the dishes in the dishwasher, and Jess curls up in the quilts on her sofa.

"I bet you get lonely. Maybe I could stay here and be company for you," she says. "At least until I find a flat."

"There isn't much room."

"You're at work most of the time, aren't you?"

I laugh. "We'll see. First, you have to talk to your parents and persuade them to accept you going to the course here."

Then I tuck them up and turn out the light and go to my room, smiling, because I have some children to look after now, and I promise myself I'll get back to Ngatirua and see the rest of my family soon. Maybe next month, after the launch.

When Ben rings I promise him, after the launch, we'll see each other then.

That night I sleep better. Sally's face was happy. Jess and Max are happy. And the end is in sight. I just have to stay focused and stay on track. In four weeks' time, I will get my life back.

In four weeks' time, we will have launched or failed.

Chapter 44

Three weeks from launch, Nicholas comes knocking at the door. When I open it, his eyes stare at me out of tiny pupils.

"What do you want?"

"You should be more polite," he says and pushes past me into the room.

"I didn't invite you in," I say. "I'd like you to leave now."

He sits down on my sofa. "I've got a business proposition for you."

"I'm not interested in doing any business with you, Nicholas."

"That winery I own part of up in the bay?" he says. "I need some money to pay the costs this quarter."

"I'm not buying a share."

"I'm not giving you a share. I want you to loan me the money."

"Hello? Why would I loan you money?"

Nicholas stares at me and then stares out the window where the wind is whipping the tops of the trees back and forth. He reaches into his man bag and pulls out a photo.

"Because I have this," he says and tosses the photograph on the coffee table.

I pick up the photograph. The quality is poor, the shapes are grainy, and the colors are washed out.

"You're asking for money?" I eventually ask. "How much?"

"Ten thousand should do it," he replies.

I gaze at his face and think about my options.

"Let me see what I have on me," I reply, rising and picking

up my purse. My iPhone is at the bottom, so I scramble for a moment or two before pulling out my wallet.

"I've only got five hundred dollars in cash."

He reaches out his hand. "I'll take that now and the rest when you get the cash out."

I hold onto my wallet. "Let me get this straight, Nicholas. You want what?"

"I've told you, ten thousand dollars in return for that photograph."

"And if I don't give you ten thousand dollars?"

"One copy of the photo goes to your boyfriend and another goes to the newspapers. So much for your brilliant career, huh, Lin?"

"This is blackmail."

"Call it whatever you want. Just give me the money."

He stands in front of me with his hand reaching for my wallet.

"Are you going to hit me if I don't give you money?"

Nicholas is shaking. "Just give me what you have, bitch."

I hand him the notes. "I'll get you the money, but then I don't ever want to hear from you again."

His eyes flicker, and I know he has no intention of vanishing out of my life. "Sure. Just been caught short this month, that's all."

He walks out the door, and I close it behind him and lean my back against it, my eyes closed.

Later that week, our first live network test does not go well. In the middle of the night, the network goes down. We send out the technicians, but it is dark and they cannot isolate the fault.

At eight in the morning, we hold an urgent audio-conference. "What's going on?" the chairman asks. "What the hell is happening down there!"

"We have a problem with the network."

"Then fix it!"

"We're trying to, but we haven't found the cause yet."

The field technicians have been out since first light examining each section of the network. Tom has his network managers at the table and they are poring over the network diagrams and the switch records.

At nine thirty I get the call that they have found the fault.

"There is a hole in the overhead fiber cable," Tom tells me over the phone. "In that stretch that runs along the edge of the forest. They're replacing the line so the service should be operational again within an hour."

"A hole? What caused it?"

Tom is silent for a moment. "Jake thinks it's a bullet hole."

"Christ." I consider that possibility for a moment. "Is someone trying to sabotage us?"

"We don't know. The boys are checking the scene."

As soon as I hang up, my cell phone rings. Alison's name flashes up on the screen.

"Hello," I say.

"Lin? How are you?"

"I'm well. And you all?"

"We're all doing fine, thanks. Oh, except Wal is complaining about his back and you know Christopher gets those bad headaches, and actually my hip aches a bit if I walk too far. But apart from that we're all fine."

"Oh, good."

The desk telephone rings, but I leave it for Helen to answer.

"Viv and I wondered if you'd like to visit for Art Deco weekend. It's such a lot of fun, I'm sure you'd enjoy it."

Helen puts her head in the door.

"Ah, um, I don't think I can decide right now."

Helen mouths, "Tom."

"Can I call you back?" I say.

"Of course. Anyway, it's in two weeks' time, so you don't have to make up your mind yet."

"Right, right. Anyway, I'll call you."

I get off the phone and pick up my landline.

"Tom?"

"We think we've worked out what happened with the cable," he says. "The boys found a dead possum beneath the line."

"So?"

Tom snorts. "We think some twit was out shooting possums and caught one sitting on our cable."

"A possum hunter. Great. I'll call Hobb and let him know the mystery is solved."

I look up at the picture on my wall of the road to Ngatirua, and I promise myself, when this is all over, I'm going there.

"So what action are you taking to make sure the cable is bulletproof?"

"We can't make it bulletproof. That doesn't make sense."

"Then make it possum proof."

"I don't think we can make it possum proof either."

"How can you make sure the problem doesn't happen again?"

"It was a freak accident, Stewart. We can't protect against freak accidents. What we can do is get the redundant route built so we don't lose service if there is a network fault."

"Why isn't there a redundant route already?"

Because you cut it out of the budget, I say, but silently, because by now I know this chairman takes no accountability for any bad decisions.

"We'll need to increase the funding allocated."

"I've already told you we won't be increasing the budget, Mere, so find yourself another answer."

When he hangs up, I ponder whether there is anything we can possibly do to get that redundant route in before we go live. We knew it was a risk. My head hurts as I try to think of where we can find the money to complete the ring.

This time I cannot find any options.

Chapter 45

I read somewhere that dreams are the result of your brain trying to make sense of the fragments of memory that flash through your mind as you sleep. Your sleeping brain strings the images together to make a story. I've always wondered whether scriptwriters have cleverer dreams than the rest of us.

Lately, in my dreams I can see no images. I can just sense danger, as if something horrible is standing behind me about to attack. When I wake, the nightmare still has me in its grasp. I can't quite recall the details, but I know there was something amongst trees, stalking me. I can't recall if I saw anything, just the feeling of dread and that I couldn't escape.

Sometimes I dream I have struck the beast before it gets me and I kill it. I don't remember seeing anything except a corner like a grave with concrete edges and darkness all around, but I think I killed something or someone, bludgeoned them, though I can't imagine what with, and I can't imagine what they looked like, either alive or dead. Maybe one of those *Doctor Who* monsters you cannot ever see. But the beast always seems to return, as if I didn't quite strike hard enough. I never feel the relief that the beast is dead and the danger is gone, until I wake up at four in the morning and my tired mind remembers it was only a dream. Then I lie awake and worry about Hera instead and the nightmare fades.

In the morning, the dread is gone, although sometimes I worry about having such dark, violent dreams. What happened to the light and gentle images of friends and lovers and hobbits?

•　　•　　•

Nicholas swaggers in. His eyes are normal today, I'm glad about that. Hopefully, he will be more rational.

"Have you got the money?" he asks.

"Have you got the photo?" I reply.

He smirks and lays a photo on the coffee table. God knows who the stupid bitch is. Can't be me. I am not stupid.

"Just a moment," I say, and then I press the button on my laptop. A recording of our last conversation plays.

Nicholas's face stiffens. "How did you do that?"

"The wonders of modern technology. Especially, Apple," I reply. "I turned my iPhone onto record while I was getting out my wallet. Oh, and it's recording now as well, so sit back down while I tell you what's going to happen next."

"Where is it? Damn you!" He teeters on his toes, his hands opening and closing in fists by his side.

But I judge Nicholas to be a weak little piffle of a man, and, sure enough, he slumps back onto the sofa.

"You won't find it. And my friends downstairs are listening on the other end. They'll be upstairs in a flash if they think you're threatening me. In fact, they only gave me fifteen minutes before they come up anyway. They'd like to—talk—with you themselves."

He stares at me.

"So, Nicholas, you've become a blackmailer. Well, I'm not taking it. That photo of yours? Which no doubt you have on file? No one will believe it's me. They're far more likely to be-lieve you've doctored an image."

"People will believe it's you! I'll make sure of it!"

"My reputation is as an uptight, sexless teetotaler. And you won't be around to make any claims. You'll be in the clink being done over by some really nasty big bastards."

His eyes widen and his skinny bottom twitches.

I give him my cool executive smile. "You see, I've checked how the police deal with blackmailers. They'll throw the book at you and go to extreme lengths to protect your victims. In this case, me."

I'm bluffing, but he won't be able to read that in my eyes. His face, however, is transparently furious. His eyebrows are lowered, his eyelids tense, and his lips are compressed.

"I'll take for granted you'll resign from your job overseeing my sisters' affairs in Wellington," I say. "Okay, the fifteen minutes are nearly up, and I really think you would be wise to leave before my friends arrive to have their own chat with you. And, Nicholas? If you ever set foot in this house again, I tell my sisters what you are, and the recording goes to the police. Understand?"

When I open the door, he gets up and goes, as fast as Joe did, down the stairs, down the path, and out onto the street.

But I worry. He still might distribute the photo. Sure I've bluffed him that no one will believe the woman to be me, but I know from bitter experience that people believe what they want to believe, especially if it's something negative about a woman in power.

And in New Zealand, especially, they like to cut the tall poppies down.

I walk in Sally's open door and collapse on her sofa. Tonight Sally's face looks less tired than mine. She opens a bottle of champagne.

"Was that Nick I saw going past the window?" she asks. "What was the matter with him?"

"He had the shits," I reply. "So he had to run."

Sally snorts and hands me a flute. "He's bad news. You know, I told him he wasn't my type and so he put some photos of me up on Facebook. Horrible photos."

"Oh, no. Sex stuff?"

Sally shakes her head. "I didn't sleep with him. But he took some nasty shots anyway, which made me look fifty and fat."

"Oh."

She sighs. "I had to grin and bear it. Anyway, let's forget the little creep. How is Ben? And Cheryl?"

"They're fine. Cheryl found out Joe was arrested last month for beating up some guy in the pub. He's out on bail, but we're hoping they'll put him away for a while."

"Is she still staying with Ben?"

"Ben tells me she's settled in too well. He's still sleeping on the sofa in the living room. Emmy's mother has taken a job in Cape Town for six months so Emmy's with Ben full time."

"Long-distance relationships are tough," says Sally. She takes a swig and turns to look at me. "Haven't you thought of moving to the mountain? Since the mountain can't move here?"

"There's no work for me in Dipton."

"Does that matter?"

"Of course, it matters. You know it matters! I'm not just the sum of my looks and personality, I'm the whole package. And the whole package includes my career, the income I make, the fact I can afford to spend money on whatever I want, the fact no one has to support me."

"You mean you don't trust him to love you without the money."

I gaze at the bubbles floating to the top of my glass and don't answer. That's not quite what I meant, but maybe it's true.

Because who am I if not the slick executive high flyer? I am no longer young, and I'm only average on the good-looks front. What else do I have to offer? What other edge do I have to say I'm special?

"Is it worth it, Lin?"

"What?"

"Your brilliant career as a chief executive."

In the background, Michael's computer makes a pinging noise as he plays a computer game, and the wind rattles the double-hung windows on the side of Sally's living room and whistles in the chimney. Polly sits up and scratches her belly with her left foot.

I examine the liquid in my glass. It is half empty.

"Of course, it's worth it," I tell her, and smile my executive smile, the one that doesn't reach my eyes.

Sally looks at me with an expression I can't fathom.

"I've bought a house!" she says suddenly. "I wasn't planning to, but as soon as I saw it I had to have it."

"Wow!" I raise my glass and clink it against hers. "Congratulations."

"It's a beautiful house," she says. "Sits on a hill facing west for the evening sun. White walls and windows everywhere and a big garden all around."

"It sounds like the house that John built."

She fiddles with her glass. "Actually, it is the house that John built."

"Oh. Does John know?"

She scrapes at a mark with her fingernail. "Yes, he knows."

"Does he mind?"

She puts down her glass and gets up to close the curtain before sitting back down. "Actually, I've asked him to live there with us."

I reach out and touch her arm. "Sal!"

Sally's face softens. "He is very happy. It's like being with a different man."

I raise my glass and toast her again. *I hope they will be happy.* "No regrets losing your exciting single life?"

"I'm forty-five," she says. "Too old to keep playing doctors and nurses. And John has become a very good cook. Apparently we're going to have pigs and sheep and a vegetable garden. He's already talking about growing olive trees and hazelnuts and avocados. And he'll drive Michael to and from school and take care of him while I'm at work."

"The magic Kiwi lifestyle."

"We're going to be the real thing."

I think they will be happy.

"I'm going to miss you all."

"Even Polly?"

"Especially, Polly! I still remember how she scared Joe away."

Sally gets up to check on our meal and to call Michael in from the garden. Polly pants her way inside as well, following the scent of the precursor to leftover scraps into the kitchen.

"Out. Out, damned dog!"

"When do you finalize the purchase of the house?" I ask.

"In two weeks' time."

"Fast work!"

"If you gotta go, you gotta go," Sally replies. "Besides, my lease ends in March. So it was either buy now or wait another six months. What are your plans, Lin?"

"I don't know. After the launch, I'll have a better idea what the future holds."

"Everything is still on target?"

"Everything is on track to what the team and I expect, although not everything is going to be perfect on Day One. There hasn't been enough time to test all the processes and to fully train the staff. We will have to hand hold every transaction for the first couple of months."

"Is that a problem?"

"Our volumes are going to be low in the beginning, so we can fix anything that goes wrong."

"Then you should be fine."

"You'd think so, wouldn't you? I've spent the day reviewing the business plans with my CFO. Everything is on target except for the network build, because the Board changed the plans to focus on the commercial areas instead of residential. That's put our funding under pressure, but we'll have enough to meet the Government's provisos."

"Does the guy know his stuff?"

"I think he's more interested in finding what is wrong rather than what is right. Just another bastard looking out for number one."

I finish my glass and hold it out for Sally to fill up again.

"But I'm probably just being paranoid."

Chapter 46

The negative press articles start appearing two weeks before the official launch. The first is in the Computer pages and talks about a network failure and insufficient testing. The article refers to Hera's system selection as having been "hasty, with poor due diligence" and the implementation as "cutting corners and definitely not by the book." The article is written by one of the Old Boys of the technology press. He enjoys himself in the final paragraphs making slighting references to our imminent services being "nonexistent weapons of mass destruction" and several other banal anti-American jokes presumably targeted at me, the American chief executive, no longer referred to as a Kiwi.

There is a nastiness in the Kiwi culture, I've noticed, that requires them to believe the worst of anyone they want to do badly by so they don't feel so bad about it. I could wish they'd feel less guilt and in turn, do me less harm.

People I know seem to look at me oddly, and my calls don't get returned as promptly as they once did. Georgette didn't meet my eyes in the last meeting, and Dr. Grey doesn't return my calls at all. Maybe I am just being paranoid or maybe the bastards really are out to get me. I shrug it off and try to joke, but it hurts. *It hurts.*

The final piece of nastiness is a caricature of me in the morning newspaper a week before the official launch date. I am shown with slanting eyes, wearing an Uncle Sam hat and a short skirt, with a whiplike cable in my hand. The balloon issuing from my mouth says, "Lie back and enjoy it!"

Marion comes in while I sit at my desk looking at the clipping, wondering how to respond, or even whether to respond.

"You've become a tall poppy, Lin," she says. "I'm sorry, but it's how New Zealand treats anyone who does things differently. They cut them down to size."

"Do we do anything about it?"

"We launch a bloody good service bloody well," says Ian from the doorway. "Don't worry about it. Just the good ole Kiwi knocking machine."

"Any idea where they got their information? Some of it seems to come from inside the company."

Ian's face is unsmiling. "It could be a disaffected staff member."

I look back at him without replying.

Marion shakes her head. "There's nothing more you can do, Lin. You should get away for the weekend. Why don't you come with us to Napier? We're doing that special Art Deco tour on Saturday, remember?"

"Do come, boss! It's our own private celebration for the launch," says Ian.

"I might need to be here to talk to the Board members before their meeting on Monday. I'm expecting a call from the chairman this afternoon. I'll let you know after we've spoken."

"Tell Scott I want to see him," I tell Helen.

After a moment, she sticks her head around the door. "He says he can't make it today." She looks embarrassed. "Apparently, he has some figures he has to pull together for the chairman."

"Tell him he can come now or he can come in two minutes. There are no other choices."

"Lin!" he says, and smiling, collapses into the chair across from me. "You're in a panic."

I freeze, angry that he is outfacing me. But I sit down and pull the chair close and lean my arms on the desk.

"I am concerned about these leaks," I say, and watch his face carefully.

His face doesn't move. "Dreadful, isn't it?"

"Do you have any thoughts about who might be responsible?" I ask.

He gives his ready smile and stares me straight in the eye. "None whatsoever."

I hold his gaze. He stares straight back, unblinking. "Not you then, Scott?"

Peake laughs and rises. "Of course I haven't spoken to the media, Lin. Now, if you've finished insulting me, I've got work to do."

Tom sits at the table fiddling with a pen while I talk about the rumors. No, it isn't good for Hera, he says, his eyes sliding to mine and then away.

"Any idea who may have talked to the media?" I ask, watching his face closely.

He looks down at the pen in his hand. "No," he says, "I have no idea."

The printout of the article sits on the table between us, in silent witness. I put the printout back inside my folder and wait for him to complain that I've unfairly accused him, but he stands and says, "Will that be all?"

When he has gone, I glance up at my painting. I haven't been back to Ngatirua since we left abruptly at Christmas. But it has helped just to know that my family is there, a haven away from all this crap.

I watch the grass growing in the paddocks and the trees waving in the wind at the top of the cliff. Although the painting doesn't show it, just beyond the trees Vivienne's beautiful house sits amongst the rosebushes and the summer flowers. The pool would be sparkling in the sunshine, cool and refreshing to dive into. Down the hill I can picture Alison's kind face and welcoming smile, and I can imagine Wal's laugh as he hands me a glass of wine. Max would walk in from feeding the dogs, and Jess would be in the corner working on something pretty and precious.

The telephone shrills, and I am returned to reality. Hobb has seen the articles, he tells me, and the Board has already held a telephone conference to discuss the situation.

"The Board is concerned our services have been jeopardized by your compromises," he says.

"Our services will work very well," I reply. "It's likely there'll be some teething problems, but nothing that can't be quickly fixed."

"We're not happy about there being any issues at all."

"The telephone and data services have been well tested, and we know they will perform reliably. We are confident we can address any issues with the support systems and processes without any negative impact."

"We don't like what the papers are saying."

"The team and I are expecting a very successful launch next week," I assure him. "That should stop further bad publicity."

He pauses as if to find the right words. "In light of the publicity, we are considering delaying the launch."

"What! Delay the launch! You're not serious. There is no reason to delay, all our systems are go. All the work we've put in to reach this date that you've told us is critical to the survival of the business—"

"We have other options that don't require us to hit the launch date."

After all the pressure that we must be part of the consortium, and to be part of the consortium we have to make this date, he's suddenly suggesting the date is no longer critical? Unless they have negotiated a delay with the Government? In which case, why didn't they tell me?

"What do you mean?"

"I'll brief you after the Board meeting on Monday. In the meantime, I want you to prepare to halt the launch."

"Is that a directive from the Board?"

I cannot believe he has a mandate for such a major decision without the Board voting on it.

There is a brief silence on the other end of the line.

"Not yet," he replies, coolly. "We'll vote on Monday. Oh, and we've decided that Mark, Pita, and I will front the press conference. We appreciate your input, Lin, but we think, in light of the negative publicity, you should keep your head down for a while. Out of the limelight."

I disconnect the call and sit at my desk clenching the telephone receiver as if it were some bastard's balls.

Robert doesn't answer my calls until the next day.

"What's going on?" I ask. "Who's screwing whom?"

"The Board is debating the future strategy for Hera, and we haven't been able to reach an agreement yet," he says. "Shall we say there are some opposing views, and I don't yet know which way the votes will fall. Talk to me Monday night. I should know by then what's going to happen."

"Hobb implied it didn't matter if we don't launch by the first of March. Has the Government given us more time or what?"

"Launch the service as agreed, Lin! You hear me? Do not accept any directive from anyone to halt the launch. That would limit the options to the one Hobb is pursuing."

"What option is that, Robert?"

And Robert tells me what Ozcom wants to do.

Chapter 47

Prepare to halt the launch, says the chairman of the Board. Don't accept any directive to halt the launch, says the director I owe my job to. The one whose support I should be able to count on.

I shiver and rub my arms to warm myself up. Damned if I do, damned if I don't.

When my cell phone vibrates against the surface of the table, I start in surprise and look down as if it is a snake about to strike before pressing the answer button and putting the phone to my ear.

"This is Lin."

"Hiya," he says. "How are things?"

"Like a shower of maggots."

"That bad?"

"The bloody Board!"

"Emmy and Cheryl both say hi."

"And those news stories are continuing. After all my hard work, I bet I'll be known for this crap in the media, not for getting Hera to the launch date against all odds."

"What can you do?"

"Nothing. There's nothing I can do now that will make a difference."

"Cheryl's met a nice accountant," he tells me. "Who has a couple of kids."

"Bloody accountants!"

"Who do you think is talking to the media? Is it this Peake guy?"

"I asked him whether he knew anything about the leaks to

the media and he didn't bat an eyelid. I asked straight up if it was him and he laughed. Laughed! Said of course he hadn't talked to the media."

"Bummer. Anyway, shall I book tickets for next weekend? Or the one after?"

"Peake would stab me in the back in an instant if he thought he could get away with it."

"Shall I come this weekend, Lin? Moral support?"

"No, no, I'm fine. We'll leave it until later on, after the launch, as we agreed."

"Okay." He clears his throat. "Well, look after yourself."

"I will, bye now!" I turn off my phone.

I stand by the window and gaze out. Gray today. Clouds hang threateningly over the city as if about to snuff out the life of the ants scurrying below. The pane of glass against which my forehead leans is cold and hard. Eventually, I turn away and sit at my desk.

My cell phone is starting to look battered, the white frame has scratches on one side, and the screen is smeared from whatever it was I grabbed as a snack for breakfast an hour ago. I wipe it on my sleeve and turn it on. iPhones are so easy to use. Anything you need pops up in the screenload of icons. Contacts are halfway down on the right-hand side. I scroll through Alison and a couple of others and barely think at all before I reach the *H*s.

"Ben," I say when he answers, "I've changed my mind. Can you come this weekend? Please? I could do with that moral support."

I scroll to the next name. "Tom?"

In the end the decision was clear.

Late that night the doorbell rings, and when I go downstairs, Ben is there. I hug as much of him as I can reach and breathe in his healthy noncorporate male smell.

He reaches his arms around me and pulls me against his

chest before holding my shoulders and looking down at me, smiling.

"I wanted to come up, but the door code wouldn't work."

"We've changed the combination."

Our lovemaking is nice, fast but nice. I curl against his back with my arm over his side, my hand encased in his. But I can't lie still. The anger in me rises and I twist and turn and face the wall while Ben's breaths slow and he starts to snore gently. I watch the moonlight sneak in through the curtain and pray for sleep because I can't stand my head being so full of argument and regrets and, yes, *rage*.

But in the morning the sun shines through the gap in the curtain, and when Ben pulls the fabric aside, the light blazes forth and bathes the room. I can feel the heat against my bare arms. In the copper beech below my window a bird twitters, and another tweets back in response, and then more join in until I can hear a whole symphony playing out in the yard.

From the kitchen comes the sound of the coffee grinder, and Ben brings me coffee in my favorite orange-and-black bone china mug and climbs back into bed.

As we lie together sharing the paper, the heaviness that has weighed me down for weeks starts to lift. After two long months alone, Ben is here, and, with Ben, I can face whatever happens next.

Ben is looking at me with a question in his eyes.

"Let's get out of town," I say. I would like to be out of reach of the chairman, just in case he tries to give me a directive I don't want to obey.

Ben is happy to go up to Ngatirua, he replies. Wal has promised to take him fishing next time he comes.

"My friends at work want me to go to some event in Hawke's Bay this afternoon. Do you want to come?"

"Nah, you go with your mates, do some bonding. I'll go fishing with Wal."

"I didn't know you liked fishing."

"What's not to like? You sit around for a few hours telling yarns, scratching your belly, sculling a few tinnies, there's a couple of frantic battles, you only have a dumb fish to fight so you win, and you get to cook it and eat it for supper. Sounds like my kind of sport."

Marion is happy I'm going to join them, and we arrange to meet at the fishing port on the north side of Napier Hill.

Alison, too, is happy we're coming to stay.

"Lin! It will be lovely to see you! Viv and I thought you'd deserted us!"

"I'm sorry, Ali, work has been so hectic—"

"And we'll see dear Ben again too! I'll call Viv. What time will you get here, Lin?"

"The bus will drop me off at the turnoff at around eight o'clock."

"I'll get someone to pick you up."

"No," I say. "I'll walk up the hill to the farm. I love to walk."

So we throw a few things in the car and drive up to Hawke's Bay once more. This time it almost feels like I'm going home.

As we near the zigzag hill, Ben starts whistling "Country Road, Take Me Home," and I add my voice to the melody, remembering most of the words.

There isn't time to stop to see my sisters so we don't take the turnoff to Ngatirua, we keep driving north, past the fruit-growing town of Hastings, and on up the bay of Napier, a pretty little town that got flattened by an earthquake in the thirties and was rebuilt during the Art Deco era. Today's special event combines touring the Art Deco buildings with the art and wineries of the Hawkes Bay region.

Ben turns into the port area and we drive slowly along the waterfront, dodging fishermen until we find the rendezvous. Hera's violet minibus is parked outside one of the cafés.

I kiss him good-bye. "See you tonight, back at the ranch."

•   •   •

Tonight I will have that talk with Alison. I will ask her why they didn't make more of an effort to contact me once they knew I was moving into their house. We're surely past the risk of ruining our relationship.

Chapter 48

"Was that the guy?" asks Helen.

"That was Ben, yes."

"He looked nice," she says.

Nice. The greatest compliment a Kiwi can make.

I smile. "He is *very* nice!"

"It's good to see your eyes, Lin. Contact lenses?" Marion asks.

I nod. "I normally wear contacts on the weekends."

We wait in the café for Tom, Ian, and Fred who spent the morning in Wellington and have taken a flight to Napier instead of the violet minibus. Our CFO is not joining us. He is in Auckland, no doubt doing his toadying best to ingratiate himself with the Board members who have been gathering. I am happy to be here instead, celebrating with the people who've been doing the real work.

Helen takes the wheel and we drive around Napier Hill and through the pretty Art Deco streets, stopping at the galleries and then climbing back on the bus. We work our way south, stopping at Trinity Hill, Te Awa, Ngatarawa, Sileni, and Te Mata, each displaying art from a local artist, before arriving at our final stop at Clearview near Haumoana where I trust Joe's children are still being well nurtured by their grandmother.

Here the art takes the form of cartoons by a guy named Dick Frizell. I buy Ben a black t-shirt displaying a character morphing from a Mickey Mouse to a Maori Tiki; "From Mickey to Tiki," it is called.

Then we sit down for an early meal before the team heads back to Wellington and I head home to Ngatirua.

I sit next to Tom.

"How are Kiri and the twins?" I ask.

"They're fine," he replies. "I gather you're staying in the bay."

"Just for the weekend. I'm staying at Ngatirua farm with my sisters tonight."

"The picture in your office."

"Yes."

"Up the zigzag hill."

"By the way, we found out who leaked to the press."

I am bluffing, the press would not give out their sources, but I am almost certain my suspicion is correct. I watch Tom's eyes.

Tom shuffles in the hard, wooden seat, stretching out his legs. He lets out a sigh.

"If you had a beef, you should have raised it with me."

"I do raise the issues with you, but you don't listen."

"I do listen. I just don't alter my decisions. And I am the boss, Tom, the decisions are mine to make."

"Yeah, and we know how you got to be the boss, don't we?"

"What the fuck is that supposed to mean?"

"You shafted me, didn't you Lin? When Adam died."

"Who told you that?"

"Does it matter? It's true, isn't it?"

"I speak the truth as I see it. I don't intentionally shaft any-one."

Tom holds my eyes for a moment, then nods as if to say okay I accept that, and picks up the newspaper.

"I should have told you about Peake," he says.

"Peake?"

"Leaking the stories to the media. What did you think I meant?"

"I was worried you did it."

Tom's eyes widen in surprise. "Of course, I didn't! Okay, I did bitch about you, but it was Scott who went to the press."

"But why would he do that?"

He smiles. "Perhaps he wants your job, Lin. After all, if we missed the launch date—"

"Then he's out of luck, isn't he."

Because that morning we launched Hera's service, five days before the official launch date. It was to have been a happy surprise for the Board on Monday. And now I know it will be an unhappy surprise for the ones who were hoping we'd fail.

"The first installs this morning went well, Lin," Ian says. "A couple of problems, but the guys got them sorted pretty damned quick."

"A couple of the accounts weren't set up correctly, but we fixed the fields so they're all good now," says Fred. "And we've changed the guide so it shouldn't happen again. The disconnection we tried didn't work properly, but we won't be handling many disconnections in the first weeks. And we've got a work-around while we reconfigure the system," assures Fred. "Here. Try calling this number."

I take out my cell phone and make the call.

A resigned voice answers. "Yes, it works," he says before I have the chance to say anything.

"Our first customer," says Fred. "Try sending him an e-mail."

"Come on, guys, leave it. Let's eat," says Marion.

Ian reaches over to offer me the wine.

"She doesn't drink," says Marion.

But today I am not Caesar's wife. "I'll take a glass," I say, and Ian pours me a Hawke's Bay Chardonnay. "Cheers!"

"Cheers!" come the replies.

"Here's to Hera!" I toast and, "Hera!" they reply.

Then Helen calls, "And to you, Lin!"
"To Lin!"

This is it, I realize. *This* is the feeling of success. When you achieve something exceptional, and the people who know best tell you you've done a good job. I sit there and enjoy that feeling and smile at them, my friends, and raise my glass again.

"To you guys," I reply. "The true heroes of Hera. You're everything good about the Kiwi can-do culture. I just helped clear a few of the obstacles from your path."

Tom reaches out a firm hand and places it on my shoulder. "We've learned a few things from you."

I let my eyes crinkle into a genuine smile.

"Ditto."

Finally, replete and happy, we start for home. Tom has to drive the rental car back to the airport, but Fred and Ian join us in the bus, and the driver turns the wheel toward Wellington. They sing songs on the way, songs I don't know, something about Aotearoa and leaky boats then something about a drive.

When we reach the turn off to the zigzag road, they look up at the steep hill and tell me I'm mad. We'll drive you up, they say. It's not far out of our way.

"No," I tell them. "I like to walk. And I haven't walked for a long time."

"Knock the bastard off!" cries Ian.

"What?"

"It's what Sir Ed said."

"Sir who?"

"Jeez, Lin! Sir Edmund Hillary, the world's greatest mountain climber! It's what he said when he conquered Everest!"

"Oops, sorry."

I get drunken kisses from Ian and from Fred and hugs from Marion and Helen.

"Good-bye!" they call as the minibus rolls on down the road.

I watch it vanish around the bend, and then I turn onto the zigzag road and start my walk up the hill to Ngatirua.

Chapter 49

I wake in darkness, curled like a fetus on my left-hand side and take a breath—and a vile sweet stench explodes in my nostrils, in my throat, and I gag and retch and thrash out with all my panicked strength, but my arms, my legs, they are caught, trapped, buried, I can't get away from it, I can't move at all—*oh God, trapped in a hole—my worst nightmare—*My mind explodes in blind irrational terror and all goes blank.

I wake again. I am still in the nightmare. Not dreaming then, for a moment I don't move, but the smell, the smell! I breathe through my mouth, panting in short gasps, whimpering, trying to escape that terrible stench, the blood pulses and my brain must surely burst! But it doesn't, I am still here, still alive. Oh, let me die now, please let me die, I am so afraid. God doesn't answer. I am still here, still here, trapped in the dark.

My lungs suck the vile air. My throat hurts, but I can still breathe. I listen to myself panting. The air is poison but there is oxygen. I tell myself to be calm, don't think about being buried—no—think about what you can feel. Be rational, Lin, evaluate your situation. Be rational, you have oxygen, you're not suffocating. Be rational, there might be a way out—

My head hurts. What does my body feel? Everything narrows to the sense of touch. I feel a wall against my neck and back. I feel something pressing down on me from above. My left shoulder is a dull ache, and I can't move my left arm at all. My right arm lifts a little, an inch. Whatever is above me is less solid and unyielding than the wall to my back. My fingers twitch and my nails scrabble and catch in some rough cloth. Can I move my legs? I try to straighten my leg, but the hard barrier is there too, *I'm trapped,* my body convulses, I scream and the stench catches my throat and chokes me—I can't breathe—*oh, God I'm going to suffocate!* All goes blank.

I wake again. The nightmare. My mind is numb. I take a shallow breath and then another, and force myself to calmness. You're not dead yet, Lin. Try to work out what happened, try to work out where you are, try to work out how to escape.

I remember crunching over the remains of the debris outside my father's studio and stepping onto the path that winds through the trees to reach Ngatirua. I remember catching sight of something out of the corner of my eye and turning, but not quite fast enough to see whatever it was, whoever it was, and then a sudden blow, and everything went dark.

Now it feels like rough-woven cloth enshrouds me, and I'm buried in a hole amongst dead things.

Don't think about it, Lin, don't think.

I push myself backward, hard against the solid wall behind me. Whatever is piled on top of me slithers around when I move. The fingers of my right hand feel some space, I move them back and forth. There is a gap in the cloth! I move my right hand as far as it can go. The gap in the cloth has been pulled tight with string. If I can just loosen it!

I pant with the effort, and the air is moist and warm and the smell is of dead things. Oh, God, where am I? *Patience, Lin, be calm, be still,* and I try again, working my fingers through the opening and ripping where the string holds the cloth. It's looser now. I raise myself an inch and then another inch. Whatever lies on top of me is soft like a rag doll.

Now my left arm can move, *but, God, my shoulder hurts!* With the extra purchase I pull the binding apart. In sudden frantic desperation for air, I push my head through the hole. Something damp spatters onto my face and into my open mouth. I spit it out. My body jerks in revulsion and I panic again, trying to escape from the corpse above me but still caught in the cloth that binds my body, and I have to let myself go still again and relax. *Calm, Lin, calm.*

I get my arm out and push aside what lies on me, and reach up as far as I can. There is space above. Thank you, God! Relief washes over me. If I can sit up, maybe stand, it's not so bad, I'm not buried, I'm just in a tight space.

The blind panic subsides and my brain reconnects.

The air is still moist but cooler now. I am lucky whoever put me here did not bury me properly. There must be a gap letting in fresh air to replace the carbon dioxide I'm panting out.

I can work the cloth open now, but I hold it tight around me to protect myself from the other dead things that have been tossed down in the hole. I reach out and touch something furry and the fur comes away wetly in my hand so I jerk back and there is a crackle and a crunch as things snap beneath me. Snapping means dry and long dead so I grope with my right hand beneath the sack and find a bone, I think, but it doesn't come free. I don't mind dry bones, I just can't stand those that have wet stuff still attached, and maggots, so I feel around for a free piece of old bone, my hand following the carcass, feeling along its body to its shoulder, I hope, groping for the front leg.

It doesn't feel like the sheep hoof I expected so I snatch my hand away, hitting my wrist on something soft that clinks in an unnatural way, *unnatural if it's a skeleton, that is.*

The soft thing feels like bare leather and has a long shape and I feel the open top with my fingers. Inside there is something long and sticklike, with a bulbous knob. Golf clubs? I pull one out, and almost chuckle, thinking I should have paused to ponder which iron to use.

I push aside the furry dead things—possums? And reach up with the club. There is a clang as if against metal. I thrust again, and the metal shifts with another clang.

There is more fresh air now, fresh misty air. It is still dark, but I know the open sky is up there. I pull myself out of the cloth I was bound in and clamber awkwardly over the dead things and raise myself up. I can just touch the corrugated iron that covers the hole with my fingers. I feel around the edges until I find a gap and push my stick through the hole and jerk the metal sideways, it catches momentarily, but then the iron shifts and there is open air above me. Oh, thank you, God, and I know I am going to be able to get free.

Then I hear the distant barking of dogs.

I grasp the rough edge of the iron sheet and twist till it swivels to one side, then I grab the earth, and pull myself up, slowly, my shoulder screaming in pain, and slither out of what I have guessed is one of Ngatirua's offal pits.

I lie panting on the safe ground above. The grass feels like silk. The air tastes like ambrosia. Shakily, I stand. Clouds must be covering the sky tonight, as the night is very dark.

What direction do I head? Over the hill lies the main house and just below lies the other. *Who has done this to me? Which house do I stumble my way to? What should I have read in someone's eyes that I must have missed?*

And then I hear footsteps, stealthy footsteps pattering up the hill, and I know that whoever it was that put me in the pit is coming back. I can't see them, but they are between the houses and me.

Do I call for help? But will anyone hear me if I do? And even if they hear me, can they get to me before whoever is jogging toward me now?

I start running blindly away from the person coming for me. *Where can I hide?* I blunder in the dark and trip but catch myself and keep going.

Branches hit me in the face, and I gasp and pause, trying to see, trying to hear where they are.

Then to my left I see a light, a small light, moving back and forth, a flashlight, it moves back and forth down below on the paddock, searching, searching for me. I huddle behind the tree and move backward into the forest.

I watch the light and I move away at a different angle, feeling my way among the trees. The ground is rising so I think I must be climbing the ridge above the studio.

Suddenly my left arm is grabbed. I scream in pain, but a hand muffles my mouth and starts to drag me backwards, higher up the hill. I kick helplessly but I can't get free. My hurt shoulder is on fire, *oh, the pain!*

The wind buffets me, we must be near the top of the ridge. Oh, God, I'm going to be thrown over the edge. *Oh, no, I'm not going to let you do that.*

Fool, you secured the wrong arm. I swing the club I still clutch backward over my head, there is a crack! as the iron connects with my attacker's face and his grip loosens, I leap sideways, free, and dart away at a tangent.

Suddenly, a full moon bursts through the clouds and trees emerge like ghosts coming to Dunsinane. Startled, I pause.

"Bastard!"

A cry breaks the silence, and I look toward a voice I recognize. The moon lights up the contorted face of Wal, my sister's husband, standing on the slope below me.

"Bloody bastard!" he cries again and lifts his gun to aim at me.

"Lin!" cries Ben's voice.

I see him running to rescue me, but he is too far away. Wal's rifle lifts higher, and I can see the look of death in his eyes.

But his eyes are not focused on me. Slowly, I turn and look behind me.

Chapter 50

The moon shines on the figure of my other sister's husband, Christopher, silhouetted against the sky at the crest of the ridge. The moonlight reflects off his dark glasses and the wind ruffles his hair.

Ben arrives and grabs me in his arms and squeezes me until I cry out in pain from my damaged shoulder.

"Thank God you're okay!" Ben holds me at arm's length and sniffs. "What happened?"

"Someone tried to kill me!"

Ben looks at Christopher's immobile shape. "Was it you? You?"

Christopher's mouth relaxes into a smile and he gives a small laugh. "Me? Of course not. I've been helping search for Lin."

I close my mouth and think. Someone must have caught me from behind as I walked home and struck me on the head. And then tied me in a sack and stuffed me down the offal pit.

I think about the fire at the studio. I think about the spring that incapacitated the brakes of our car. I even wonder about the chocolates that arrived for me, which the dog ate and then was fortuitously made to vomit back up. I recall the railing that fell, nearly taking me with it.

Could a blind man have done all these things? Stolen softly through our lives and engineered those attacks without us having any inkling?

Then I think about the sheer ineptitude of the attempts. Even when he hit me, the blow must have glanced off my shoulder and knocked me out rather than killing me.

"Maybe it was you, Wal," says Christopher. "You have as much motive as me. Or Max. Yes, Max! He's a dark horse. He likes killing things."

"Liar!" yells Wal. "You're a damned liar as well as a rotten swine!"

Christopher shakes his head. "I am blind. How could a blind man attack anyone?"

As he shakes his head, the light splinters, and I see that both of the lenses of his glasses are broken and the frame skewed, smashed by the blow I gave him. I can see his eyes now, but they hold no expression.

"I know for sure it was you, Christopher," I say. My blood starts racing. "You hit me and then you buried me in a pit. And you were going to throw me off the cliff, I know!"

He shakes his head again. "Actually, now I come to think of it, they're far more likely to believe my wife did it," he says.

Christopher's mouth smiles, but there is nothing in his dead eyes. "It would be easy to believe Vivienne went berserk when I told her you made a pass at me. She's always hated you, and that would be enough to tip the balance."

"You bastard! No one would believe that!" cries Ben.

But I flinch and a whimper escapes from my throat.

"With Vivienne's mental history?" Christopher snorts. "If you don't want her back in the psych ward, then you'd all better pretend that nothing happened."

Wal slowly lowers his rifle and turns his head to look at me.

"What do you want to do, Lin?"

My pulse is beating as I think about this man who hit me over the head and stuffed me down an offal pit. I think about the bones in the pit. He has a taste for it now. He tried to kill not only me, but Ben and Cheryl. Who else might he attack?

But if we try to bring him to justice, he threatens to lay the blame for the attacks on my sister. What would such a betrayal do to her? I think about Viv's adoring eyes following Christopher's every move. I think about her mother, Rose, who killed herself when my father betrayed her. I think about my father's mistakes.

Both options are unacceptable.

Christopher laughs as he stands there, on the edge of Ngatirua ridge, the magic place where my sisters live. He thinks we will let him get away with murder. He thinks he has won.

There is a third option, although it too is unfavorable, but, like Sally says, sometimes you have to make sacrifices for the people you love.

Fleetingly, I think about my brilliant career back in Wellington, but the lesson I draw upon is of the farm, not the city.

The head of the golf club catches him full on the chest. With the weight of my rage behind it, the blow knocks him over the edge.

We don't hear a sound as he falls.

Chapter 51

Wal is a big man, a strong man, a warrior, the epitome of stalwart Maori manhood, but he stands with his rifle pointed to the ground, gaping at the empty space in front of him. My Ben, the rugged Southern man, stares at me in astonishment.

"Shit!" says Wal.

I am small and slight and no epitome of anybody. "Remember, Wal? You told me you have to destroy dangerous dogs," I try to explain.

The space in front of us where Christopher was standing moments before resonates with emptiness. My pulse slows.

My God, what have I done? What have I become? My right arm suddenly weakens and I drop the golf iron.

"Where did you get that?" Wal asks sharply.

"The offal pit. That's where he put me."

"Christ!" says Ben. The men are not very eloquent tonight.

My head hurts and my shoulder hurts and there is blood dripping down my cheek. "Why did he do it, Wal?" I ask.

"Let's get you back to the house," Wal says. "We'll talk then. Alison has been frantic."

"Who do you know who plays golf?"

"First things first, Lin."

So we walk back up the hill and down to the house where Alison waits anxiously. When she flings her arms around me, I relax into her embrace, feeling the softness of her chest and the beat of her heart beneath her sensible sweater, smelling the lavender she uses on her hair. She doesn't seem to mind that I stink.

In the distance, or so it seems, Wal is telling her what happened. Alison hugs me again before taking me to the bathroom. I stand under the warm shower and clean away the remnants of the dead while she runs me a bath.

"Can we keep it from Vivienne?" I ask. "All of it?"

Alison sighs. "I don't know."

I lie in the water and doze. Alison returns and dresses my cuts and anoints my bruised shoulder and then folds me into her dressing robe.

"We have to keep what he threatened from Vivienne," I say when we rejoin the men in the living room.

Ben helps me into a chair, his kind face gentle, but there is a crease between his eyes whenever he looks at me. He glances over at Wal who is standing by the fireplace, looking grim.

"We went back to the offal pit he threw you in," Wal says. "It was one of the old ones." He hits the stone of the hearth with his fist. "That bastard! Fergus was in there."

"What?" I ask. "Who is Fergus?"

"We thought he went back to Scotland," Wal explains. "But he didn't. His body is in the pit along with his pack and the rest of his golf clubs."

"Max's father!"

"Christopher told us Fergus left by taxi early in the morning. When we never heard another word, we just assumed he'd decided to give up and move on. But Christopher must have killed him and buried him in one of the old offal pits."

"Viv is so fragile," says Alison. "I don't know how she's going to handle it."

"Max needs to know his father is dead and he needs to know his father didn't desert him," argues Wal.

"Fergus wanted half of Vivienne's property," Alison explains. "They didn't have a prenup and so by law he was entitled to it. Vivienne was frantic about losing her house, and so was Christopher."

"But why did he try to kill me?"

Wal looks at Alison. She gives me a faint smile that vanishes almost before it appears.

"We wanted to tell you, but Vivienne wouldn't hear of it."

"Tell me what?"

"We thought we had persuaded her, but when we saw you on television, she got hysterical—she said you must be getting paid a fortune and that it wasn't necessary to tell you. She refused point blank, and Christopher got angrier and angrier—"

"We should have ignored them and gone ahead," Wal says. "All this might not have happened."

Alison's face flinches in pain. "I know. But I thought if she got to know us first—"

I sit in the armchair and wait for Alison to tell me now. She meets my eyes briefly before wiping the already clean table with her sleeve and straightening the cloth. She picks at a thread dangling from the corner and snaps it short.

"When our father left Mum, they agreed he would take nothing with him," she says, bringing her hands together in her lap and clasping them as in prayer. "The arrangement seemed fair since it was Mum's family's farm and Mum's family who lent them the deposit for the house in Wellington, and it was Dad who was leaving."

"Yes, I knew that," I reply.

"Mum hoped he would come back to her, that he would tire of your mother and come back to Ngatirua and the home she had created for him."

Alison is wringing her hands, the left tugging on the right.

"He never came back. She couldn't bear that he had—" Alison looks away. "And one day she walked out of the house to the top of the ridge and threw herself over."

"Oh, my God," I say. "The same as—"

"It's going to be hard to tell her. But it would have destroyed her to discover Christopher was prepared to save himself by casting the blame on her."

"Christopher tried to kill me because your mother killed herself because our father wouldn't leave my mother and return to her?" I shake my head.

"No it wasn't that, Lin. You see, Rose never changed her will. So when she died, Dad inherited everything she owned."

"I thought your grandfather was alive? I thought you inherited directly from him?"

"He died a year earlier. Gran was still alive, but he'd left the property awkwardly. She took this house and the new farm, and Rose got the rest."

"But Dad can't have known that! Or he would have stayed."

"Gran destroyed the will. He never knew he owned the main estate and when he died, he left everything he had to you."

I stare at her in wonder. I own this magical place?

"Wal and I are okay. We took over Gran's house, and Wal used his own money to buy out Viv's share of the new farm. But Viv spends all her income and she spends all the money we've paid her, and she's put it all back into the damned house."

A little gurgling gasp breaks from my throat. "He didn't have to kill me!" I say.

"He was a twisted man," breaks in Wal. "Something broke in that crash and never got mended. Viv saved him from destitution by marrying him and bringing him here and giving him a comfortable life. But I knew he was rotten."

I gaze into the fireplace with its vase of dried flowers and seedpods. My head hurts. I've stopped thinking about the why and wherefore. My shoulder is on fire and my nose is running and my eyes seem to be trickling water.

"What do we do now?" I ask.

Ben stares at me. I don't understand the expression on his face. He looks away.

"Wal and I have been thinking it through," he says. "This is what we're going to say—"

Chapter 52

The men carry Christopher's broken body home the next morning and an ambulance takes him to the local funeral parlor where they will mold him back together and patch up his face as good as new, they say.

The police come and go and come back again and are now planted around the offal pit, carefully extracting the contents.

I never expected to get away with murder. I made the choice and I expected to bear the consequences. All I wanted was to keep my family safe.

But when Ben suggested an alternative version of the truth, I agreed.

The police didn't disbelieve me when I told them I slid into the pit looking for a shoe that had slipped between the sheets of iron. They didn't disbelieve me when I told them I fled screaming after I picked up what seemed to be the bones of a human hand. They didn't disbelieve me when I said I ran and fell and hit my head and knocked myself out.

They didn't disbelieve Ben when he told them how Christopher had reacted to my description of what I had found. After all neither Ben nor I could have had anything to do with the death of Fergus, ex-husband of my sister Vivienne.

And yet the police inspector isn't happy. A blind man committing murder? He can't put his finger on what triggered that sixth sense of his, but he knows something is not quite right.

Wal takes him aside and admits that Christopher was not just blind, but had spent time in a mental health institute.

Now a madman committing murder, that was comprehensible. So the police accept our stories and if there is a lingering doubt in the inspector's mind, he clears his conscience by reporting Wal and my sisters to the Accident Compensation Commission. Too many accidents, he says. First, your sleep-out has no fire extinguisher and then you have an offal pit without a secure cover!

The irony didn't escape me. Rose had killed herself and my father had been accused of her murder. I murdered Christopher, but we convinced the police it was suicide.

I hadn't expected to so closely mirror my father's fate.

Ben has brought my purse. It smells and I don't want it any more, but I retrieve the contents of my wallet. Wal says he'll burn the woolsack Christopher wrapped me in. We don't know where my cell phone went. Perhaps Christopher was smart enough to smash it and throw it down the cliff where its signals couldn't be traced.

"And we found this too," Ben says, handing me a plastic bag. Inside is a men's t-shirt with Mickey Mouse morphing into a Tiki on the front.

"It was by the wall of the studio. He would have known to search for your purse, but he didn't know you were carrying anything else. When we found it, Wal and I knew you must be somewhere on the farm."

Then again, Christopher hadn't been that smart or perhaps I was just lucky. We think he'd expected people to believe I must have fallen victim to some random assault on the main highway.

No one had ever followed up Fergus's disappearance. The friends he had in New Zealand thought he'd left for Scotland. Presumably, the friends he had in Scotland thought he had changed his mind and stayed in New Zealand.

•   •   •

When I let myself in through the French windows, the rooms still glow with beauty. Christopher's absence has not made the slightest difference to the house.

Alison is in the kitchen preparing food. Vivienne is in her bedroom, but she's awake, Alison tells me. She holds my gaze and then nods her head to the doorway.

When I take in the tray, the face peering back at me from the bedclothes is pink and puffy. Unlike the house, her beauty has dimmed.

"I am sorry, Viv," I say, taking her hand in mine. "So very sorry about Christopher."

I am sorry about Christopher. Sorry he was such a monster, sorry that she loved him, and sorry she is hurting now.

"He was such a handsome man," she says.

"Indeed, he was a very handsome man."

"I want to remember him as he looked yesterday, wearing the jeans I'd bought him for Christmas and that blue shirt. He never saw the color, but it was his favorite. He used to say it smelled like summer."

"Summer?"

"I dried it on the line down in the garden. He always said he could smell the scent of honeysuckle on the laundry in summer."

"I guess blind people rely on their other senses a lot more."

"It was uncanny how he knew where I was in the house. He could sense where I had been by the perfume I wear. And his hearing was so sharp! He knew by the sound of people's footsteps who it was even before they spoke."

"I didn't know him well."

"He didn't like strangers much. He preferred being here in the house with just me." Vivienne's face crumples and her eyes start leaking tears. "I can't bear to think of him running away through the dark and then, oh, I can't bear to think of him at that ridge!"

"You must eat something. Alison has made your favorite soup."

"Why didn't he wait and talk to me? I would have stood by him, I would have made sure people understood it wasn't his fault! How I wish you'd never fallen in that hole!"

"At least now you and Max know why Fergus never replied to any of Max's e-mails."

"I would rather Christopher was alive!"

"I guess he couldn't face being blamed for Fergus's death."

"But it was an accident! It must have been!"

Her eyes lock on mine, but I glance away, casting around Vivienne's bedroom, desperately seeking to distract her. Unlike the rest of the house, here there is but one picture, of a Maori warrior with feathers in his hair and a *moko*, tattoo, covering his face.

"What a beautiful painting! The detail is so intricate."

Vivienne's sobs stop and her swollen eyes stare fixedly at me. "It's a Goldie."

"Ah? I don't know anything about New Zealand artists."

"That's my favorite of all my pictures," she says.

"I'm not surprised. Oh, I have seen it before! Didn't it used to hang in the studio? I think it's in the photograph I have of Dad."

"Bitch!" she suddenly shrieks and the next instant the bowl of soup bounces off my cheek, its contents sliding down my face like duckweed.

"I hate you! It's all your fault, you and that Chinese whore who stole my father!"

Her face is contorted and her mouth sprays saliva. "I hate your stupid face and I hate your horrible eyes!" She screams hysterically and flings the cutlery at me.

I retreat and slam the door shut. Alison comes running down the hallway as I lean against the door, shaking.

"Lin! Are you all right?"

"All I did was admire that painting she's got by her bed. Then she starts screaming and calls me a bitch."

"Oh. You saw the Goldie."

"So what?"

"That will stain," she says. "I'll put it through the wash for you."

"No more fricking secrets, Ali!"

Alison's kind face is resigned, but she is silent. I awkwardly pull the damp shirt back on around my injured shoulder and wait for her to speak. She hands me a clean towel to wipe my face and lets out a sigh.

"Mum gave the Goldie to Dad for their first anniversary. She loved that picture and Viv loves it too. Now it's worth a small fortune. And there is no doubt the Goldie belongs to you."

We can hear the sound of Vivienne keening, louder and louder. Alison's eyes flick toward the room and back to me. Vivienne is her twin; they have been inseparable since they were born. I am merely the bastard latecomer.

"You'd better go to her," I say. "But first, let me tell you what I'm going to do."

Afterward, I trace my way back through the beautiful house, leaving wet footprints on the polished floor. The works of art shine forth their messages of beauty and wonder, the living room glistens in its pristine shades of cream and brown, the garden sprawls alongside the walls in a splendor of colors and shapes.

There is a sharp pain in my chest. I cannot imagine facing Vivienne again, Vivienne who hates my stupid face and my horrible eyes. How much more would she hate me if she knew what I'd done?

I'd done it for her. But we couldn't tell her that.

I pause on the path and look back at the beautiful home she and Rose created. Ngatirua. A sacred place.

•   •   •

A brilliant career, a close family, a great love—it is a woman's trilemma. You might get one, and if you're lucky, two; but few of us can have it all. I should have known I wouldn't get to keep my sisters.

I turn back onto the path and walk away.

Chapter 53

Red velvet curtains frame the stage, chandeliers drip from the ceiling, and cables festoon the corners of the room in which Hera is holding its press conference.

Stewart Hobb stands at the podium gripping the microphone, behind him the portly figure of Mark Stanton and the plump shape of Pita Lane.

The journos balance laptops on the papers they've been given, faces turned to the stage, waiting to hear what they've been enticed here for. The photographers focus on capturing images of the important people and ignore what is merely spoken. There are a few coughs, assorted buzzes from cell phones, and scraping of chairs as bottoms shift to seek comfort.

So far there have been no surprises. Hobb has announced the launch of our new broadband service and he has placed a call to the minister of broadcasting via our new network. That had required a few mirrors and a lot of smoke, but we made the connection.

"Mr. Hobb, can you confirm the rumor that Ozcom is buying out the other shareholders?"

Hobb's face freezes; he looks down at his notes and then raises his head and looks across the floor. "There have been discussions about a potential buyout, but nothing is confirmed."

Hobb stretches his mouth in a smile, and the audience buzzes back at him with interest.

"Mr. Hobb," calls another journo. "Would this be an amicable buyout?"

Hobb's smile evaporates. "No decision has been made. There is some disagreement over future strategy that we expect to resolve after further consultation and discussion."

"What strategy is that?"

"We can't divulge Hera's detailed plans," Hobb says, shaking his head.

"Mr. Hobb, are you still expecting Hera to be a partner in the consortium?"

"We expect Hera to be a player in New Zealand's broadband future," he says. "But the form remains to be seen."

"What does this mean for your chief executive, Linnette Mere?"

Corporate psychopaths don't need to use their hands to murder people in order to get what they want. There are plenty of opportunities in the ordinary and legitimate power they have.

They do kill things though, if you let them.

At the Board meeting three days before, Hobb had proposed to halt the network build, sack most of the staff, and use the remnants of the company to support Australian business in New Zealand. Ozcom had always been more interested in protecting their trans-Tasman business than they were in investing in New Zealand's residential infrastructure. What they wanted were business connections for the New Zealand branches of Australian companies. They certainly didn't want to spend money on anything that would be purely for the benefit of New Zealanders. Mark Stanton, always more interested in minimizing risk than in creating something new, voted with Hobb.

They had expected us to fail to hit the launch date. With Hera's ability to compete in tatters, Ozcom expected to be able to buy out the other shareholders for a pittance. And I have no doubt my unloyal CFO Scott Peake expected to see himself at the helm of a new branch of Ozcom. Twig, really.

But because we made the launch there was a choice over

Hera's future. Hera could join the consortium and become a real player in New Zealand's broadband future.

The American and Asian shareholders voted to continue with the network we'd started building and to join the consortium.

Pita Lane held the casting vote.

Pita called for a *hui* at very short notice to discuss what the *iwi* wanted to do with their investment in Hera. The Maori elders came from all the regions the *iwi* held. We watched them troop into the Marae, the Maori meeting place on the waterfront across the road from Hera's offices, and we ferried documents out to them whenever they asked for more information. Ian and I worked on models to show different financial scenarios whenever they came up with a new angle.

It is a difficult time when your Board is in fundamental dispute over the very existence of the company as an independent entity. I kept Peake out of it, even though as CFO, he should have been the man to present the finances. But we didn't trust him.

Tom's people laid on a *hangi* to feast them. He brought food back to Ian, Fred, Marion, and me, slaving away in my office. We feasted on packages of vegetables and meat, slow cooked for hours on hot rocks, buried under flax and earth. We nibbled on fresh crayfish from the southern coast, and clams from the beaches to the north. I didn't eat the rotten corncobs, but I developed a brief, unlikely to be repeated, taste for muttonbird, the oily swamp fowl of New Zealand.

By Wednesday morning, the Maori elders had reached a consensus: they would not support selling out to Ozcom, and they wanted to keep building the network. They wanted the jobs created by Hera. Both the jobs and the competition would be better for New Zealand.

Lane's vote killed Hobb's proposal. At least until the next

pool of funding was depleted, and by that time, money should be coming back into the accounts and Hera formally confirmed within the consortium. The buyout price would be a lot higher, and the prospect therefore rather less attractive to Ozcom.

Or so Robert and I thought.

There was something else Lane wanted before he cast his vote to save Hera. He wanted control over the appointment of the chief executive. He wanted a better cultural fit, he said. A local.

Robert argued, no, that wasn't fair.

"Fair?" Lane had asked. "What's fair got to do with anything?"

In the end, the survival of the company is more important than any one individual. I could have pushed to stay, but I decided to step aside.

Besides, I could still feel the rage I felt when I knocked Christopher off the cliff. What had I become that I could so easily kill a man?

I was no longer fit to be a leader.

Hobb does not glance at me when he opens his mouth to reply.

"Ms. Mere's job was to launch Hera. We will be appointing a new chief executive to oversee the ongoing operation."

Hobb calls for Tom Heke to stand. I reach out to shake his hand. He has a good heart, has Tom, and he's the right man for the job, now. He grips my hand and looks at me.

We're quits. I smile and he smiles back, his warm brown eyes vanishing into the folds of his cheeks. Then he climbs onto the stage and I slip away.

And so the psychopaths lost out this time.

The hotel is around the corner from Hera's offices. I climb the stairs one last time to my office, now as bare as when I first took over, sit down at the PC, close my eyes, and wait for the feeling of loss.

Instead, I feel—numb? I open my eyes and type out my farewell e-mail.

Thank you, I tell them. *We knocked the bastard off.*

Chapter 54

It is one of the good days in Wellington. People sit at the outside tables taking in the sun. As I walk up Cuba Street, the singers are out, singing "How Bizarre." The girl singer's face is alight with what might be love for the boy she is with or maybe just happiness from the warmth of the air. As I pass the fountain, water splashes from one bucket to the next. A small brown bird sits in the pool fluttering its feathers.

I look around and memorize how pretty this place is. Already I feel nostalgic for the soul of Wellington, clouds rampaging across the sky, the green and blue of the hills and the sea, and Cuba Street sparkling in the sun.

I wonder whether my father grew to love this quirky town as I have grown to love it.

Did he miss it, as I know I will?

Did he miss his family? As I know I will?

My father had it all: a rich and beautiful wife, twin daughters, and a top job at the university. But he'd lost them all and lost my mother too.

I know how he must have felt.

Inside the apartment, my niece sits at the table, a half smile tilting those full lips, eyes downcast, thumbs flying.

She completes her text and looks up. "Hi, Auntie Lin. Ben dropped me off."

I drove back for the Board meeting, and Ben stayed behind at Ngatirua. We didn't get a chance to talk about anything other than pulling wool over policemen's eyes. When I told him I planned to leave New Zealand, he went very silent.

"Is Ben coming back?" I ask Jess.

"He didn't say."

My heart sinks. *He left without saying good-bye?*

"I'm meeting a friend for pizza downtown, and then we're going to the Library Bar. Can I borrow some money? Student loan hasn't come through yet."

"Is a hundred enough?"

"Sweet." She stretches like a cat and bounds to her feet. One of my favorite scarves seems to have got caught up around her neck.

She vanishes out the door. "See you!" echoes up the stairs.

The house is empty. Dirk and Jiro are still hard at work, creating their world-beating Hobbit movie and Sally and Michael are staying at the new house tonight, Sally's nirvana, the lifestyle block up the coast. She told me to visit any time. "Plenty of room," she said.

I smile, suddenly realizing there's nothing stopping me visiting her whenever I want. What I have, finally, is plenty of time.

I'll call her. I might even let her look after me this time.

A bottle of Kiwi bubbles is in the refrigerator. I take it out and stare at it. I don't recall putting a bottle in to chill. Then I take out two plastic shopping bags that weren't there this morning. One contains a rack of lamb and the other seems to be some kind of shellfish.

Oysters. I split open the bag and count one dozen of the little beauties. On the bottom shelf is a dish containing a mess of potatoes and cream. Ben's pièce de résistance.

I hurry into my room. On the far side of the bed is Ben's scruffy old pack, and he has already managed to leave a trail of clothes across the floor. In the bathroom his toothbrush sits next to mine.

Back in the living room I fetch a flute and hold the cork still while I twist the bottle free. A champagne cork popping is supposed to resemble the sound of a lady's fart. Much the same as the sound of my own, I've always thought. I wonder if that makes me a lady?

The wine hisses down my throat. Probably not. Ladies don't kill.

And I sit at the table and wait.

The door latch rattles and Ben comes into the room. I raise my eyes and examine his face, trying to read his intentions. My face feels naked without the executive mask I lack the energy or the inclination to pull on. This is Ben, who knows me.

"I had to get some butter," he says, waving a small packet.

He looks the same as he always does: relaxed, unhurried, focused on the task at hand. He takes the lamb up to the terrace and puts the rack on the barbecue. When he comes back, he turns on the fry pan, slips in the butter and the potatoes, and then carries the plate of oysters to the table.

He tips an oyster into his mouth and licks his fingers. "How did today go?"

"In the end it was almost a relief."

"I guess you'll have to go hunting another job. Are you sure there are no prospects here?"

"Perhaps in a few years time I could come back, but now I have to leave."

"The tall poppy thing."

"Not only that." I flinch. "I killed a man. You can't just kill someone and carry on with your life as if it never happened."

I don't know why Christopher became a killer. Perhaps he was born a killer. Perhaps it was the culmination of what happened to him, the disaster when he was so close to success, his rage at all he had lost, his fear of losing everything else.

He was a crippled thing, vermin, a dangerous dog who

threatened me and threatened the people I loved, and the world was better rid of him. All of those thoughts went through my brain in that split second when my arm moved.

Was it the best decision? Were those reasons enough to justify a murder? I don't know. Whatever, I chose to give up the job and give up Ngatirua.

Penance, you might say. I have wrestled with psychopaths and I am *not* one of them.

Ben's face wears the uneasy look it wore after he saw me knock Christopher off the cliff. "The worst moment was when we found his body. I was so afraid."

"Afraid? He would have been in no state to hurt anyone."

"Afraid he was still alive and I would have to decide whether to let him live or die."

I reach out and touch his hand and his face relaxes.

He says, "You shouldn't have had to—that is, I feel I failed you."

"One killer in the family is enough."

Ben grips my hand briefly before rising and taking the empty dishes away. He returns with two plates of creamy, buttery potatoes and lamb chops, and a perfectly dressed salad.

As he puts the food on the table, he catches sight of my picture of *The Road to Ngatirua,* propped against the wall.

"You're still giving up your claim to the family farm?"

"It just seems like the right thing to do. Getting this apartment is all I want."

When I chose to gift their land and Vivienne's precious Goldie back to my sisters, Alison's offer to give me the penthouse in return had been perfect. I loved this apartment. I loved the way I could see all of Wellington sprawled at my feet.

"Jess was rapt you're letting her live here while she's studying."

"That seems right too."

A smile slowly breaks over my face. *I will be luckier,* I think.

I might lose my family for a while, but not forever. Alison promised to keep in touch and Jess might even follow in my footsteps. Like Sally told me, sometimes a bit of family is enough.

"Will that jerk find you another job?"

"Which jerk? Oh, you mean Robert? Maybe. And Dao told me to look him up if I'm ever in Hong Kong. But I want to take a break first."

My hands are no longer automatically reaching out for the next rung of that ladder. My hands are reaching instead for the people I love. And for a glass of wine. Ben holds out two bottles of red. I nod at the Pinot, although, come to think of it, I am growing tired of Kiwi wine.

He fills our glasses. "Where will you go?"

I look out the window to the north and then back to Ben's face. "I haven't decided."

"Do you think you could—" He lifts his glass and swirls the wine slowly. "Do you think you could—maybe—live with me?"

My heart swells, even as I remember Ben's tiny studio miles away from anywhere. Miles away from any prospect of my sort of work.

Sometimes you have to make sacrifices. So I smile at him, my mouth wide enough to show my crooked tooth.

"Yes."

His eyes crease and he takes a deep breath and looks around the room. When his gaze returns to my face, he smiles back.

"I'm sure I can find something to do in Dipton," I say. "Perhaps I can help market your furniture. Or maybe," *horror of horrors*, "teach?"

Ben's face slackens and for an instant he looks appalled. "Oh, Lin, I wouldn't ask that of you!"

I shake my head. "I will never ask you to leave Emmy. It's what our father did to my sisters. Vivienne never got over it."

My thoughts have been flying somewhere else too.

"And it's what my mother did to me."

• • •

Ben looks down at his plate in silence. Outside the birds twitter amongst the branches of the copper beech, and the last of the sun floods through the western windows.

"Emmy's only staying in Dipton for my sake," he says suddenly. "She wants to join her mother in South Africa for the rest of the year."

He lifts his head and smiles. "Maybe it's time to put you first. So, where shall we go?"

I pause for a moment's thought. I remember coming to this land of hope, following my instincts, hoping to find my sisters, and hoping to find a way back to Ben. Okay, so I took a couple of diversions, but I was proud of what I had achieved at Hera even though I wouldn't be around to reap any of the harvest. And, although I had to leave Ngatirua, I still held onto some small parts of my family.

And I had Ben. I felt lucky.

Now my instincts are telling me something else. You might say what I decide to do next was fated, but I know it was logical.

I reach over and take Ben's hand and smile back. "I have another address. I'd like to see where my mother was from. How about a trip to Macau?"